Contents

The Syndicate: Volume 1
1

The Syndicate: Volume 2
175

THE SYNDICATE: VOLUME 1

Loose Id

ISBN 10: 1-59632-134-2
ISBN 13: 978-1-59632-134-2
THE SYNDICATE: VOLUMES 1 AND 2
Copyright © 2005 by Loose Id, LLC
Cover Art by April Martinez
Edited by: Raven McKnight

Publisher acknowledges the authors and copyright holders of the individual works, as follows:
THE SYNDICATE: VOLUME 1
Copyright © March 2003 by Jules Jones & Alex Woolgrave

THE SYNDICATE: VOLUME 2
Copyright © May 2003 by Jules Jones & Alex Woolgrave

Printed in the U.S.A. by
Lightning Source, Inc.
1246 Heil Quaker Blvd
La Vergne TN 37086
www.lightningsource.com

Prologue

It took Allard precisely ten seconds to diagnose why "the screen thingy went all black."

"That's the fifth power-cable out of its socket I've seen today," he snarled gently. Time to go through the job ads. It could be very therapeutic to reassure himself that there was a vast market out there for sysadmins who had got tired of the current bunch of morons they were working with. He tried not to remember that the vast market was largely composed of *other* bunches of morons who had recently pushed their previous sysadmins beyond the point of tolerance. If nothing else, if he found a job on another planet, at least it would be a change of scenery.

He glared out of the window. He could think of so many better colours for a sky to be than orange. On the other hand, at least he had a window. His last workplace had been a hundred feet underground to get away from the weather.

Just as he was putting his feet up and reaching for his second cup of coffee, he heard a beep. The prats hadn't even given him time to open the bloody job ads.

He reached for the com unit, wishing he had the nerve to bury it under his paperwork, so it would never be seen or heard from again.

"Yes?" he snapped, in a tone that meant "No!"

"My screen's gone all dark!"

He gritted his teeth. "Have you checked all the cables?" Standard procedure, when he wanted to say "fuck off!"

"Yes!" the voice on the other end squeaked. Allard recognised it now. He had given it a lecture last week after the third time in one day it had done something stupid.

"Prescott, isn't it?"

"Er, *yes.*"

"Don't run away. I will not be pleased if I get there and you are not around to explain exactly what you have done to your machine."

He expected to have ten minutes of Prescott denying he had done anything, followed by a red-faced admission that he had installed the latest "game" going the rounds. He did hope so. It would put him ahead in the company's IT sweepstake, with the most common "stupidities" this month. Collecting stupidities was excusable. You had to derive warped amusement from them *somehow.*

He was wrong. "Prescott, why do you have a portable heater in your office?"

"They're doing building work and they switched the heating off."

Reasonable. "Why have you got it right next to your computer?"

"I wanted to keep my legs warm, and the computer's main box is under the desk. It gets in the way if I put it on top."

Allard refrained from using any four-letter words, because last time somebody had actually taken it as an invitation. Instead, he explained that Prescott's computer would be taken away for repairs, and Prescott would not be getting it back for at least a week. He did not mention that Prescott could have his machine back within the hour if he were not so annoying that it was a public service not to give him a computer.

"But what shall I do about my files?"

"Restore them from the frequent three-generation backups we have been explaining for the last two years you should make."

"No. No. My *personal* files on that computer."

Allard rubbed his hands together. Personal, embarrassing files? He might get some entertainment out of today, after all.

He took out the drive unit in seconds (with Prescott looking at him as if that were a black art, as usual) and pocketed it. "With my equipment, I can probably access the files and move them across to the main storage for you. You'll be able to access them from your officemates' machines. *Won't* that be helpful?"

Prescott went white, and said, "Er…"

"A job well done, I think," said Allard. "Of course, it may be quicker just to repair the computer and bring it back to you."

Prescott looked fidgety.

Allard picked up the computer and walked out with it. It went on his "to do eventually" table, and he returned to his coffee and job ads. With any luck, he'd never have to repair it, because he would have left the company. What a good argument for leaving the company.

* * *

Allard picked up his coffee and took a long swig. He could feel his brain-cells stretching under the stimulation; when he was talking to Prescott, he could feel them shrinking.

The job ads. Surely he would find something there to offer him the promise that not *every* IT person had to deal with people like Prescott all the time?

Logging onto one of the better sites, he set a search running and left it to its own devices. He could finish his coffee break with Prescott's private files, presumably a porn collection, and check the selected ads over lunch.

It was quite an extensive porn collection. Not particularly to his taste, but very thorough. Prescott had a thing for little white socks. He could have happily gone through his whole *life* without knowing that. Little white socks on airbrushed pretty-boys, posed beside vehicles or stallions or outdated edged weapons in an unconvincing way.

Allard preferred women to men, and men to boys. When he *was* thinking about men, he liked them large and freshly sweaty, not gleaming with carefully applied baby oil. He also liked them old enough to have a bit of personality. Prescott liked a personality-vacuum in his pretty pictures.

The models also all appeared to be sharing a single brain-cell between them. This was doubtless utterly unfair on some of them, because at least one or two of them must be quite intelligent in the real world. It was just, he liked the intelligence to show.

All very boring, really. There was no need for Prescott to have been quite so embarrassed, other than for his lack of taste. This was extremely tame. No orgies, not even a hint of kink, and the pretty boys were all well over the age of consent. In his years as a sysadmin, Allard had learnt quite a lot about human sexuality. Some of it he would rather not have known, including things like colleagues with a penchant for little white socks. Prescott was deeply, wearyingly normal. He felt his eyes closing even thinking about it. There certainly wasn't anything here that he'd be remotely tempted to add to his personal collection. He preferred pictures of real people.

That little lot really was depressing. Back to the job ads. An unusual advert caught his eye. *WANTED: IT SPECIALIST FOR SYNDICATE CREW.* There was a word you didn't see every day. Syndicate? Oh, yes, a political philosophy advocating worker-control; a sort of left-wing capitalist thing.

He put "syndicate" into a search-engine and got back reams of nonsense (including some alarming stuff about pirate ships, back in the days of wood and sail) which seemed to imply that his guess was more-or-less correct.

A quick e-mail query later, he had the appropriate loony-fringe e-mail land in his inbox, explaining why it would be a really good thing to have a part-share in a ship. He sighed. He liked clean, well-paid jobs (where he could *get away* clean and well-paid); this sort of arrangement sounded messy.

On the other hand, the work sounded interesting, and being his own boss could only be an improvement on his current boss. This lot didn't believe in management, obviously, but from where he was sitting, neither did his current employer.

He sent off his résumé.

* * *

He was mildly surprised to find an invitation to an interview sitting in his inbox the next morning. He hadn't expected the determinedly political bunch to show any interest in a faceless capitalist when there were doubtless so many of their own lot interested in joining.

The interview was tomorrow. Not a lot of notice, but as they said, they would be in the neighbourhood.

He didn't bother to hide the message. In fact, he left it open on the screen. Even if nothing came of it, he could happily annoy various people by letting them know he was looking for a job elsewhere.

* * *

The ship was somehow larger than he'd expected, given the impression he'd had of a fairly small group of people. Of course, his previous experience was with passenger ships, and this must be a freighter. It looked good, reasonably trim and well-cared-for, not that he was an authority on such things. It was rather let down by the name *Mary-Sue* in purple letters with a rose painted beside it. Taste obviously wasn't these people's middle name.

"You don't have to tell me," murmured a tall, curly-haired man who could evidently read his expression. "It was Harry's idea, and he's like that."

"It just seems a curious name for a ship," said Allard. "Who are you, by the way?" *Now this is more like it,* thought a part of Allard's mind still shuddering from Prescott's taste in porn. *Big, friendly, sexy, and not airbrushed-to-death.* This man was in his early thirties, probably around Allard's own age, ordinarily attractive without being 'pretty', and untidy without being a mess. He also had an impressive mane of brown curls that, with the long face and dark-honey-coloured eyes, actually made him look leonine.

"Vaughan." The man held out his hand. "Ship's engineer. I take it you're the IT expert who's due for the interview."

"Allard." Allard held out his own hand politely, despite worrying about what a large engineer's grip could do to a precision tool like his hand. "Will you be taking me to see the captain?"

Vaughan winced visibly. "I *am* the captain, but it's not a way of thinking we encourage. This is a community of equals; I just tend to sign the paperwork if I don't happen to run away fast enough."

"What an interesting outlook on life," said Allard, hoping that avoiding signing paperwork did not extend to paycheques.

"What would you like first—see what the job is? Tour of the ship? Meet the other members of the crew?"

"I'd like to do the job, not move in and marry it," said Allard.

Vaughan looked slightly hurt. "You've never done a ship-based job before, have you?"

"I should imagine it's fairly similar to any other, apart from the scenery."

"Well, in a manner of speaking, you *do* have to move in and marry it, or at least move in."

It showed how desperate he'd been to leave the current— no, previous—job that it hadn't actually occurred to him that this job would involve living with his colleagues as well as working with them. "I see what you mean." He thought about it. "You can explain the job to me as we tour the ship. I'm going to have to look at your equipment anyway."

Vaughan spluttered slightly. "Sorry. Too much exposure to Harry. For a second, I thought you were referring to something else."

This made no sense to Allard. "Equipment, tools, tech," he said impatiently, waving a hand.

"This ship," said Vaughan, stepping through the door and leading him down a corridor that somehow didn't seem quite to scale, "is second-hand, or more than that, from a bunch of aliens. It's passed through a number of hands, tentacles, whatever…" he waved airily, "and we've landed up with it. Its systems are a little strange, and since we're—you might call us an accumulation of specialists—we want to find the best IT expert we can."

"Oh, you're a group of consultants." Allard was pleased to finally find a normal handle on this group. The ship looked rather less battered than he'd expect from a 'communal-property' bunch of weirdos. Since all of them owned a share, it was *their* money, paintwork, and furniture; he supposed it made sense it wasn't shabby. The corridor, at least, was clean and well-maintained, just a few minor scuffs and chips on the paintwork from daily use.

"More or less," said Vaughan. "Everyone on this ship has a skill that's useful to the ship itself and can be hired out. We do some trading and cargo-running, but we also act as consultants."

This is a definite improvement on my previous job.

"So you want me to handle ship's systems and act as a consultant?"

"That's the general idea."

Just as Allard was beginning to wonder if the corridor actually ever came to an end, Vaughan led the way into the computer room. Allard was pleased to see that this, too, was clean, moderately tidy, and well-lit.

"Yes, that might be acceptable. I won't stand for having a share in the ship, though. Nothing personal, it's not the way I work. I want a salaried position."

"Owning shares in the syndicate is the way this ship works," Vaughan said. "I thought that was clear from the ad."

He'd better get this point clear from the start. "It's not the way *I* work. If I decide you're all a bunch of..." *wankers,* he thought, and decided to wait to say that until the contract was signed, "...idiots, I want to be able to pull out without having to stop to disentangle my capital."

"We do actually know how to run a business," Vaughan said. "We've been doing it this way for some time, and been quite successful. We are not about to lose your capital for you."

I should have used 'wankers.' It makes it a lot clearer. But business sense would have been the next point to address. He assembled what little tact he had. "I was actually thinking more along the lines of working compatibility, whether you would suit as colleagues, but I'm glad to hear that you're as attached to your money as I am to mine."

"Well, we haven't had any other suitable applicants from this system," Vaughan said rather doubtfully.

How dare he suggest I might not be good enough, Allard thought for a split-second, before catching up to the point that *he* knew how good he was, but he hadn't actually proved it yet.

"If you're as good as you seem to think you are, perhaps we can come to some sort of arrangement," Vaughan went on.

"Give you until the next planetfall to make up your mind. Of course, if you left the ship at that point, we'd want you to pay a fare."

It was good to see that at least one member of the crew was very hard-nosed about money. He'd thought they might be a bunch of woolly-minded idealists, but Vaughan, at least, seemed to have his head screwed on the right way 'round.

"As long as I get paid a reasonable salary for the work done in the meantime," he said.

"We'll be fair about that. Now, can you actually work with these systems?"

Many of them looked fairly unproblematic, although they clearly had been used by members of several different cultures and at least three different species. He noticed that an AI appeared to have been part of the original fittings—or at least that's what he'd *thought* that particular unit was. "What's your main AI like?" he asked, slightly preoccupied with a little preliminary button-pushing.

"Shy," said Vaughan.

Allard stopped pushing buttons and looked Vaughan in the face.

"Shy, I said," Vaughan repeated.

"That's not a disposition I remember encountering before."

"Nor had we," said Vaughan.

He filed that for future consideration. Well, it was an alien system.

After prodding a few more devices, he said, "I can probably manage most of this. The rest would take a bit more work. On the other hand, I can't think of many people who could do any better than that."

"I'll show you the engine room," said Vaughan. "Then I can take you up to the flight-deck, and you can meet the rest of the crew there, as well as look at the remaining systems."

"If you're the engineer, doesn't that mean you are adequate for taking care of the engine room? Certainly better than an IT expert."

"It's always useful to have some degree of backup," said Vaughan.

This is certainly better than the situation at my last place of employment now I've left. Allard hugged himself in silent glee at the thought of the amount of mess he would not be expected to clear up.

He followed Vaughan into the engine room.

"Just look at this engine!" Vaughan enthused.

Allard looked at it. It was an engine.

"This is quite an old ship," Vaughan said, stroking the engine-housing, "and this is the original engine. Not as sophisticated as some of the ones available today, but this one is actually far more reliable. It's easy for one person to manage. It manages itself most of the time. That's far more important than an extra percent efficiency."

Allard looked more closely at it, then he asked to have the housing taken off so that he could see it properly. Vaughan was right; this was actually a rather nice piece of technology, even if it wasn't new and shiny.

Vaughan picked up on his interest and started wittering on about it in detail. It was a pleasure listening to someone who knew his subject, and Allard couldn't help noticing that Vaughan had rather a nice voice. Especially when he started making love to his engines. Unlike Allard's last employers and colleagues, Vaughan was actually interested in what he did. This job was looking better all the time, even if the people involved had strange politics.

Eventually, Vaughan broke off from what he was saying. "I'm sorry, I got a little carried away."

Allard said, "Don't be. It's a pleasure listening to someone who's genuinely enthusiastic." *Particularly when he's enthusiastic in a warm, flowing baritone that's a pleasure in itself to listen to.* "My last colleagues left any interest in the job behind when they left work."

Vaughan looked at him appraisingly. "I can safely say we don't have that problem here. We do things because we're interested in them."

"This job seems more appealing all the time," Allard admitted.

"So how much notice do you need to give your current employers?" asked Vaughan.

"Just as long as it takes me to clear out my desk." *Not very long. Since I got used to taking jobs as bad as that last one, I'm making sure I can strip every trace of my presence out of a building in twenty minutes or less.*

"You're not going to give them any notice?" Vaughan sounded slightly shocked.

"They wouldn't give me any notice if they decided to dispense with my services." And that certainly didn't endear them to him. He'd have shown them a good deal more loyalty if they'd behaved better to him or others. "They *didn't* give two of my colleagues notice when they decided to dispense with their services and make me do both their jobs. I owe them nothing."

"I do hope this tit-for-tat mentality extends to giving notice to people who *would* give you notice," Vaughan said.

"I treat people precisely as well as they treat me." Which was, as far as Allard was concerned, the plain truth. So many people over-complicated social interaction.

"Are you flirting with me, Allard?"

Including him, apparently. "If I've got to do *that* to get a job, I'm not interested."

"Well, that put me in my place," murmured Vaughan, sounding slightly regretful.

Time to think about un-squashing Vaughan later, if necessary, Allard thought. He could do with a few weeks concentrating on work before he started considering recreational activities. Vaughan was the sort of person that would probably bounce back quite well if Allard decided to un-squash his ego later.

"I suppose I'd better take you to meet the others," said Vaughan, leading the way into the corridor.

"How many are there?" asked Allard.

"Three more humans, plus Master Control Unit 93."

"The shy AI?"

"Yes. He's got a bit more personality than your average AI."

"In other words, he's as weird as the rest of the crew."

Vaughan faked a huge double-take. "Who told you about the rest of us?"

Allard smiled politely.

"But seriously," Vaughan said, "why the hell would you apply to join us if you have no interest in what we're doing?"

"You may have gathered that I do not enjoy my present place of employment."

"Somewhat," agreed Vaughan.

"Even a slightly cuckoo job with people who are at least marginally intelligent would be a big improvement. I can stand a few political speeches for the sake of a decent job. And if you can stand the odd ideological disagreement for the sake of a decent worker, we may be able to come to some arrangement."

Vaughan said, "That's not the point."

What a pity. We were getting on so well until now.

"This is not a lunatic-fringe operation that substitutes verbiage for work," said Vaughan rather firmly. "It's a serious way of getting people to work together on a long-term basis in a way that benefits both the group and the individuals. This co-operative has been running for about five years now, with changes in membership as people found they were suited to a larger or smaller group. We *do* have provision for people to leave, whether to join a group more suited to their tastes or to leave syndicalist ship-running completely." He looked at Allard with intense dark eyes. Allard was interested to see that Vaughan's eye colour shifted with emotion. "But it's a serious operation, and we ask that our members try to take it seriously. We cannot run on the same basis as short-term contracts for a large corporation, if that's what you're used to."

"I find that quite understandable," said Allard, "but it's not my way of working." He paused. "Look, I'm not the easiest of people to get on with. I don't get on with other people easily. I function best where I have the security of knowing I can walk out, if necessary."

"All of us," said Vaughan quietly, "have probably worked for large corporations at some point. We appreciate the freedom to make our own minds up."

"Who exactly *is* 'we'? You were about to tell me before we got sidetracked into political debate."

"Well, here we are at the flight-deck," said Vaughan. "You're welcome to come in and meet the rest of us."

Allard followed Vaughan through to the flight-deck. It was spacious, well-equipped, and clearly old but well looked-after. It was also not designed by humans.

A balding but quite young man was trying to sprawl in an alien chair and put his feet up on the desk. Obviously, it was quite *difficult* for humanoids to lounge about on this ship, but he looked as though he was putting in the effort. Despite the casual, nondescript clothes and thin fairish hair, he wasn't bad-looking. An expressive face, and Allard liked the look of the laugh-lines around his eyes.

He got up when he saw them come in. "Harry Chance. Valuations man. Are you the one who's going to throttle our computer systems into some sort of shape?"

"Possibly," said Allard non-committally.

"Harry's already introduced himself," said Vaughan. "Over there we have Karen Bright, our weapons tech..." A rather attractive woman with dark, curly hair glanced up at him, smiled, and then looked back at her console. "And our pilot, Claire Steele." The striking blonde did not look up at him. That was all right. If he'd been busy when somebody had strolled into his office, he'd probably have waited until he'd finished what he was doing, as well.

"And, last but not least, Master Control Unit 93." Vaughan indicated an arrangement of geometric shapes on the wall that Allard had taken for a piece of art. It didn't say anything.

Allard politely faced it, feeling slightly silly. "Hello, Master Control Unit 93. I am Allard."

"Say hello, MCU 93," said Vaughan.

It still didn't say anything.

"This may be your new personal physician," said Vaughan. "You might say hello to him."

An androgynous voice (tilted very slightly towards the male end of the spectrum) said, "Welcome aboard the *Mary-Sue,* Allard."

"Now we've been introduced," said Allard, "may I approach you with a probe at some point? I've been known to get unpleasant showers of blue sparks from AIs who do not consider me properly introduced."

"I like this one," said MCU 93 to Vaughan. "May we keep him?"

"We haven't decided yet," said Vaughan.

He turned to Allard. "You're doing a lot better than the last one we tried. He did his best to rewire MCU 93, without bothering to ask first. MCU 93 took it personally."

"I'm not surprised," said Allard. "In case you didn't know, changing an AI's circuitry can actually affect their personality. It would be roughly equivalent to somebody spiking your drinks. Or, in extreme cases, a lobotomy."

The blonde (ah yes: Claire Steele) looked up. He noticed she had brown eyes—unusual combination with what he was ready to swear was a natural blonde hair colour. She gazed at him thoughtfully, and then said, "At least you seem to know what you're talking about. There aren't that many people with much experience of AIs. Let alone alien ones."

"I know enough not to treat them like ordinary computers."

Actually, the opportunity to handle an alien AI was an attractive feature of the job. Living on a ship controlled by that AI was less appealing. AIs weren't that common, for a good reason. They were just as capable as humanoid intelligences of going insane. For some reason, people were far more bothered by that when the life-form in question was silicon. This was irrational. Allard wanted to keep as far as possible from mental disturbance, whatever the physical make-up of the circuits containing it. But it was easier to overpower something if it wasn't built into the fabric of a ship; that particular worry was sensible enough.

However, MCU 93's personality seemed pleasant and likeable, which was a good start. Allard wouldn't be surprised if insanity had warning signs like brooding or paranoia, and the 'feel' of MCU 93 was quite healthy.

"We do have a slight problem, everybody," said Vaughan rather hesitantly. "He's not a syndicalist."

"What's he doing *here,* then?" said Claire, staring at him. "The advert was clear enough. We don't want any time-wasters."

"If I might join the conversation at this point," said Allard, "there are more important things than minor political squabbles. Like finding out if the work I can do is necessary, and if we can work together."

Harry exchanged a 'full of himself, isn't he?' sort of glance with Vaughan.

Vaughan said, "That point didn't become clear until he was already touring the ship, but I believe he may have something to offer us."

"The last non-syndicalist we tried," said Claire, "was an industrial spy who ripped off all the technical details he could take back to his corporate home."

"I don't like working for corporations any more than you do," said Allard flatly, "but I need my freedom."

"Why should we take you instead of somebody who believes in the same principles as we do?" said Harry.

"Because I'm very, very good."

Vaughan sighed. "And he's not flirting when he says that. I've tried."

No, Allard agreed, *I wasn't flirting, and I don't intend to. At least not just yet. However, this crew provides considerably more inspiration for flirting than the last lot.*

"Are we supposed to take his abilities on trust?" Claire said. "This is a second-hand—well, tenth-hand—ship bought from aliens. It has special requirements. Can you deal with alien computers?"

"Probably better than most. Oh, you want a free sample, do you?"

"You must see our position," Karen said. "We don't know anything about you."

"I've been discussing this with Vaughan," Allard said. "He seems to think that a form of consultancy work might be fair on both sides."

"As a probationary period," Vaughan hastily put in.

At the end of the probationary period, Allard thought, *I will have left if I don't like it. If I do like it, I can always threaten to leave. And if they don't care if I leave, I haven't been doing a good enough job anyway.*

"I've never worked on a ship before," said Allard. "As Vaughan has already pointed out to me, it involves living as well as working with my colleagues. I don't think it's unreasonable for me to find out whether I'm suited to that before making a long-term commitment."

Harry said, "Yes. If you go stir-crazy after three days in space, we probably *don't* want the hassle of trying to untangle you from the contract before you can leave."

"I think I can manage three days," said Allard. "I have, after all, travelled on a number of occasions."

"Just how many jobs *have* you run away from?" said Claire.

She's a bitch. But so am I. I can cope with that. At least she had a personality. It might be no more pleasant than his own, but compared to Prescott and his un-charming stable of pretty-boy photos, it was a big improvement on 'bland'. She was better-looking than Prescott, as well.

He grinned at her. "I didn't run away from all of them. And no, I wasn't sacked, either. I've worked as an independent consultant as well as in a salaried position."

"I'm still not happy about this," said Claire.

"Just think of me as a consultant who just happens to be on board," said Allard. "If I was a planet-based consultant, I would expect to go and stay in the area. The area in this case happens to be your ship. If nothing else, you may care to employ me short-term to sort out your ship's systems. We can worry about long-term contracts after that."

"If you're happy with a short-term contract, why do you want to leave your present position?" asked Karen.

"Because they're a bunch of wankers, and I can't stand them," admitted Allard. "But *don't* tell them that until you've offered me a job."

Claire started to snigger. "At least he's honest. You can say that for him."

"There are two ways to take that from someone I don't know," said Karen. "Either they *are* a bunch of wankers, or you're a shit-stirrer. Without knowing you, I can't say for sure," she added demurely. Allard took a second glance at her. Yes, she was much politer than Claire, but she was quite capable of coming out with her own blunt style of remark—very decorously. He suspected that the quiet voice and sweet smile covered up for that rather well.

"There is always the possibility that I am a shit-stirrer *and* they are a bunch of wankers who set me off," Allard said, with a helpful smile.

He paused, and decided to deal with the query seriously. He suspected that that, rather than stupid jokes, was the way to impress Karen. "Look, they really are a bunch of jobsworths. They arrive on the dot of nine and leave exactly at five, whether or not they've finished what they are doing. Nobody has any idea what anybody else is working on, or why; and the senior management treat us like dirt."

He thought about that. Vaughan had been more sympathetic to his attitude when he'd explained why he had that attitude. "Two of my colleagues were sacked, and I was expected to do their jobs. I resent that, but I also resent the fact that they came in on a Monday morning, were told to go to the office, and came back with a security guard to stand over them as they cleared their desks into a black bag, and were then marched to the door. They happened to be two of the few people I actually *liked* at that firm, but I would also like to be clear that it isn't a good way to treat anybody."

"This is the sort of thing we're trying to *stop!*" said Vaughan, eyes alight with fervour. "We are all co-owners. Nobody should have to deal with that sort of behaviour just because there are bosses."

"You'll have to excuse Vaughan," Harry said lazily, returning to his default sprawl. "We all take it seriously, but Vaughan takes it *very* seriously."

Allard thought he could probably put up with the evangelism, as long as he was merely expected to share a room with it and not pontificate as well. At least Vaughan had a rather nice voice, even when he was talking complete bollocks. It could always be considered background music.

"If you can put up with me, I can put up with you. I think." He decided, on a provisional basis, to like these people. They were weird, true, but they were intelligent, and even good-looking, which might be a consideration later on in the long distances between planets. "As long as I can decide to leave later if I'm wrong about that, or you can decide to put me down on the nearest planet sooner than actually strangling me."

"Is that what passes for diplomatic from you, Allard?" Claire said.

"Yes. If you can cope, this may be a fruitful relationship." He looked at Vaughan. "Do I have a job?"

"Hey!" said Harry. "The rest of us have a vote in this, too."

"Sorry," said Allard, meaning it. "It'll take me a while to get used to the way things are done here, but it'll probably be more interesting than the sort of job with a boss who decides everything." *Whether he's competent to or not.*

"Show of hands?" said Vaughan. "Hands up, everyone who's willing to try this arrangement with Allard."

To Allard's complete amazement, everybody raised their hands. *That's not how it works. People drew lots not to sit next to me at the last place but one.* "Are you absolutely sure?" he asked. "Remember, you will be living with me, and I might not manage even the most cursory façade of pleasant behaviour over my own personality on those terms."

"We're weird, too," said Harry.

"He certainly knows of what he speaks," said Claire, with a cynical grin and a toss of her bright blonde hair. "Quick, Vaughan, get him to sign the contract before he finds out about Harry's idea of personal entertainment."

"What *is* Harry's idea of personal entertainment?" asked Allard quickly.

"We're it," said Claire. "He's a voyeur, and we can't keep him out of our data-files or his audio bugs out of our bedrooms, try how we might."

"*You* can't," said Allard, rather smugly, thinking that at least Harry seemed to have a more lively taste in porn than Prescott did.

"And you can, if you're capable of doing the job we hired you for," said Karen. Allard was moderately surprised—she'd kept fairly quiet until now.

"Where are you going, Harry?" asked Claire, over the sound of Harry getting up with more speed and animation than he'd shown in half an hour.

"Running a backup!" said Harry, over his shoulder.

"Tut, tut," said Allard. "You should already have one in a safe place. I can see I will have a lot to teach you about data security."

"When can you join us, Allard?" Vaughan asked.

He glanced at his watch. "My employers—may they rot in hell—are still at work at this point, so I should be able to clear my desk and get back to you within the next hour or so. It'll take me a little longer to clear out my flat, but I'm a consultant—I'm used to knowing I may need to move at short notice. I don't seem to have collected a lot."

"Want a hand packing stuff?" Vaughan asked.

About to refuse, he stopped and thought about it. With two of them, he could get away with shifting the stuff himself rather than getting professional help. And Vaughan was reasonable company when he'd dismounted from his particular hobbyhorse.

"Thank you. I'd like that," he said.

* * *

A discreet distance from the front door of his erstwhile employer, he finally gave vent to his feelings. He'd bottled it up until he'd left the premises, on the grounds that he *might* one day need a job with the same bunch of morons again.

Vaughan politely let him rant until he'd run out of steam. "Do you need help finding further synonyms for 'wanker'?" he asked, after a while.

"No. Thank you for listening to me get that off my chest."

"Even my brief exposure to that establishment," said Vaughan, "tells me why you were so eager to leave. It reminds me of why I became involved in the syndicalist movement in the first place. Let's move on quickly before I succumb to the temptation to set fire to it."

Allard could quite understand why Vaughan felt that way, having been subjected to a security check for unannounced visitors. Allard led the way to his flat. One of the few enjoyable features of working for that company had been that he was within easy walking distance of work, and still living somewhere pleasant.

Now it had the benefit that he'd never bought a car—one less thing to get rid of.

"You do travel lightly, I see," said Vaughan. "I suppose if you've been working as a consultant on short-term contracts for the last few years, you've needed to be able to move in a hurry."

"Not usually this much of a hurry," said Allard, opening his front door. "Why did you accept me? I was expecting a lot of talking-around-the-subject."

"We *are* quite practical," said Vaughan. "We have sound business reasons for needing a very good person to handle our computer systems. And although we would have preferred to have a full member of the syndicate, we would have needed a short-term computer consultant anyway." He grinned cheerfully. "And there's always the hope that we'll have converted you by the time you've finished the work that needs immediate attention."

"And besides, your AI likes me," said Allard, smiling back, and mentally dividing his possessions into those he wouldn't mind a casual acquaintance handling and those he was going to pack himself, in private.

"This is a nice flat," said Vaughan. "With windows. Are you sure you'll be comfortable on a ship?"

Allard thought about it. "I don't see why not. You showed me the cabins are nice and big, even if it's because they were designed for eight-foot aliens. If it comes to a view, I can always look at the stars."

Delivery Boy

Allard was six hours into a ten-hour job. He wanted a pizza, but wasn't within a thousand light-years of a delivery round; he wanted intravenous caffeine or, conversely, the time to take a good rest; he wanted the damn thing finished, and it wasn't shaping up. Six hours of fighting the technology into submission, and he was beginning to wonder if there was enough caffeine in the ship's stores to keep him running until the end of the job. The computers were better-fuelled than he was. He hated it when that happened.

He did not want Vaughan, the engineer and the closest the ship had to a central authority (which, in practice, meant that everyone came and argued with him first before arguing with everybody else). More particularly, he did not want one of Vaughan's late-night specials in the way of philosophical conversation, about Honesty or Liberty or whatever damn thing it was this week.

It might be other people's idea of how to pass the time between planets, but he preferred a good book. And he *meant* good. Vaughan had lent him some god-awful syndicalist thing about *Non-Structured Decision-Making,* and he used it to prop his wonky chair-leg. Allard still hadn't managed to get through to Vaughan the reason he was on a syndicalist ship, which was that it was the furthest he could get from authority while still being paid.

Anyway, he'd like to know how Vaughan would cope with his idea of bedside reading, which was something on algorithms.

He prepared himself to fend off some teeth-grindingly dull speech on philosophy.

"What've you said to Karen?" asked Vaughan.

Damn. It wasn't even the philosophical variant on his back now, and he wasn't any too interested in gossiping with Vaughan, either.

"It started with a polite 'no' and she asked me to expand on it," Allard said.

"Dear me, you *do* have exacting requirements," Vaughan murmured. "What would your Ideal Lover be like, as a matter of interest?"

Allard, without turning round, snapped, "Dynamite sex, no conversation, and turns into a pizza afterwards. With extra-strong coffee."

"All right, all right, I can take a hint," Vaughan murmured. "Good night, Allard."

* * *

Two nights later, Allard had finished that job and had one good night's sleep. Unfortunately, the job had reproduced before it died, and littered that corridor with equally urgent necessary-things-to-do. So he was deep into the next when he heard Vaughan's footsteps again. *Doesn't he ever sleep?* he wondered, annoyed.

"So, you ordered 'dynamite sex, no conversation, and turns into a pizza'," Vaughan said thoughtfully.

Allard's nose twitched. There was something distinctly savoury in the air. *Had* Vaughan managed to…no, that was silly. It was definitely too late at night for this conversation.

"Will 'arrives bearing pizza' do as well?" Vaughan asked him.

Allard backed clumsily out of his work. Anchovies, olives, plenty of cheese, all the extras. And he had missed dinner because he was busy. "Yes. As for the rest, I suppose two out of three isn't bad," Allard said, thinking about the 'no conversation' and the 'pizza'. He took a slice and bit down. His eyes half-closed. Delicious.

Vaughan leered at him. "*Three* out of three, if you please." He fumbled in his pocket as Allard took another big bite of pizza, and handed Allard a very large silk hanky. It looked familiar. It looked suspiciously like the one he'd bought because it was large enough to use as a scarf. "I took the liberty of rummaging in your drawer for something suitable."

Allard frantically tried to remember exactly which drawer the hanky lived in, and decided he was probably safe. He chewed, swallowed, and took another mouthful. He'd like to know how Vaughan had programmed the kitchen for decent pizza—he'd been trying for days, and all he'd got was cheese indistinguishable from industrial glue, on a base indistinguishable from cardboard. Perhaps he *should* have admitted that he didn't know everything there was to know about the ship's systems. He took a huge gulp of coffee.

Industrial-strength verging on dangerous, as if Vaughan had brewed a big pot of extra-strength and stirred a caffeine pill into it. He could almost feel it running through his veins and invigorating him.

"This should be big enough, I think," Vaughan continued, gesturing at the hanky. "No matter what you may think about me having a big mouth."

Allard said, "Can I use it whenever I like?" hopefully. He could think of a few speeches that could have been helpfully or even profitably muted.

"Well, if you're *that* eager, we can skip the pizza and go straight to bed," Vaughan said, with an airy wave of his hand.

Allard spluttered. He ought, by all that was right and proper, to knee Vaughan in the balls and leave the room on a tide of righteous fury at this point, only (he didn't actually want to)...only it was a damn good pizza, wonderful coffee, and service of this standard ought to be encouraged. And there would be a certain amount of additional therapeutic value in being serviced by Vaughan. Vaughan was tall, well-built, well-hung and had lots of lovely curly hair he could run his fingers through. All of this didn't exactly make him an impossible prospect. The expressive brown eyes weren't bad either, and that rich, deep voice would sound wonderful if only it were whispering sweet nothings instead of politics or commerce. He might even be tempted to forego the gag. Eventually.

"I think I'm going to need the energy, if you want me awake."

"That's a tough choice," said Vaughan, "but I do want you to be able to come out with enough ardent praise for my efforts. So, nice as it would be to do you when you're half-asleep *and quiet,* I do want you awake."

Allard mumbled something through the pizza, about how dare Vaughan have the bloody nerve to ask for him to be quiet.

Vaughan waved the hanky, and said, "*You* were the one to specify no conversation, Allard. I'm just going along for the ride." The hanky fell fluttering to the table beside the pizza.

"I hope the ride's worth it," Allard murmured, through more cheese-and-anchovy topping. Actually, he was beginning to get distinctly interested. The cheese-anchovy-and-caffeine mix was beginning to invigorate points south, as well as cheer him up mentally.

"You'll have to decide that," Vaughan breathed intimately, and stroked him delicately between the legs, not precisely *on* or precisely *away from* any of the parts of his anatomy that might be presumed to take an interest.

Allard moaned through a mouthful of pizza.

"Good," said Vaughan, patting Allard's crotch lightly. "I can manage to contain myself for long enough for you to refuel; don't know about you."

Allard passed him the gag. "I've been fantasising about this for weeks," he told Vaughan, unable to stop himself smiling as the ambiguity winged neatly home.

"Before I put that on," Vaughan said, "I'd better help you with the pizza so we can get started quicker."

Allard mumbled a polite 'go ahead' noise through his third slice, and watched Vaughan bite happily into his first. He liked a man with an appetite.

Soon, there was nothing left but a round mark on the box.

Vaughan licked the grease off his fingers.

"It's traditional to lick one's *own* fingers, Vaughan," Allard murmured, for form's sake.

"Oh. Do mine need licking clean, then?" Vaughan murmured, and got up to trail them over Allard's face.

"No," said Allard, licking and sucking happily. "Which is a good thing, as you've still got to put that gag on."

"Can't it wait until we get to the bedroom—and, incidentally, your room or mine?"

"Your room, Vaughan. You can get the grease on your sheets. And, incidentally, I quite like the idea of leading you through the corridors gagged."

"Oh. Well, if you want to wear it, it's fine with me and, I suspect, the rest of the crew. One or two of them have mentioned the possibility."

Allard decided the pizza must have cheered him up. It was the only possible explanation for finding that amusing rather than annoying.

Vaughan pulled him to his feet. "Let's get on with it, then."

In short order, Allard was clearing a lot of engineering texts, tools, and hardware off Vaughan's bed.

"I sleep on the chair if I can't be bothered to clear up," Vaughan admitted, rather apologetically.

"But the chair is covered with junk as well."

"Yes, but I can just tip it up and it all slides off," Vaughan told him.

"Don't try doing that with me." Allard gave an enormous fake yawn as he finished clearing the bed. "What were we doing, again? I may be too tired."

Vaughan kissed the back of his neck, trailing the kiss over to his ear. "I believe you mentioned something about 'dynamite sex'," he murmured. "It probably involves a good big stick of dynamite stuck into a narrow crevasse, and then it explodes all over the place."

Allard was in no possible doubt about the narrow crevasse, not with the way Vaughan's hands were all over his buttocks. "It sounds rather high-speed to me," he said doubtfully, turning round to face Vaughan.

"Oh," said Vaughan. "If there happened to be a stick of dynamite left over when the main one had gone off, one would just have to set a controlled explosion. Blow the lot to kingdom come," he added thoughtfully, licking his lips.

"Mmm," said Allard, finding the idea strangely appealing. "What do you mean 'the main one'?" he snapped suddenly. *I wouldn't mind it up me,* he decided, *but there's nothing to say I have to take the attitude along with it.*

"It's a matter of point of view," Vaughan said airily.

"Maybe you need a little attitude readjustment. I have a Luser Attitude Readjustment Tool," Allard said. He snorted gently. The 'Tool' was generally not that literal, and certainly not inserted, but there was always a first time. And it was practically his duty to go on top and eradicate any possible misconceptions Vaughan might have about dominance. And, his cock reminded him, it would feel good.

"What?" said Vaughan. He did look confused.

"A tool with which you adjust the attitude of a luser. 'Loser' crossed with 'user.' That is, a computer user who has just done something stupid. Again. Beating them about the head with a clue-by-four often does the trick. Most of my tools are in my toolkit, but I think I've got one in my trousers."

"Four inches, eh?" said Vaughan.

Allard felt a Bastard-Operator-from-Hell mood beginning to creep over him. "The four refers to the cross-section, Vaughan," he snapped. "As in two-by-four."

"I'm not *that* much of a size-queen," Vaughan told him. "Maybe I should be on top if you're actually deformed."

Allard began to reach for Vaughan's back pocket, where he'd last seen the hanky. It really was time to stuff something in Vaughan's mouth, and tempting as the idea of using his cock was, he intended to use his cock on the other end.

Vaughan seemed to enjoy that, until Allard whipped out the hanky and applied it to Vaughan's mouth with a cry of triumph. Thinking of whipping out the hanky, he *did* remember which drawer it had come from and, yes, it was the one with the whip. Damn. The whip had been a present from an admirer, a present that he hadn't actually used. He never expected to have a situation where he might want to put it to use. He could only hope Vaughan hadn't noticed the colour of the hanky.

He applied it firmly yet gently, and tied it in place. Vaughan's eyes were practically emitting sparks, the same way his own would be if the situation had been reversed. Vaughan wanted to talk back nearly as much as *he* did. Good. Although he would never entertain the concept that he might have been losing an argument, however light-hearted, he did enjoy the idea that Vaughan's desire to speak had been frustrated.

"Cat got your tongue?" murmured Allard. "I could have sworn that you'd have *something* to say about this situation. Even if it's just 'Unhand me, you villain!' That's the traditional response, isn't it?" He bit Vaughan lightly on the neck, enjoying the way Vaughan moved, as if he were trying to speak and nothing could come out. "Is that it? I can feel you struggling to escape."

He fondled Vaughan's cock, which was definitely trying to escape from Vaughan's trousers.

Vaughan reached up, presumably to remove the hanky.

Allard grabbed his wrists. "You promised," he said reproachfully. "No conversation."

A rather muffled number of words managed to make their way free. They might have been, "Do I get the dynamite sex, then?"

"I'm sorry? What was that?"

Vaughan appeared to try to mumble. "I *eh,* 'o I 'et the—"

Allard kissed him lightly on the hanky and grabbed him firmly on the cock. Vaughan fell backwards onto the bed. "I was thinking of having you on your knees, but since you're offering so kindly, you may stay on your back.

That would have been very erotic if Vaughan had not started giggling. Allard decided to stop trying to take it too seriously, and made a grab for Vaughan to ascertain that part of him was taking it seriously enough. It was. Good. He undid Vaughan's trousers, just to make sure he was right. Definitely not a couple of socks down there, although it was best if Vaughan lost the underpants. Yellow polka-dots just weren't his colour. He was rather impressed. He'd have bet a serious sum of money that yellow polka-dot underwear would put him off having sex with *anybody.* They didn't, but he'd better not push his luck. He removed the boots, dragged off the trousers, and finally, with a sigh of relief, took off the underpants and pocketed them.

"'Ot are 'ou 'oing?" said Vaughan.

"Call it a fashion statement."

Vaughan gave him to understand they were all that colour; he liked yellow. Allard shuddered. "All right, I'll dispose of *all* of them," he said wearily, thinking that if he'd known it was this much work, he'd have declined the offer.

Vaughan's eyes were incandescent with sheer ferocity.

Then again, maybe it would be worth it. He could always make sure it was.

He got up, found a tape measure on the small pile of things discarded from the chair, and took a few measurements. "Vaughan, could you try not to move? I'm trying for some degree of exactitude, and it keeps growing."

Vaughan growled through his muzzle.

"Something white and pure to go with the naïveté, I think," Allard said thoughtfully, once he'd got the measurements. "Or to go with any little fantasies I might have of deflowering you. But I'll have you naked, for now. I just want to make sure you aren't going around without any underwear once I've destroyed the yellow ones. I'd find the thought altogether too enjoyable for work hours."

He addressed the ship's computer, and some fresh, white, untouched-by-human-bottom underwear fell softly down the requirements chute. At least that part of the software was working. He put those in the wardrobe, making absolutely sure that the yellow dots, yellow ducks, and yellow fluffy chickens were safely on their way down the disposal chute.

He turned back to the bed, to discover Vaughan, having fully undressed, was hastily stuffing a pair of fluorescent green socks down behind the mattress.

He decided that a naked Vaughan was interesting enough to make it worth not getting into a fight about the socks. Or even a

Vaughan dressed only in a hanky, which seemed to be a very fetching accessory. He said so, his voice descending into a low purr without any conscious decision.

Vaughan mumbled something about "'ot on 'e 'igh' eh!" Allard paused, decoded that as "not on the flight deck!" and said, "Of course not, Vaughan. I want to keep this little treat entirely to myself."

Vaughan grabbed his hand and pulled him onto the bed. "Yes, Vaughan, you have my permission to undress me." Whereupon Vaughan began to fiddle with Allard's clothes. To Allard's fury, with little effect. He appeared to be pushing the decorative buttons on Allard's shirt; first serially and then in combination.

Allard put up with this for five minutes, and then said, "What the hell are you doing?"

He listened to Vaughan's reply, which was extensive enough not to travel through a bunched hanky very well. "You have my permission to speak, Vaughan. Therefore, you may take a minute out of the scene to tell me."

Vaughan removed the hanky, worked his lips a bit, and said, "We've all been looking at that shirt and wondering what the buttons were actually *for*. I mean, they could be a little peepshow thing, one part of your body going on show when you press the right button. Sort of 'left nipple, right knee, cock, elbow', one by one. On the other hand, Harry thinks there's one jackpot combination that makes the whole lot fly off at once!" He was laughing too much to continue.

"Minute's up," Allard said repressively, replacing the hanky. "Now take my clothes off. Carefully."

Now that the joke was over, Vaughan seemed to have no trouble finding the fastenings on the shirt. Soon it was on the floor. Unfortunately the trousers were still at half-mast, because Vaughan had neglected to remove the shoes first. Allard could forgive this, as it appeared to be due to Vaughan's eagerness to get him naked.

"Do the job properly, Vaughan," he sighed. There was no point in letting Vaughan know his low standards were forgiven at this point.

Vaughan apparently thought that 'properly' involved nuzzling Allard's legs as best he could while taking the shoes off. The nuzzling was done well enough for Allard not to give him permission to remove the hanky to do it properly. His own less repulsive socks followed them, and then finally Vaughan disembarrassed him of trousers and underpants. Vaughan seemed to wrinkle his nose up slightly. Allard decided he must be imagining that his own clothing was perfectly practical, unlike things with horrible yellow patterns on them.

He lay down, with an ostentatious yawn. Vaughan took the hint, and began to wake him up. Fingertips flew, darting and dancing over his nipples, his thighs, the head of his cock, and a number of areas that shouldn't have been erogenous zones. He'd never heard of arousing the inner elbow, say, or the back of the knee. Not that he felt like complaining. Damn. This was the sort of foreplay that went even better with added kissing; he'd forgotten that point when insisting on Vaughan being muzzled.

Vaughan lay down, too, and lifted his knees.

Good idea, thought Allard. Getting on with the main event would distract him from worrying about the lack of kissing, and (his eyes glanced smugly downwards) nobody could say he wasn't ready.

Vaughan's eyes flicked sharply left. Following his gaze, Allard discovered a bedside-table, presumably full of all the usual useful bedside-table things.

"Inattentive of me," he said, and reached out. Sun cream, paracetamol, Philips screwdriver, hairbrush, half-dismantled thing…and, right at the back, a tall container of hand-lotion on its side, only slightly leaking. He poured himself a handful, rubbed it briskly in, and began to apply it.

Unfortunately for the fantasy, although fortunately for the reality, Vaughan probably wasn't a virgin. He squirmed enthusiastically, then frantically, moaning through the gag and grinding himself down against Allard's invading fingers. Allard slid them out, while Vaughan told him not to stop (quite clearly, although without bothering to use consonants) and prepared himself, making a display of that. He stopped making a display of himself just short of making a fool of himself, luckily.

"Aha, my pretty!" Allard said, pretending to twirl a moustache he didn't have. "Now I have you at my mercy." A perfectly judged pause. "That *is* the traditional thing to say, isn't it?"

Good. Vaughan was still laughing so hard, almost swallowing the gag, that he was not in any condition to be coherent, or tense. Vaughan cracked up, and Allard crammed in. It was an odd sensation, fucking someone who was laughing. It *did* mean they were unlikely to clamp down in any unpleasant way, but there were certain tremors which seemed to follow straight through from the muffled laughter to the heat enclosing him. He slid nearly out, then shoved in a lot harder. Oh, that was—that was—that was going to make him make a variety of embarrassing noises just about now. He buried his face in Vaughan's neck to silence them, and heard one seep out around the edges, altogether too much like a pleading squeak to suit his purposes. He'd better do something about 'no conversation' on his own account, before Vaughan noticed. Since they only had the one hanky between them, he'd have to improvise. He fumbled unhandily at the knots until they gave way. Hanky out, tongue in. That kept both of them busy, and quiet.

His hips jerked into a sudden ferocious thrust. And again, and harder. He hoped it felt as good for Vaughan's arse as it did to his cock, although he doubted that was possible. Shouldn't he be thrusting his tongue suggestively, fucking and mastering Vaughan from both ends, about now? He didn't have the coordination, or the will-power, to do anything but keep fucking, hard, while Vaughan sucked and stroked at his tongue. Asserting his power by fucking Vaughan? It was more that he was watching while Vaughan's arse swallowed him whole. Oh well, if he'd got the basic dominance parameters wrong for this relationship, Vaughan had definitely better fuck him next time. It was the last coherent thought he had before he was coming, fast and hard. He was enclosed by pure sensation, mouth and arse clamped onto him so that nothing could escape as he reached melting point. He was almost howling into Vaughan's mouth as his cock jerked, stopped moving, poured helplessly and exquisitely into the other end of Vaughan.

He had needed that very badly, he thought, opening his eyes and glancing blankly at the clock. All three minutes of it. He had also done it very badly, if one considered the three minutes and the fact Vaughan didn't look precisely ecstatic.

"I told you the trouble with dynamite is it's too quick!" he snapped, only just holding himself back from apologising by main force.

"All right, Allard. You were right and I was wrong. Now do something about it," Vaughan ordered.

Allard raised an eyebrow. "You mean I have to ruin this lovely, languid afterglow by actually doing something?"

"Yes!"

"All right then," Allard said peaceably, sliding off Vaughan and letting him get his legs down. He fondled Vaughan's cock appreciatively. "What, for preference?"

"We were discussing a controlled explosion, which sounds fine," said Vaughan.

"Not sure I can manage it with a stick of dynamite this big," Allard said.

"Try," said Vaughan.

Allard sighed, grumbled (not entirely seriously), and decided this was the sort of unreasonable demand from Vaughan he could learn to like. He bent down to get a better view of the problem. He enjoyed that, as well. He licked quickly all the way up from the base, back down, and up again slower. He liked the feel of a hot eager cock against his lips and tongue just before it went in.

"Please!" said Vaughan, rather throatily.

Ah. The magic word. *Now* he felt dominant; there was the sense of mastery over Vaughan's pleasure he'd been hoping for, and even if it had turned up late, he could enjoy it to the full. He opened his mouth and sucked the very tip. Oh, he could spend time with this. Maybe it might be worth drawing this out for a while until he was up for another go.

Vaughan groaned, sounding desperate.

He decided to be merciful, and wait until tomorrow. He sucked, hard. Honour would be satisfied by making Vaughan go at it as fast as *he* had, and he could manage that. Mouth on cock, tongue busy with a few little refinements, one hand steadying the impressive length of the rest of it, and the other playing with Vaughan's balls. He sucked, and *sucked,* and here came the explosion, here came Vaughan, noisy and hard and copious. Very copious; Allard still had quite a mouthful left once his 'stick of dynamite' had subsided. He moved up the bed and passed it neatly back to Vaughan in a long kiss.

Vaughan seemed to enjoy the kiss, infusing it with a languid sense of endless possibilities. Damn. He'd *meant* it to be a way of handing back Vaughan's by-product and remaining coolly uninvolved.

He stopped kissing. "I just like the taste," he said, and glared downwards at his not-quite-erection, which was showing signs of coming back.

"Yes, I know," said Vaughan in a soothing rumble.

Allard decided it *was* a rather nice voice for whispering sweet nothings. He did not say so. Then he rolled onto his belly and said, "I need a wash." *Preferably in cold water.*

Vaughan went to the bathroom and ran a hot bath. When the steam had reached a certain degree of pleasant-smelling approachability, Allard padded in its direction, irresistibly drawn. The bath was big enough for two, which was fortunate, as it was already occupied by one. It was just not *quite* too hot. He liked that. He eased himself in beside Vaughan, with a sigh.

Vaughan said. "Well, 'dynamite sex', 'no conversation', and 'pizza'. How well did I do, then?" His tone was distressingly bumptious.

"I will take an equal share of the responsibility for the sex not being as 'dynamite' as it might have been. The 'no conversation' was adequate. You were supposed to turn into a pizza afterwards, but bringing a pizza with you is an acceptable substitute, especially as I was hungry first. You forgot the ice cream."

" *What* ice cream?"

"The ice cream for after the pizza."

"You've already had your dessert, and you didn't mention ice cream. In fact, you didn't even eat the cream I provided."

"For that, one should slowly savour the taste, as at a wine-tasting," Allard told him, kissing him again. The flavour was still delightful. Allard glanced down, just to make sure he wasn't doing a visible 'periscope' act with the bathwater. Luckily, a mass of bubbles can cover a multitude of sins.

Vaughan grinned beside him. "Checking to see you're not enjoying yourself too much?" he said, doing his best to grope beneath the bubbles. He found something. "Is that all you can manage?" he asked, doubtfully.

"Actually, Vaughan, it's late, and I'm tired, and you're doing well to get that much. The libido is willing, but the flesh is weak. Take it as a statement of intent, post-dated to tomorrow."

"Want a cuddle till then?"

Allard considered this. The sample of 'cuddle' he was getting at the moment seemed to be particularly adequate, and although if Vaughan kept cuddling him until tomorrow morning they would both have to cuddle asleep, that was acceptable.

"Yes. As long as we don't have to spend *all* the time until tomorrow morning in a cooling bath." A thought struck him. "Do you need to change the sheets?"

Vaughan gave him a mistrustful glance. "What do you mean, *you?*"

"Exactly what I said." He might feel wonderful, but if Vaughan had turned up willing to provide services from pizza to bed and all points in between, Allard wasn't going to say no to any useful service.

"No, I'll be a lazy slob and sleep in it," said Vaughan cheerfully. "Although it might be nicer to sleep in you."

Allard groped for Vaughan under the bubbles. "You're tired as well, aren't you?" This was, he thought, a good explanation for why Vaughan hadn't got insistent. Vaughan wasn't *quite* half-way up.

"Didn't say I wasn't," Vaughan murmured. He was lying back with half-closed eyes, and looked entirely too comfortable, considering it would probably be sensible to go to bed and he couldn't lug Vaughan.

"Kneel up, Vaughan," Allard said.

Vaughan was evidently tired enough to do this without making any comment.

"Hands and knees." Vaughan flopped forward. Allard admired the view for a while, then started slopping some bubbles about. It was an attractive bottom, and he wanted to be sure he hadn't carelessly mistreated it during three very fast-moving minutes. He hadn't, apparently. It was now clean and unhurt. He slapped Vaughan's rump. "Up you get, Vaughan!"

Vaughan glared at him.

Allard used the "instant dry" function; the one that instantly vaporised a bathful of water and blasted the occupant with hot air. It wasn't the most pleasant way to finish one's ablutions, but it was undoubtedly the quickest known to man or alien.

"*Warn* a chap before you do that, Allard!" Vaughan muttered.

"I wanted you awake enough to stumble to the bedroom. I'm not going to lug you," said Allard.

Vaughan, grumbling, got to his feet and followed.

Allard got in, making sure to leave the damp patch for Vaughan. It wasn't too damp; they'd managed to get most of their enthusiasm inside each other.

"Good night, Allard," Vaughan said, reaching for him and closing his eyes.

"Good night, Vaughan," Allard said, grateful that Vaughan wasn't going to be embarrassing, and very grateful to go to sleep.

* * *

He hadn't slept quite that deeply for some time. What had he been doing? He rubbed his eyes hard; he could remember a lot of hard work, and a pizza, and…

He rolled over, and found the bed occupied by a large, warm, naked Vaughan.

…and a lot more hard work, in fact. His cock sprang instantly to red-alert, and told him it had forgiven him for putting it off at two o'clock in the morning, but he had better come up with the goods soon.

He prodded Vaughan.

Vaughan said, "Mmm?" and went back to sleep.

He prodded Vaughan harder.

Vaughan said, "Fuck off, Allard!"

This was good—Vaughan knew who was in the bed with him. It was also bad—Allard had just been told to fuck off, which was one word longer than what he'd been thinking about.

He tried again. Vaughan muttered and hid under the pillow.

Allard considered the situation more seriously. Last night, when he had definitely not been in the mood for socialising, Vaughan had provided calories and caffeine, and he had *got* in the mood. Therefore, he needed to provide calories and caffeine.

He borrowed Vaughan's dressing-gown and went and had a word with the food machine. Statistically, Vaughan's breakfast-of-choice appeared to be a pot of strong tea and a plate of hot toast with an assortment of marmalade and jam. Apart from the tea, that sounded acceptable to Allard, too.

He prepared a pot of tea and a pot of good coffee, both in one-person quantities.

Then he prepared a very large plate of toast, added some honey to the selection of marmalade and jam, grabbed the pots, and set off. Vaughan had retrieved his head from under the pillow to lie more comfortably, but appeared asleep.

He dumped the tray on the floor beside the bed. Vaughan twitched crossly at the sudden noise, and Allard waved a piece of toast-and-honey under his nose. Vaughan muttered something about liking to start with blackcurrant jam, and Allard made him a piece of toast-and-blackcurrant, passed it over, and started happily on the scorned honey.

Caffeine and sugar were a good way to start the day, he decided, and he hadn't given up hope of Vaughan rejoining the human race after enough toast and tea had been applied.

He licked a smear of blackcurrant off the tip of Vaughan's nose.

Vaughan looked at him, but didn't actually glare. This was progress.

The blackcurrant tasted quite good. He prepared a slice of toast-and-blackcurrant for himself, and guessed marmalade for Vaughan's next slice. This appeared to be acceptable, although Vaughan did mutter something about preferring the more acid things at the end.

"You'll get that," Allard told him.

"Back to normal service, then, I presume," Vaughan said. "Talking of which, breakfast in bed *for somebody else* isn't like you."

"Ulterior motives," Allard said. "I felt a lot less grumpy and a lot more interested in fucking you after caffeine and calories last night, and I am simply applying the same general principle."

"I'm not grumpy."

"Not any more," Allard said. "Do you feel interested yet?" He investigated.

Vaughan said, "At least I let you finish the pizza first. Good thing, too, I suppose, or I would have been served cold pizza for breakfast."

Allard shuddered at the idea, and reached for a slice of toast-and-strawberry to comfort himself. Cold pizza for breakfast was taking the computer geek stereotype a little too far.

"I thought you were investigating my condition," said Vaughan reproachfully.

"When I know I've got enough to work with," Allard told him, "I can get on with whatever's next on my list. In this case, breakfast."

Since Vaughan was now awake enough to deal with the toast himself, Allard lifted the tray from the floor and placed it on the bed between them. A slice or two later, he thought this might have been a mistake. Or perhaps he should have just tripled the normal amount of toast rather than merely doubled it. Well, at least Vaughan would have no excuse for low blood sugar putting him off.

They finished the toast, and Allard insisted they use the napkins. Vaughan would quite cheerfully have wiped his fingers on Allard, but Allard did have some standards. And besides, he knew what it was like to have crumbs in the bed, and other places.

Allard set the tray down on the floor and then pounced on Vaughan.

They might, of course, switch roles, which would have the benefit that he could indulge himself and let Vaughan do the work. But on the other hand, his disgraceful failure of control might have left Vaughan with the impression that Allard couldn't really manage it. It was his duty to disembarrass Vaughan of that, and switch roles later, once he'd established the general situation.

He was going to, he decided, have Vaughan properly, and thoroughly, and take about ten times longer than three minutes. Of course, his plan for last night had been fairly similar, but his control had been weakened by sexual deprivation and tiredness. He flung the bedclothes off to take a good look.

A marmalade-flavoured kiss, first, while he decided which way to approach the problem. Slow. He simply went still every time Vaughan tried not to let him lead, and let Vaughan figure it out. Once he'd got to the stage where Vaughan was waiting for him obediently, he showed off everything he'd ever learned about how to kiss, and then some. Suck, twine, curl, lick, keep kissing; deeper, then gently; a light quiver, suck and slide; some hard tongue-fucking; a momentary retreat to breathe; more suck-twine-curl-lick, going back in; more deep kissing, unfairly co-ordinated with tugging viciously at Vaughan's nipples; and finally an unhurried glide of Allard's mouth down to Vaughan's neck, leaving him panting and begging.

"You're ready," Allard murmured into Vaughan's ear. "I do like that."

"So do something about it!"

"Oh, I intend to," he purred, and ran a fingertip over Vaughan's cock, doing his best to achieve a level of stimulation that was irritatingly insufficient.

"Do something else about it!"

Allard fished a silk handkerchief from under the pillow.

Vaughan shut up.

There were certain benefits to Vaughan's lack of body-hair, Allard decided. In particular, one could rub and stroke and tongue all over him without having to stop and spit out awkward little hairs. Smooth, hot skin felt very, very good, and his cock started to suggest that rubbing against that plentiful expanse could be satisfying. He told it that that wasn't going to give Vaughan the impression he was in control, and to shut up. He couldn't stop touching all that skin, though, which was quite all right, as he didn't have to. Instead, he rested his hot face and lips against the smoothness of Vaughan's chest, using his hands in stereo to tug Vaughan's nipples to eager, greedy peaks. Down a bit, biting evenly and softly on one nipple after the other, and licking down the side of Vaughan's body where Vaughan wouldn't be expecting it, then running a fingertip lightly down the middle, stopping just short of touching his cock. He could hear Vaughan's heartbeat, flatteringly interested, and was glad this position did something to hide exactly how desperate *he* was getting.

He sat up. "On the other hand," he told Vaughan, "maybe I should approach the question from another angle."

"Allard!" wailed Vaughan, as Allard turned clumsily, wriggled, and began to suck at Vaughan's toes, trying to suggest that Vaughan had five stiff little cocks on each foot and all of them wanted to be sucked. After that, he trailed his tongue over the arch of the foot, circled Vaughan's ankles with his hands, and began to work his way up. Since Vaughan had more body-hair from the waist down, Allard did most of the work with his fluttering fingers rather than his tongue, but appeared to be doing a satisfactory job of making Vaughan really desperate. By the time he got to the interesting bit, the thighs, Vaughan was pleading with him.

"I'll do anything you like, Allard, just let me—"

"All in good time. Which is, incidentally, what I intend to have. Slowly and very thoroughly." He kissed Vaughan softly on the inner thigh as he worked one stroking hand up the other. "Now, where was I?"

"About two millimetres too far from my cock!" Vaughan replied crossly.

"All right. Two millimetres coming up." Allard did his best to move exactly two millimetres.

"Two inches!" Vaughan snapped.

"You see how useful it is to be exact."

"I don't care," Vaughan wailed. "Just suck me!"

Allard did so. However, Vaughan had not specified which bit of him was to be sucked, so Allard was sucking a patch of soft tender skin on the inner thigh.

"Allard!"

"Don't you appreciate that?"

There was some incoherent whimpering, then Vaughan said, "Please suck my cock."

Allard did so. He was very careful to get this *just* right, tongue flicking over all the most sensitive parts, sucking just hard enough for his own pleasure and not *quite* hard enough for Vaughan's, one hand playing with Vaughan's balls. He needed to have one hand on Vaughan's balls to be able to judge exactly the right moment to stop. Vaughan's balls quivered, reaching a certain moment...

Allard stopped.

Vaughan used a few words he must have learnt from Harry, or possibly Claire. They sounded like something the pilot might have picked up in a bar with her low-life friends.

"It's for your own good," Allard told him, hastily shifting so that his own cock and balls were out of easy reach of any aggressive intent.

Vaughan used even more words. Allard didn't know some of them.

"The longer the build-up, the more the delay, the better the orgasm," Allard said reasonably. He started looking for the lubricant. Where had he dropped it last night...ah, there it was beside—and luckily not under—the breakfast tray.

"You're not thinking of some sort of time interval involving weeks, I hope?" Vaughan asked, in a rather nasty tone of voice.

"No, just twenty minutes."

"Well, I suppose it's an improvement on three minutes."

"Exactly!" Allard said happily, rubbing a handful of lotion to warm it, and slapping it between Vaughan's legs. "Mind you, it will probably be more comfortable for you if you roll over. For that length of time, it will probably give you an unpleasant stiffness in your legs—"

"I've got an unpleasant stiffness in my *cock*—get on with it!" Vaughan snapped, although Allard noticed that he was rolling over and, as he'd noticed in the bath, presenting a rather attractive bottom. In fact, he couldn't help thinking, Vaughan *was* a rather attractive bottom, even if he'd ruined Allard's approaching pun. Obedience should be rewarded, so Allard worked the lubricant up and in with slow, thorough, and suggestive attention to detail.

"It's only fair to warn you," Vaughan said breathlessly, "that I can probably come from that, if done well enough."

Allard stopped immediately. He made Vaughan comfortable on a pillow, prevented him from being *too* comfortable on the pillow, and applied himself to the job at hand, or possibly in hand.

He'd loosened Vaughan up just the right amount. It felt very comfortable indeed. Too comfortable—this was not going to last twenty minutes. Still, he was a reasonable man, quite capable of adjusting the parameters of whatever he was doing to meet requirements. Call it twenty minutes including foreplay, and that would be just about right. On the other hand, going by the way Vaughan was bouncing up and down underneath him, and squeezing him, and generally encouraging him to get on with it…

He pulled back and slammed forward again. Yes, that seemed more to Vaughan's taste, without all the fancy extras.

Actually, it was more to his taste, as well. Vaughan was making a sort of '*now* you've got the idea!' noise. He abandoned twenty minutes as a target and went for broke, every hard thrust making Vaughan howl with pleasure, and he'd be howling, too, if he could spare the breath *(god, what was wrong with three minutes, anyway?)*. Being bigger, Vaughan managed to scramble to his knees, despite Allard's opinion on the matter. Allard decided the improved angle of attack was worth it. Not that he'd last out to enjoy it for long; not like this. Three long, violent strokes; he just had time to bite Vaughan as a gentle hint, and get his hand under. He yelled as he brought both of them to orgasm in one last blinding second.

He blinked. That last second had lasted about five minutes; long enough for them to collapse sated on the bed, breathing easing back to normal.

"Ten minutes, including the foreplay," he muttered disgustedly to himself.

"God, but it was worth it!" Vaughan told him. "*That* was dynamite, if you like. I haven't come that hard since I joined this crew." His tone made it clear that this was quite an honour.

Allard wasn't thrilled. Six months wasn't *that* good as a standard of comparison. However, when he looked at Vaughan's face, he decided he was probably nearly as good a top-man as he wanted to be, judging by the results.

"You didn't have to leave it *that* long, mind you," Vaughan said.

"Well, Vaughan," Allard said, nudging Vaughan so that he looked at the pile of clothes on the floor. "Last night, you spent five minutes pushing every button I had, so it was well-and-truly your turn."

Vaughan sniggered. "Can I go on top next time?" He followed that with a yawn.

"If you're very, very good," Allard whispered.

"That's all right, then. I just was," said Vaughan, and fell asleep.

Allard didn't like letting Vaughan get the last word, but for the life of him, he couldn't think of an answer to that, because Vaughan *had* been very, very good.

* * *

Half an hour later, he noticed it *was* half an hour later, and Vaughan was also awake.

"We are going to do it again?" he asked Vaughan.

"Isn't that my line?" Vaughan said. "Only if you get some better underwear, as well."

"You're the one with yellow polka dots and fluorescent socks. I'm normal," Allard said.

"You're so normal, you keep a whip in your underwear drawer, buried under all the grey flannel knickers. Which is the real you?"

"The grey flannel knickers, of course," Allard told him. "I'm not a pervert, even if I have had the odd unfortunate present from a friend. That, I may add, has never been used."

"Maybe it was a subtle hint about the grey flannel knickers. Too subtle, obviously. *You* may be sexy as hell, Allard, but you cover it up too much. Who wants to grope grey flannel? Or grey socks with little Daleks on?"

"What would you like to see me in?" Allard asked him, because of course Vaughan was just winding him up and wouldn't have any better ideas.

"Black silk, well-cut, and not much of it," said Vaughan promptly. "Under loose trousers."

"Oh."

"In fact," Vaughan said thoughtfully, "there's a tape-measure round here, isn't there? I'll just take a few measurements and tell the computer."

"Is this what they call topping from below?" Allard asked him.

"Yes." Vaughan grinned at him as he went to fetch the tape measure.

Allard didn't put up much resistance to being measured. A new fantasy had just popped up in his mind, where he was wearing perfectly ordinary outer clothes, but as the others went out of the room for a moment, Vaughan slid a hand into his grey trousers and over his black-silked buttock. A large, hot hand. He certainly shouldn't be enjoying the thought already, but then Vaughan seemed to have unusual effects on his own time management.

"Silk," he said firmly, "for special occasions. Otherwise, grey flannel." Give Vaughan an inch and he'd take a light-year—and he'd had six inches this morning already.

"Yes, Master," Vaughan said.

"Tone of voice, 9. Leer, 0," Allard remarked. Something occurred to him. "Next week, I'm going to have a couple of unpleasant late-night jobs to do. I am going to be in serious need of pizza. And I'm going to be too tired for any hard work after the pizza."

Vaughan's face fell. "You only want me for one thing."

"Deliver me a pizza, then deliver me anything else I might need while I lie back and enjoy it," Allard clarified.

"Bastard," Vaughan muttered. "You do realise I'll be thinking of that all week now?"

"Of course," said Allard, and smirked.

A thought seemed to occur to Vaughan. "Er…you didn't actually mean ice cream, did you? I just thought I'd check."

"Try putting the ice cream in easy reach of the bed, and then fucking me," Allard suggested. "Don't mix the two. It's delicious, but it's hell on the sheets."

Special Delivery

It was useful having a partner who knew what was required, Allard thought, sinking into an anchovy-flavoured haze and permitting Vaughan to undress him. He opened his legs and relaxed.

Vaughan tied a loop of cloth 'round one wrist, and secured it.

"I didn't specify anything elaborate," Allard said.

"Have some coffee, Allard. I intend to keep you awake for a while." Vaughan's voice was rich with more than its normal complement of smugness.

Allard opened his eyes, reached out, and gulped at the coffee. "This doesn't mean I agree with your suggestion." He put the mug down.

"You don't have to agree," Vaughan said, doing the other arm. "You're tied up and can't escape."

"Unhand me, you villain." Allard gave an ostentatious yawn.

"Where did I put the handkerchief we used the other time?" asked Vaughan.

"If the proponent of non-hierarchical decision-making and mutual consultation feels he can't out-argue me unless I'm muzzled…" Allard said.

"No, that's not it. I just remember how much you enjoyed having me unable to speak."

"It's such a rare delight," Allard said.

"Quite," Vaughan replied.

"Bastard," Allard said, annoyed to find he was too comfortable to work up much indignation.

"Yes, you are. But I love you anyway…"

Allard tried to decide whether he needed to panic.

"…or at least I want to fuck you," Vaughan concluded.

Allard decided he didn't need to panic. He twitched his arms, wondering what exactly Vaughan had secured him to…

"You've been fiddling with my cabin equipment, haven't you?"

"Yes. I like fiddling with your equipment," Vaughan said, fiddling with some more of it as he spoke.

Allard sighed, enjoying that. He supposed he didn't really mind Vaughan having made a few adjustments, or at very least, he could save up really minding for later.

Vaughan fumbled in a pocket (his own, of course, since Allard wasn't wearing any) and brought out a thing. What sort of thing it was wasn't entirely obvious. It was red, but apart from being red, looked more than anything like a piece of cord, doubled over on itself to form a loop, with a bead holding the loop closed and a lot of softly frayed ends trailing down.

"What's *that?*" Allard asked, deeply suspicious.

Vaughan held up his hand where Allard could see it, folded it into a fist with the middle finger extended, slipped the loop over the extended finger, and ran the bead up the cord to tighten the loop onto the finger.

Allard yelped and tried to cover his most important assets. All he achieved was discovering why Vaughan had tied him up before showing him the…the…the *thing.*

Vaughan found that hilarious, for some reason. "It's also a little, tiny whip for whipping those areas that have to be treated delicately, but I must admit I haven't used it that way. Perhaps you're the expert on whips."

Allard yelped harder, and wrenched painfully at the ropes. "I *told* you, I've never *used* it!" he shrieked, approaching a degree of utter panic he had probably never shown Vaughan before.

Vaughan looked at him. "Why weren't you bothered about being tied up?"

"It was a new and interesting experience, and oddly enough, I trusted you!" he spat.

"All right, no whipping. Don't think I'd be that comfortable with whipping your tender parts even if you liked having it done," Vaughan told him calmly.

Allard relaxed a bit. "Why did you get that…thing, then?"

"It does make a very nice cock-ring, and the nice soft lashes are very enjoyable used that way. Allow me to demonstrate."

He reached down and secured the item around Allard's cock, which was beginning to recover, particularly when Vaughan stroked it. The soft cords fell delicately into place between Allard's legs, tickling and tingling at him. All those sensitive places appeared to be very grateful not to be whipped.

"Isn't it nice, used that way?" Vaughan murmured.

Mmm, thought Allard.

"Keeps you ready and interested until I'm prepared to let you come," Vaughan told him.

Allard's cock leapt at the thought of using it on Vaughan, although he was considerably less pleased with having it used on him.

"Looks as if you like the thought," said Vaughan.

"I was thinking of trying it on you sometime," Allard told him.

"So you really hate this…" Vaughan stroked the length of Allard's cock, which increased, "…and wish I wasn't doing it?"

"You can keep doing that as long as you like. It's the equipment that concerns me."

"Oh, so I can keep doing it as long as I like, then. Twenty minutes, I think. And I've never seen a better piece of equipment," Vaughan murmured, fondling Allard's personal equipment.

"That equipment would prefer to be naked," Allard told Vaughan, with what he thought was a creditable attempt at his flattest tone of voice.

Vaughan bent and kissed it. "I'm sure it would," he agreed, licking it from base to tip.

Allard looked desperately at the clock. Nineteen-and-a-half to go. He considered his position: flat on the bed. But apart from that, he could try kneeing Vaughan, since only his hands had been tied. However, Vaughan might then become upset and go away, leaving Allard to try to undo his wrists using his feet. On the other hand—he gasped in pleasure—he could just permit Vaughan to do that again. And again. All he wanted to do was guide Vaughan to achieve an exact perfection of position that wasn't quite…

Vaughan stopped.

Allard decided: *I will not beg, I will not beg.* He glanced back at the clock. Eighteen-and-a-half. *I will beg.*

"Nothing to say for yourself, Allard?" Vaughan grinned. He fondled Allard's inner thighs and balls.

"Please?" said Allard hopefully.

"Not good enough."

"Pretty please with sugar and cream on top," Allard said wearily.

"No, the cream comes later." Vaughan smirked. "In eighteen minutes."

"Seventeen-and-a-half," Allard corrected.

"Who's counting?" Vaughan said airily.

"You'll be counting your teeth if you're not careful."

"Maybe I'll just count your balls. One, two." Vaughan fondled as he went. "I think you're normal, but just to be on the safe side: one, and two," he said, returning in the opposite direction. He cupped them in his hand. "They seem to move if I do this."

"I'm not surprised," snarled Allard through gritted teeth. He tried to look at the clock without Vaughan noticing. They were obviously going through some sort of temporo-spatial anomaly. Time had slowed down.

"I said twenty minutes, and I keep my promises, unlike some people."

"I didn't notice you complaining at the…ah!" gasped Allard. "You could let me finish my sentences before you do that."

Vaughan let go of a nipple. "Well, you didn't seem to be that happy with the idea of me using a gag to keep you quiet. I don't know, never satisfied."

"That's what's bothering me!" snapped Allard. "And stop fiddling with that!" he added as an afterthought.

"Which?" asked Vaughan, working away with both hands. "I like the idea of fiddling while Allard burns."

"Well, thank you for admitting that you're a dictator—" Allard's voice trailed away as he tried to jack-knife off the bed, without much success.

"Time to tie your feet. Not that I mind, but all this kicking is getting a little untidy."

Fifteen-and-a-half minutes. Fourteen, by the time he'd been spread open and tied into his undignified position. He wasn't even flat on his back any more, but tied with his knees up and his legs apart for easy access. The thought was strangely intriguing. He even seemed to be enjoying the way he was exposed for Vaughan's viewing pleasure. Not that he would tell Vaughan that.

Vaughan stroked a gentle finger down his thigh. "This was a really good idea. But I must admit, when I thought of it, I didn't realise you'd enjoy it quite this much."

Allard realised that he didn't need to talk to express what he was feeling, so he might as well be honest about it and not wait for the lie-detector between his legs to come up with the truth. "Nor did I." He sighed. "Wish I'd tried it years ago."

"I wish I'd tried you years ago, too," Vaughan told him, equally honestly.

There was a silence. Thirteen minutes.

Then Vaughan bent down and began to suck at Allard's toes. Allard cursed, writhed, and tried to levitate out of his bonds, before realising that wasn't going to happen and settling down to work on neurally rewiring which parts of one's body got an orgasm and which parts didn't. He was just beginning to think he was getting somewhere by sheer force of will, when Vaughan withdrew his mouth. "Actually," Vaughan said, "it's just as interesting from this side."

"Twelve minutes," said Allard.

"You're the clock-watcher, and I'm something one consonant shorter."

Allard groaned, partly because Vaughan had started touching him again, and partly at the truly dreadful pun. "I can't watch yours, because you're wearing too much!" he snapped. "Strip!"

"You said you were letting me go on top this time. I've been looking forward to it all week."

"I'm ordering you to get your clothes off and do it. Now."

"As a point of interest, what would you do if I didn't?" Vaughan obediently began to undo a few buttons, making a languid display of it.

"Explode in sheer frustration!" Allard snapped.

"Well, we can't be having that. I'm working on having you explode in sheer satisfaction."

Allard closed his eyes and groaned.

When he opened them, the clock showed eleven minutes, and Vaughan was nude.

"That was quick."

"Large, baggy clothes and desperation," Vaughan said, lubricating him briskly and efficiently. Allard complained— efficient was deficient when one wanted to be thorough.

"I like to do it with someone stretched but not over-stretched," Vaughan told him. "I like to know they can really feel the distinction between my finger," which slid out, "and my cock."

Allard could. It had been a fairly large finger, but it was a fairly large cock, as well.

Vaughan looked at the clock. "We've got ten minutes for the actual fuck," he announced smugly.

Allard wondered how Vaughan could spare the neurons to either read the clock or be smug about it. All of his seemed to be fully occupied, as indeed was he. The bastard wasn't even moving. He clamped himself onto Vaughan as a gentle hint.

"Yes, I know it's nice," Vaughan murmured soothingly.

How the fuck is he managing to stay still?! Allard thought, incandescent with admiring fury. He moved, clutched, clamped even harder, if possible. "How-the-hell-did-you—" he gasped.

"I'd like you to appreciate the trouble I went to for this, Allard. I had a wank earlier, just to make sure I'd last out for the full twenty minutes, since you seem to like a nice, long, leisurely fuck."

Allard wished he'd thought of that, as well. At least it explained things. He'd hate to have to put it down to Vaughan's naturally better self-control and staying-power.

"Of course," Vaughan explained, "it was a bit of a risk, because I couldn't be sure I'd get it up twice today. But when I thought of what good inspiration you are, I was fairly sure I'd—" he gave one hard shove "—manage it.

"Eight minutes," Vaughan told him. "That was two minutes with me just staying still and making sure you could really feel it."

"I can feel it. I can feel it—just *not enough!*' he snarled, biting Vaughan, which was not a sufficient relief, considering the relief he was thinking of.

"Am I really not big enough for you?" Vaughan withdrew nearly all of it. "Shall I go and find a dildo? Twelve inches might be difficult—might actually have to go down to a shop and find you one. I find seven inches perfectly comfortable for recreational use."

The only good thing about Vaughan having withdrawn most of it was that a higher percentage of Allard's brain had come back on-line now that it wasn't so busy with the 'getting fucked' subroutine.

"There's nothing wrong with the size. It's the velocity I'm concerned about."

"Oh, I forgot. You're the three-minute wonder."

Allard had to collapse back on the bed, panting with rage. "What do I have to do to make you forget about that?"

"Look incredibly appealing all panting and flushed, and desperate to have my cock up you. What three-minute fuck? Forgotten it already," Vaughan said.

That was a slight comfort.

Allard glanced at the clock. Seven minutes to go.

"But I'm a man of my word," said Vaughan. "I promised you twenty minutes, and twenty minutes you shall have. I'm not one to hold a grudge and insist on giving you even less than you gave me." He replaced his cock in Allard. "Of course," he said thoughtfully, "I could give you exactly as many strokes as you gave me."

Allard moaned. It felt even better now he'd been waiting for it, and it was driving him even madder to do something. He panted. Then he thought he might as well distract himself by talking.

"You weren't counting, were you?" Allard gasped, some small part of his mind panicking at the thought that maybe, just *maybe,* Vaughan had been.

Vaughan apparently took pity on him. "No. You were better than that."

Then Vaughan leaned down, kissed him, and actually started fucking him properly. Allard made a number of forgettably embarrassing noises into the kiss, and cooperated enthusiastically. Then Vaughan stopped again.

"No!" Allard wailed.

"Sorry. Forgot to untie something." Vaughan untied Allard's wrists. "I do like a cuddle during as well as after."

"If you stop again, you will discover how it feels to get strangled," Allard told him.

"I'd better not stop again." Vaughan started moving, this time very slowly.

"What's the *matter?*" Allard snapped.

"We've got to keep an eye on the time. Four minutes to go," said Vaughan.

Allard began to cuddle Vaughan, hoping to encourage him. Also, it felt good. "I'm not sure I can keep going for another four minutes."

"I am," Vaughan told him, with another hard, slow stroke and hard, slow kiss.

Allard decided that (oh-fuck!) Vaughan was going to last out, and (oh-fuck, oh-fuck!) he wasn't sure *he* was.

Vaughan appeared to divine something of his state of mind. "You're quite safe." Another thrust. "You can't come until I untie your little decoration." He kept shoving in and dragging out, slow and hard and giving plenty of pressure where Allard needed it.

Allard stopped just short of begging.

Vaughan rammed in again, and stopped still for a moment, fondling Allard's balls gently.

Allard begged, loudly and repeatedly, if rather incoherently.

Another dragging backstroke, and in, and Allard was nearly...*nearly*...

Vaughan pulled halfway out and kissed him hard. It was wonderful and it wasn't what he wanted. He tried to make a grab for his own cock, and Vaughan pushed full into him so hard that he forgot even about what his cock was trying to do.

Then Vaughan stayed still and looked at the time. "That was two minutes. Another two, and I can let you finish off."

Allard gave up on begging and made another grab for his cock. He didn't expect to actually *reach* it, but if he could trigger Vaughan into giving him a serious fucking, the result would be satisfactory. He couldn't reach it. He'd forgotten there was a Vaughan in the way. Vaughan smirked at him, and wriggled just enough to remind him that his cock was pressed tightly between his belly and Vaughan's. Not that he actually needed a reminder. He tried to rub himself frantically against Vaughan.

"You could try asking," said Vaughan. "It's better manners."

He started counting. "One-hippopotamus, two-hippopotamus..." How many hippopotami would he be up to by the time Vaughan let him finish the job? Two times sixty, minus however many seconds it had been since Vaughan had said "Two minutes to go".

"Well, *I* usually count sheep, Allard. If you're too tired, we could always stop." Vaughan sighed, and stopped what he was doing, becoming heavier on Allard in a way that did interesting things to Allard's cock.

Allard began to talk his way out of trouble; fast, as usual. "It's a way to count seconds. Use a pentasyllabic word plus the number word, and you take up about a second saying it."

"And you do like using pentasyllabic words, don't you, Allard? Why don't you just try counting thrusts instead?"

"You haven't given me any for the last fifteen seconds," Allard told him.

"Ah. That must be why you're still capable of using pentasyllabic words. I knew I was doing *something* wrong." Vaughan shoved into him hard.

"Oh, that's…do it again; I want another one!" Allard growled.

Vaughan stopped, shifted slightly, and turned to look at the clock. Allard was positioned so that he could not see the clock past Vaughan's head. "Why have you stopped, and how long have we got to go?" he asked, desperately trying to work out which of those questions was most important.

"Just waiting for my mark."

"*What?*"

"And on the mark, it will be ten strokes to—" And Vaughan's pendulum swung.

Allard groaned. He had never enjoyed timekeeping this much.

"Nine," Vaughan announced. He was giving it to Allard hard and heavy. Just a little too slowly, Allard thought, but it was beginning to look as if escape velocity might be achievable by the specified time.

"Eight," Vaughan was no longer looking at the clock but at Allard, who found the rhythm extremely satisfying, even if it wasn't backed up by instruments.

"Seven." Allard groaned, hard, and collapsed back on the pillow. He couldn't talk, couldn't move, and he didn't even need to keep count, because it was being done for him.

"Six." Vaughan stopped to pant.

"More!" Allard snarled, trying to shove himself forward at Vaughan to get more into him.

"Five, four," Vaughan told him.

"Three!" Allard panted.

Allard suddenly panicked as he realised that Vaughan had not undone the thing imprisoning his cock.

"Two—and we'll just make it!" Vaughan reached for Allard's cock. Instead of undoing the thing, he merely stroked the silky threads over Allard's aching cock and gripped it firmly.

"One!" Vaughan commanded.

Neither of them said, "we have lift-off on schedule!" but Allard managed to think it, just the microsecond before he went off like a rocket, a whoosh of heat right up his spine as Vaughan's squeezing hand somehow wrenched a powerful gush of come from his cock, possible or not, and kept going, more and *more,* and he was coming *inside,* too, quivering as Vaughan's orgasm seemed to rub and stretch at the sensitive inner flesh.

He sobbed with relief; that had been enough, and he'd been beginning to wonder whether enough was possible after waiting that long.

"You *said*," he accused Vaughan, "that I wouldn't be able to come if you hadn't undone the…thing."

"I lied," Vaughan said cheerfully. "My morals must have rubbed off on me from my associates."

"I don't lie," said Allard, huffily.

"Did I mention any names?"

"If lying, or anything else, is rubbing off on you from *Harry,* you'll have to sew your balls back on when I find out about it." Damn. That should have come out much more threatening—if he'd been physiologically capable of being threatening.

"I think I quite like you being possessive," Vaughan told him.

"Sod!"

"Yes, you are. And a very good one too."

Allard tried to stop smiling. It didn't work.

Vaughan stroked his hair gently.

"Why am I still tied up?" Allard asked.

"Because you're such a bloody good fuck," Vaughan said, "that I have only just remembered." He sighed, and got up to undo various parts of Allard.

"That tickles," Allard told him.

"Yes. Thought you liked it."

Vaughan moved down to free his feet.

"At this stage, if you had miscalculated my enjoyment of the proceedings, I could kick you in the face," Allard told him. Vaughan began to look a little worried. There was a silence.

"Luckily, you didn't." Allard liked his partners to be quite aware of what a terribly difficult job it was to please him. However, there was no need to frighten them out of trying it again.

Vaughan kissed the sole of his foot, which was slightly ticklish and surprisingly enjoyable. It was very nice. A little more worshipping at his feet, and he might even forget that he'd been on the bottom this time.

"Up here," he said, and stretched his arms out. Oddly enough, he didn't *quite* want to forget that he'd been on the bottom this time.

Vaughan accommodated him with a long, thorough cuddle.

A thought struck him. "I suppose my other treat has melted?"

Vaughan glanced down between them. "Yes, seems to have."

Allard clouted Vaughan with a pillow. "I meant the *ice cream.*"

"No, actually. I put it on ice. Twenty minutes is a long time to keep a tub of ice cream waiting."

Allard thought it had been a fairly long time to keep *him* waiting, but decided not to gratify Vaughan's vanity by saying so.

Local Manners

"Only a complete idiot would have set this system up this way in the first place, and then invite somebody in to un-botch it," said Allard without thinking.

"Pardon?" said Baker, the local yokel.

Even Allard could see that what he'd just said was not the best thing to say to the people who were ultimately paying their wages. Which was, of course, Vaughan's fault. He knew Allard well enough by now (carnally and otherwise) to have some idea why it wasn't a good idea to invite *Allard* down-planet to make nice to the customers. Or at least Vaughan damn well ought to know Allard well enough. Most of his previous colleagues had taken rather less than two months to find out what he was like, and he hadn't been sharing living quarters as well as an office with them. Or screwing them for the last month.

"I apologise for my associate," said Vaughan. "Unfortunately, the best Bastard Operator From Hell we could find conforms entirely to the stereotype."

Baker asked Vaughan, a little helplessly, why they allowed Allard to stay with them, given his personality. Allard decided that, for once in his life, he should be diplomatically silent and actually let Vaughan answer that, instead of butting in.

Astonishingly enough, the others also refrained from butting in.

Vaughan said, "Well, he's completely brilliant with computers."

"That can't be all of it. What's he like politically?"

"I haven't given up hope of *one day* convincing him of the syndicalist cause, however hard he tries not to be convinced."

Baker looked slightly shocked. "But there must be hundreds, or at least about twenty, people who can use a computer and have The Right Attitude. What's the real reason?"

"Not that it matters to the others, it's a purely selfish reason, but he's a *bloody* good fuck," Vaughan said.

Baker looked slightly more shocked, and as if he were trying not to be.

Allard tried not to laugh, but didn't bother to hide the fact that he was trying not to laugh.

Baker turned to him. "All right, why do *you* stay with *him?*"

"Well, he pays me on time, if I remind him, and the work's not too boring."

"No personal reasons?"

"Well, he's the best fuck I've had all month," he said politely.

"Allard, I'm the *only* fuck you've had all month!" Vaughan put in indignantly.

"Ah. That's probably why, then," he said calmly.

Baker looked around as if searching for an island of sanity in a perverse universe. "How do the rest of you feel about him being kept on as the captain's whore?"

"How dare you call me the captain!"

"How dare you call me his whore!"

"So you're not the captain?" Baker said doubtfully. "Who is, then?"

"Actually, he is. But he won't let us mention it," said Allard.

"No, actually, the truth is that we have joint ownership," Claire said. "If we need a decision reached in a hurry, Vaughan takes responsibility for it as often as not."

"And you're not sleeping with him?" Baker sounded equally confused by that.

"Sleeping doesn't necessarily come into it. I *meant*," said Allard, with heavy patience, "that you seem to be making an unjustified assumption about sexual dominance that it took me about a night to fuck out of Vaughan." He paused, and then said thoughtfully, "I quite thoroughly enjoyed doing that." He checked Vaughan was within reach, and patted his property.

"So," said Baker doggedly, "what do the rest of you feel about it?"

"Well, it explains why Allard hasn't been the way he usually is—a vicious, sarcastic, frustrated bastard," said Harry. "I can't believe I missed that!" he muttered under his breath, "I went on night shift and forgot to set my bugging devices before I left. There's always something bloody *on* when I forget!"

Allard was quite surprised at that. He would have thought that Harry would have noticed by now that Allard had been carefully un-setting his bugs, even if he hadn't been able to bypass Allard's tricks.

Baker stared at Harry. "So—you're a voyeur?"

Claire rolled her eyes. "Give the man a cigar," she said wearily.

"Strictly equal opportunity," said Harry. "Men with men, women with men or women—if it moans, I'll listen!"

"And," said Baker, bemused, "you lot put up with this?"

"As long as they do the work," said Karen, "we don't feel we need to make a fuss about their personal lives. He's an appraiser—he values things," she added at Baker's blank look. "He's very good at it, and Allard's extremely good at his computer work. Why *wouldn't* we put up with their personal habits?"

"In other words, they're irritating but harmless," said Claire.

"Rather a good description of Harry," muttered Allard.

"A better description of you would be bloody annoying but harmless," said Claire.

He bowed slightly. "Accurate, apart from the 'harmless' part."

"Fuck him more often, Vaughan," Claire said. "It does wonders for his disposition."

His smirk slipped. It *did* do wonders for his disposition, but it would never do to have people notice that. Anyway, all this bitching was putting him in a bad mood, and it was approaching time to take Vaughan behind that bush and…just take Vaughan, in fact. "Can we get on with it?" he snapped.

"Wait until we've finished our business," Claire said. "He can fuck you later."

He would have said 'that's not what I meant', but in fact it *was* what he'd meant, apart from the difference in position. He turned his attention to business, and tried to be nice and not mention the fact that the set-up was an appalling mess too often.

Vaughan glared at him every time he wrinkled his nose and shuddered.

Allard decided that Vaughan hadn't realised that the glare was enough of a turn-on to make him even *less* likely to behave. Except badly, of course.

* * *

Two hours later (it had been two hours even if it felt like two months; he'd checked on his watch), he was grateful to hear Vaughan declare a refreshment break.

Considering what needed refreshment, Vaughan would be lucky to have time for a cup of coffee. Afterwards.

They left the main picnic behind and picked up the basket with the tea and coffee. Allard wasn't impressed by the idea of a picnic, but kept quiet. He'd actually mentioned that on the ship, and Claire had said, "We know you don't like going into the big room with the blue ceiling, Allard, but the rest of us want some fresh air." This was unfair. He didn't have anything against fresh air. Just ants, wasps, caterpillars and anything else that wanted to crawl inside the sandwiches. Not that that would put him off rolling around on the grass with Vaughan. Vaughan would be underneath; he could worry about the ants and the grass stalks and the putting-his-back-out.

"There's a rather nice bush there," he whispered to Vaughan.

"Yes, and Harry's already noticed you noticing it," Vaughan whispered back. "Do you want an audience?"

It was a rather more intriguing thought than he felt entirely comfortable with. "By this point, I don't think I care."

"Could I point out that equally attractive haystack a few yards beyond it? If lust hasn't narrowed your vision too much, of course," said Vaughan.

"Prickly," snapped Allard.

"So are you. And it's a traditional trysting-place—where's your sense of romance?"

Allard sneered. "Strangled at birth, I hope."

"It's a good thing I only like you for the size of your cock," said Vaughan.

Allard was glad that was at least partly true, and secretly glad it wasn't entirely true. To distract himself from this line of thought, he started considering the technical aspects of fucking in a haystack. "Won't work: nowhere to put the lubricant. And above all, it's prickly."

"Didn't think you minded the odd prick here and there," Vaughan said on cue. "Anyway, who says we've got to fuck?" He moved up even closer. "We can fantasise about having to do it quick and quiet because we've just *got* to, never mind about it isn't sensible."

"Where's the fantasy in that? That's reality, if you hadn't noticed."

"Exactly!" grinned Vaughan, and grabbed Allard's hand. "Come on, then."

Allard considered resisting just to teach Vaughan a lesson, and decided that it would be more enjoyable to go along with it for now and show Vaughan the error of his ways later.

Vaughan, who had the luck of the devil, managed to find a ladder. When they had climbed up, they found a nice warm dent in the haystack where someone else had obviously been doing much the same thing as they were thinking about. "See?" said Vaughan. "It *was* a good idea!"

They crawled off the ladder and into the dent. It was a warm, if prickly, place.

"Now," murmured Vaughan a moment later, pulling a straw out of his mouth, "I've dragged you into this haystack completely against your will, Allard, and I'm going to have my wicked way with you whether you like it or not."

Allard hoped Vaughan didn't know quite how much effect that low voice had on him. He could always try going on top later.

"And you're not going to scream…" Vaughan murmured, although Allard was slightly unsure about that.

"You're not going to make a sound as I ravish you," said Vaughan, "because there are loads of people a few feet away from this haystack, and you don't want them to know what's happening to your maidenly virtue."

Allard did his best to remember when he'd had maidenly virtue (about twenty years ago) and decided that being quietly ravished had distinct possibilities.

Vaughan poked one finger into Allard's shirt and rubbed a nipple.

Allard tried not to make any noise at all.

Vaughan crooned. "There's a sweet little thing now. I'm not going to hurt you. Well, not much."

Allard remembered that Vaughan was a couple of years younger than him, and instantly filed-and-forgot that datum.

For the purposes of this fantasy, the facts that he wanted to remember were height (Vaughan had at least three inches on him) and weight (at least three stone heavier, which by all reason should feel uncomfortable rather than erotic). There was one sense in which he had an inch's advantage on Vaughan, but he'd probably remind Vaughan of that next time they reversed roles. There was a time and a place for everything.

This was the time and the place to 'fight back' against his 'ravisher'. He did so. As he bucked and swore (very quietly) and wriggled, his cock rubbed again and again against Vaughan, and he moved more and more rhythmically.

"You've forgotten I'm ravishing you, Allard," said Vaughan smugly. "Can't even get decent virgins nowadays."

"Think of it as a compliment to your manhood that you have overcome my maidenly fears and transformed me into a raving slut," murmured Allard, licking Vaughan's ear.

"I think I'll break you in for the white slave trade and sell you on to a brothel."

For a fair price, I hope, thought Allard, but decided this wasn't in character and just squeaked. Then he squeaked again, as Vaughan demonstrated just how his resistance was to be broken down, with a good hard grip on Allard's cock through his trousers.

This made Allard lie down with no resistance at all, and Vaughan took the opportunity to undo Allard's trousers. "Mm," he said appreciatively. "Not exactly maidenly grey flannel any more, is it?"

"Your poor, endangered virgin is on the way to his wedding night, and you're going to steal the benefit of the clothes he put on to tempt his husband."

Vaughan stole a grope immediately. "Mm. Silk."

Mm. Silk, thought Allard, and, *It's not only prettier than flannel, it seems to magnify every caress so that I can feel it all over me...* and, *Keep doing that, Vaughan!* and...

"You're getting quiet, my little debauched maiden," said Vaughan. "I'll have you confessing that you're enjoying this before I'm done with you."

"Please, sir," whimpered Allard, carefully not specifying whether he meant *please stop* or *please don't stop.*

"No," said Vaughan. "Your tears won't sway me. I mean to have you, and what I want I get."

"Where did you get this script?" murmured Allard, to distract himself from the fact that he felt he was enjoying even such corny dialogue.

"I always thought it ought to be my turn to gag you, next," Vaughan muttered. "But I never got 'round to it. Even when I was fully prepared. But luckily I've been carrying a hanky in my pocket just in case you'd let me..."

"I hope that's not a used—mmph!" said Allard indignantly.

"Well, if you're going to critique my script, I can critique yours. Shut up, Allard."

Allard decided he couldn't bite through the hanky.

"Now you can try to scream all you want. Nobody will hear you now. Not even when I do *this.*" Vaughan gave him a very thorough grope.

Allard bucked violently but silently. Vaughan nearly lost his grip.

"You're not going to escape that easily," whispered Vaughan.

Good, thought Allard.

Vaughan kneeled up a bit, leaving Allard flat on his back, and started to undo his own trousers. He was certainly enjoying this, even if he *was* a terrible scriptwriter. Allard stared greedily at the result, and noticed Vaughan noticing.

"Yes, take a good look, my pretty one. Bet you've never seen a real man before. Not like that fool you were going to marry." He grabbed Allard's hand and dragged it to his cock. "Feel that. Nice handful, isn't it?"

Allard had just about enough time to realise that Vaughan had indeed improved his underwear, and that it was now a sensible colour rather than fluorescent yellow, before he noticed that it was silk. Mm. Silk. Why had nobody told him it felt just as good to touch from the *outside?* Actually, somebody probably had, but this was quite…

He did a quick dimensional check of what was under the silk. There was plenty of it. It slid and moved interestingly in his hand. He moaned quietly.

"No, I will not have pity on you," said Vaughan.

He's enjoying this fantasy rather too much, thought Allard, looking at Vaughan's face. *If it wasn't for his basic decency, he'd quite like to actually do this to me.* He wasn't entirely comfortable with that, nor was he entirely comfortable with how interested his cock was getting. Vaughan wasn't touching him now, and he was aching, and rubbing at Vaughan so that he got the most peculiar tactile echoes in his own cock, and…

"That's enough of that," said Vaughan. "I'm not going to rape you."

Allard panted into his hanky. *I do hope he's going to do* something.

"I'm going to show you," said Vaughan, stroking Allard's wrist as he kept moving, "how much of a pleasure sex can be." Vaughan's other hand went unerringly to Allard's cock and began to rub it through the silk. "You can keep doing me," he said. "I'm just giving you an incentive."

Allard liked that. He liked the way silk moved against his cock—and against Vaughan's. They'd tried playing games before, but he hadn't had that true illicit thrill of the real possibility of getting caught since he was a teenager. Nor had he done much with silk (although he was now wondering why). He was by no means a virgin, but this *was* a new experience.

He whimpered softly. This time it wasn't for effect.

"Yes," murmured Vaughan. "You like that, don't you?"

Vaughan wasn't saying that for effect, either.

Allard whimpered again, and spread his legs a bit.

"You will enjoy it," said Vaughan. "I'll see to that." He gently, teasingly, released Allard's cock from the silk underwear and equally gently pushed the silk down under Allard's balls, displaying them and taking the opportunity to fondle them. "That's more comfortable now, isn't it?"

Allard was uncomfortably aware that back when he had been some approximation of a nervous virgin, this sort of forced seduction from an older, more experienced man would probably have worked.

Vaughan seemed to pick up on that. Taking his hand from Allard's bits, he reached to stroke his face gently with a fingertip, as if to say, *yes, there's a person in there, not just a sex toy.* "I will be careful with you," he murmured, quite seriously.

How dare he notice, Allard thought crossly. It made this more real, and it was too real already.

Then Vaughan moved abruptly and slightly clumsily, bending down to suck the very tip of Allard's cock. Allard stopped caring about what was real or not.

Vaughan was good at this. *Why did we always waste so much time fucking?* Allard thought, slightly dizzily, as Vaughan gave him the benefit of a virtuoso performance. First the tip, very delicately, and then about half the shaft—if it wasn't so good, he'd be trying to move to get himself further down Vaughan's throat, but he was at the stage where he couldn't really move. It felt wonderful. It would be good manners to— but he couldn't reach anyway, and all Vaughan seemed to want him to do was lie back and enjoy himself, so he did. Vaughan tightened the suck, sort of moaned around him, quiet but very noticeable, and Allard gave himself up to pleasure. A little more of this, and he'd...

Vaughan stopped, and moved away.

Have you lost your mind! snapped Allard's brain, while his mouth came out with yet another bloody whimper.

"Shh," soothed Vaughan. "I will take care of you."

Come here and let me kill you with my bare hands for stopping! He whimpered again.

Vaughan tucked him back inside his silk underwear. *He* has *lost his mind!* Allard decided furiously. He moaned, and tried to get Vaughan's hands rubbing him instead of tidying him up. He moaned again, rather plaintively, when he felt the silk move against the heat of his cock. It felt good—of *course* it felt good— but the idea was to get him out of his clothes, unless this was Vaughan's idea of a joke.

"I told you that you'd be begging me for it by this time," Vaughan murmured softly. "You're not the first, you know." He lay down on Allard, silk against cock against silk. "I like to hear them say it. Tell me you want me."

He took the handkerchief off.

"Please fuck me," Allard begged quietly, before his brain caught up with what he was saying.

"It will be my pleasure." Vaughan kissed him. "Although I think fucking had better wait for another day, no matter how eager you are for your innocence to be defiled." He began to move against Allard slowly. "You'll have to content yourself with this, for now."

This shouldn't be so good, Allard thought. They were hardly doing anything, and the weight and heat and satisfying armful shouldn't be quite enough to make up for the fact they were in the wrong place (he thrashed and shuddered helplessly) and were still in their clothes (silk slid against his cock) and were only a hedge away from the rest of the party getting horrifically embarrassed at what they were doing.

At this point, Vaughan prudently clapped a hand over Allard's mouth.

Allard would have either protested or bitten him, except that he was too busy coming to think of doing anything else, and there was nothing but wet silk and frantic silence and the feel of it.

* * *

When his brain rebooted, he realised that Vaughan had come, as well.

Vaughan moved his hand.

"That," murmured Allard, "was quite intense."

"My god," said Harry. "I didn't realise *this* was what you did together."

Allard and Vaughan looked at each other, and then peered over the edge of the haystack.

Harry looked slightly shocked.

Allard was as annoyed as was physically possible, which wasn't terribly. Well, they all knew what Harry was like, although he'd like to know what gave Harry the right to feel shocked, considering what he liked doing. Being Allard, he said so.

"Isn't it a little hypocritical to look that disturbed, considering you undoubtedly *came* looking for us." He looked pointedly at Harry's crotch.

"All right, I liked it. Wasn't expecting it to be that…kinky, is all."

"What a very vanilla voyeur," Allard alliterated.

"I was expecting you to just feel each other up or something."

"Harry, that was frottage. If you think that's disturbing, maybe you have a future as someone's maiden aunt."

"It's not the bits," complained Harry. "It's the fact you were both wittering on about raping virgins."

"No virgins were actually harmed in the making of this fantasy," Vaughan put in. "I can assure you that Allard was not a virgin. Though I rather regret not meeting him when he was."

Harry thought that one through for about two seconds before looking even more shocked. Then he seemed to settle for changing the subject. "Anyway, I just came to tell you two that your tea and your coffee are getting cold."

"So am I," said Allard regretfully, doing up his trousers.

"Have you got a hanky?" asked Harry. "I'd hate to have people think I was doing something peculiar with both of you."

"Harry, you *were* doing something peculiar with both of us, even if we didn't know it at the time," Vaughan said. "In fact, we have a handkerchief, slightly chewed…"

Harry squeaked.

"…although I don't think it'll go round among three of us," Vaughan concluded.

Allard contemplated the hanky, which he'd forgotten, and decided that the silk knickers would do a very good job of confining any messiness. Nothing at all to do with the concept of his cock sliding against wet silk every time he moved. "Be my guest," he said, and tossed the hanky to Harry, who tried to catch it between fingernail and thumbnail.

"It's only spit," said Allard crossly.

Harry wiped himself up, and looked as if he wasn't sure whether to give the hanky back.

"No thanks," said Vaughan. "But cleaning up would be a very good idea." He started picking bits of straw out of Allard's hair rather tenderly.

"Oh, sweet!" said Harry.

"No it's not!" snapped Allard. "Vaughan is merely grooming me like a pet monkey—which is about the level of his social behaviour."

"You *did* enjoy it, didn't you," said Vaughan, just as Harry said, "I thought fucking him was meant to improve his disposition."

"It did," said Vaughan. "You saw what he was like first."

Allard considered this as a serious point. In fact, he thought, he was capable of going back to deal with the abominable level of tech on this planet for the next two hours without making *any* rude remarks about it. He'd need caffeine, though.

He slid down the haystack, and Vaughan slid after him. He was halfway towards the siren scent of the coffee-pot before he noticed that Vaughan had taken hold of his hand and he was therefore hand-in-hand with Vaughan.

This didn't bother him as much as it should have. Apparently, sex really *did* do something for his disposition, although he wasn't entirely sure it was an improvement.

He didn't even snarl when he realised that everybody else was smiling idiotically at the sight.

"You'd never guess what they were doing," said Harry.

"They can guess what you were doing," said Allard. "Would you like me to give them all the details?"

"Er, no thank you," said Harry, a man who, for a voyeur, could be amazingly shy about the details of his own sex life.

"All three of them," complained Claire. "You'd have thought the odds were in favour of me finding at least one straight man on this ship."

"Technically, we're all bisexual," said Allard. "You're just unlucky."

"I do like doing as well as listening," said Harry.

"I'm not *that* desperate," said Claire.

Harry muttered, "Why mention it, then?"

Vaughan said, "Back to work, ladies and gentlemen," very firmly.

Allard thought that was the nearest approach to firmness Vaughan could manage at the moment. He also wondered if any of them quite counted as ladies or gentlemen. From the look on

Baker's face, none of them had been exactly polite about their rather idiosyncratic approach to personal relationships. "Actually, Baker," he said quietly, pitching his voice so that only Baker would hear, "there is a good reason I hang around with this lot. It's one of the few workplaces where I can feel normally socialised in comparison to my colleagues."

Baker looked at him, seemed to be about to say something, and then visibly changed his mind. "Yes, I see what you mean."

Play-by-Play

Allard sat down with a cup of tea and a bowl of cereal, and reminded himself to finish both before he got onto the newsgroups. First, there was e-mail. He could have lots of fun with offers of money and offers of sex, even though, in point of fact, his life with Vaughan was actually interesting enough that he wasn't going to take any of them up. And even though most of them were spam.

He liked being on the sort of working ship where people didn't make a fuss about breakfast; they had one sit-down meal a day, and otherwise, it was quite acceptable to have snacks while working. He approved of this. For one thing, it meant that he actually *had* more meals than he would have if he'd had to go and sit down with other people.

There was a sizeable e-mail from Harry. What was Harry doing sending him an e-mail? They were on the same ship. The last time that had happened, he'd had a row with Harry, and they weren't on speaking terms. But in this case, they hadn't had a row. It was too long for the usual quick memo or report about the job they were on.

He opened it. It had two attachments. Oh, wonderful. Which virus was it this week? The first one was, as he expected, the virus executable. The second was whatever confidential file had been sent out to Harry's entire address book. He opened it. Better know the worst.

He heard a voice panting and gasping. A very familiar voice. It was saying, "Oh *yes,* Vaughan, more!" He clicked it off.

"Harry!"

He heard the stumbling footsteps of the new candidate for Least Favourite Crewmember.

"Er…Allard?" Harry had obviously learned that that tone of voice never preceded anything nice.

"Harry, I put up with your particular habits without comment most of the time, but that presupposes that you actually have some vague economic use to this ship. Which presupposes that you have some minimal awareness of data security…" He saw Harry open his mouth as if to ask 'what's that', and went on. "Which, as any child might know, involves *not* downloading a virus, and *not* letting the virus send confidential files to everybody in our address book. Even you, my little user, should understand that."

Harry said, "But how can it send files out? What sort of information can it send out?"

"Banking details. Passwords. Commercially sensitive reports that our rivals would simply love to get hold of."

Just to make Allard's joy complete, Vaughan came in just in time to hear the tail-end of that conversation. "Ah. Is Harry giving you a refresher course in basic economics?"

Allard counted to ten, and gave him a suitably expurgated account of what had been going on.

"Confidential files being sent out?" Vaughan said crossly. "Well, you'll just have to write a worm to go after it and delete it. Which file is it, by the way?"

Without comment, Allard played it for him.

"And that is your first priority, Allard."

"And my second priority is to give Harry a refresher course in how to download porn safely. I presume that *is* how you caught the virus, Harry?"

He went into the admin account and locked Harry's account. "Don't bother denying it. I'll find the evidence later."

He looked at Vaughan, who still seemed annoyed. *Oh, lovely, no more sex until I've cleared up the evidence of the last lot of sex...* "I suppose you want me to do it now and eat breakfast later."

"No. You can eat your breakfast while you're doing it, as long as it doesn't slow you down. I've noticed you're capable of doing that."

He assumed that was a comment on two mornings ago, when Vaughan had brought him breakfast-in-bed for their three-month anniversary, and had seemed annoyed while celebrating it. This was unreasonable. He hadn't actually *stopped* Vaughan fucking him—he'd just continued eating his breakfast. And the whole reason he was being so ill-mannered was that he'd been overworked and missed dinner.

"Can I get dressed first?"

"No."

He settled down to type one-handed. Vaughan did the decent thing and fed him more slices of toast. Within about ten minutes, he'd finished creating a counter-worm ready to follow in the tracks of the worm and file all sensitive data in the bit-bucket. He sent it on its way, remarking, "You do realise this won't help if somebody's already opened the e-mail."

"I'm not the person who's going to be embarrassed," said Vaughan.

"It's a long file," said Allard. "I think there's quite a bit of heavy grunting recognisable as you on there, as well."

"Heavy grunting?" muttered Vaughan indignantly.

"And besides, the way this virus works, that won't be the only file that's sent out."

Harry went white.

"We'll only kill you once each," said Allard reasonably.

"It's not you," confessed Harry. "It's the girls. I mean, Claire doesn't *know* I've been recording her."

"Yes, she does. She just doesn't know you're so stupid as to broadcast it to the rest of the galaxy."

"I *didn't!*" Harry wailed.

"I think we'd better find out exactly what you're harbouring on your share of the storage space."

Allard picked up a file at random. It was called SHOPPING-TRIP. He pressed 'play'. "Well, you were discussing ship's discipline the other day," said Vaughan's voice conversationally. "I have a little catalogue here, and I'm trying to decide what we might go in for. You like leather, don't you?"

"Yes, I like leather clothes," said his own voice.

Oh. He remembered that evening.

* * *

Allard looked at the catalogue. It wasn't any sort of leatherwear he'd ever worn before. It took some effort to keep his face calm and unmoved.

Vaughan just looked lecherous.

"Vaughan," Allard said uneasily, "you know when you found that whip in my drawer, and I said it was a present from a friend, that wasn't a euphemism."

"So why did your…friend…give you a present?" asked Vaughan.

"One of my friends gave me a whip and said it was for taming my computer with."

Vaughan collapsed in hysterical laughter.

"It's not *that* funny," said Allard.

"No, it's just so—you! Somehow I have no difficulty in believing that story."

"So you'll put the catalogue away?"

"No. I'm going to teach you the other recreational uses for whips," said Vaughan. Allard *thought* Vaughan was winding him up. Then he remembered what sort of games Vaughan had enjoyed to date.

"Don't worry, Allard," Vaughan said. "I'm not heavily into that myself. Just a bit…curious. It's a nice fantasy."

Allard sneaked a glance at the catalogue, and hastily flipped it back from the more exotic later chapters, which were definitely not his thing.

The more decorative items, on the other hand—he might even consider wearing one or two himself, as well as putting them on Vaughan. Decorative straps and harnesses might be a possibility.

He found a page of interesting-things-to-put-on-one's-penis. He flinched. He looked again, prepared to flip the page at the first sign of danger—no, they all looked entirely removable and, in some cases, rather interesting. In fact, those little rings had definite possibilities. And little leather *coats* to put on one's—in case it got cold, he supposed. He looked again. Yes, he'd have to believe that people modelled that part of the body.

"I'd wear one if you did, Vaughan. Dare you!"

"So you're interested," Vaughan said thoughtfully. An impertinent hand groped Allard. "Yes, you are."

"Don't get too enthusiastic. I might try it and decide I don't like it."

"So," said Vaughan, undoing him, "you're not too sure whether you like something wrapped round your cock like this. Tightly."

Allard gasped. "You already know what I like wrapped tightly around my cock, and your arse will do, for preference."

"Does that mean you want to go on top today?" Vaughan asked cheerfully.

"Bugger foreplay. Get your clothes off!" Allard ordered.

"Oh, you do want to bugger me, then?"

"How difficult is it to get simple instructions through to you, Vaughan?" He started undressing Vaughan himself. Fortunately, he quite enjoyed this. Vaughan wore loose, comfortable clothes that didn't get in the way too much. They were also pleasantly tactile; good-quality cloth that was always nice to handle.

"Well, get yours off, too," complained Vaughan. "This is a bit one-sided."

"Yes, isn't it? I decided to indulge your leather fantasy," said Allard, without removing his clothes. "Since I happen to be wearing leather trousers and jacket today."

"Yes, you are, aren't you?" said Vaughan thoughtfully.

Allard started wondering whether his normal clothes were giving undesirable impressions to other people, then decided that as long as they were giving desirable impressions to *Vaughan,* he wasn't going to worry about it now.

When Vaughan was naked, Allard said, "On the bed with you, and hurry up about it."

Vaughan scrambled to obey. Obviously he *did* quite like leather—on other people.

Allard admired the view. Vaughan had a lovely arse, especially quivering with anticipation like that.

Hastily grabbing the pot of lubricant beside the bed, Allard slapped some on.

"Sadist. You know that's cold."

"Yes. I know."

Vaughan wriggled. "Get on with it."

"No. I'm enjoying the anticipation." To his surprise, he was. Perhaps he should look at that catalogue with an eye to finding pretty decorations for Vaughan. Ones that would involve Vaughan not being able to move until he was given permission.

Right. That was it for the anticipation.

"Stand on the floor. Bend over the bed," he ordered. "I've had a good look, and I'm in a hurry now."

Vaughan muttered something about "don't forget to fetch a book to stand on."

Allard felt quite glad about the heels that he was wearing and Vaughan wasn't.

Vaughan seemed quite surprised that Allard could get all the way in without having to stand on top of something. He clamped down. It was a lovely sensation for Allard.

"I must try surprising you again," said Allard. "Frequently."

"You little bastard!" spluttered Vaughan.

"Obviously not quite as little as you expected, whether in height or in length," said Allard, as he proceeded to plough away with a will.

Apparently, he had distracted Vaughan from replying. Quite understandably. This was very enjoyable. Lovely, tight squeezing around his cock, enthusiastic grunting from Vaughan, lovely view of Vaughan's naked back bent in front of him. Yes, he would probably enjoy that view accented with light touches of leather.

He made sure he was comfortably mounted, hands grasping Vaughan's hips as he rode him hard. Only one thing would make the experience better, and once he was sure he wouldn't embarrass himself by falling over, he groped desperately in front for Vaughan's cock and began to pump at it mercilessly.

Vaughan gave a sharp, surprised cry.

"I like being able to control my mount," said Allard, working away at him.

Vaughan didn't seem to mind that, to judge by the way he thrust enthusiastically into Allard's hand. Allard liked that— Vaughan wouldn't be able not to make some sort of annoyed remark normally, if he wasn't too worked-up to think of one. Now, Vaughan couldn't think of anything to say. Well, nothing involving words, anyway.

Allard was getting closer to orgasm, too. Grinding himself in, swearing and gasping and enjoying the decadent feel of his fully-clothed body pushing urgently against his naked opponent.

"Ought to get myself…soft leather gloves," he panted. "Just to let you…feel that on your cock!" And squeezed, feeling Vaughan come in his hand as he flooded into Vaughan's equally tight arse. He was dizzy—enervated—happy—and definitely in need of something to collapse on. Vaughan, for preference.

He pushed. Vaughan collapsed on the bed. He collapsed on Vaughan. He would have to admit that he missed the usual warmth of skin-to-skin contact, but it felt very good all the same. He liked a good cuddle…

* * *

Back in the present day, Harry was looking nervous, and Vaughan was looking interested.

He never *had* got the leather gloves, and rather wished he had.

"Not quite as vanilla as you used to be, Harry, if you're keeping that one to listen to again. But then neither am I," he said.

Harry looked even more nervous, whether at the comment or the grin that went with it.

"We must make time to go to an appropriate shop. We still haven't bought any of that stuff yet." Vaughan rubbed absent-mindedly at his cock.

"Don't get too excited, Vaughan. There's rather a lot of this stuff to go through."

"Well, don't listen to all of it next time."

Allard sighed and settled down. The quickest way to sort this out would probably be to check the log of outgoing material, and make sure there was nothing that his own counter-worm would have missed.

He was happy to see that it hadn't been active very long. The virus hadn't worked its way through the entire address book, although it *had* selected a variety of files to send out. Fortunately, it wasn't just himself and Vaughan that were in line to be embarrassed. And fortunately, it *was* just embarrassing files and not commercial or financial ones.

He wondered whether he could get rid of Vaughan for long enough to take private copies of some of the dodgy files, since Vaughan was unfortunately sufficiently computer-literate to see what he was doing if he tried it in front of Vaughan.

"Weren't you about to go and get us some cups of tea, Vaughan?"

"Harry can do it."

Well, yes, Harry *was* still hanging around looking nervous.

"Harry. Two teas." Harry scuttled into the galley.

Vaughan leaned closer to Allard and whispered, "While he's out, shall we make some copies of these for ourselves?"

"What a reprehensible suggestion," Allard remarked, as he copied files to both his own and Vaughan's directories.

"If it is, why are you doing it?"

"You're the one with the morals, Vaughan. I don't need to explain myself, because everyone already *knows* exactly what I'm like."

"Yes, they do. Anyone who's too stupid to put proper security on their files *deserves* to have them read out."

"I don't know why you're smiling, Vaughan. That's completely accurate."

"Allard, dear, we hired you because *we* don't know enough to put proper security on our files."

"Yes, well…" Vaughan did have a point. It wasn't entirely sporting, under those circumstances. People who realised they were too stupid, and got outside help, did deserve marks for trying.

"I'll just have to give Harry remedial classes," said Allard. "In the meantime, where were we?"

"Well," said Vaughan, "I'm fairly sure we've cleaned up the mess. All of the pilfered files seem to come from the directory C:\NAUGHTY on Harry's machine. Shall we do a quick check on some more random files just to check that he *has* only got porn in there?"

Allard thought about it. Yes. He deserved a bit of a rest after all that work, and they could both enjoy "checking" the files.

Harry came back in with a tray of tea.

When Allard and Vaughan said what they'd be doing next, he seemed resigned. "Can I watch you listening to them?" he asked.

"Harry," said Vaughan, "don't you *ever* learn?"

Allard kept his thoughts to himself. They were along the lines of, "it might be interesting".

Vaughan flipped down the directory listing. "Ah. STORYTIME. What's in that file, I wonder? I've always liked being told stories."

Harry spluttered into his tea. "Er, you won't like that one!" he protested.

Allard smirked. That probably meant it was something they would both enjoy.

Vaughan apparently agreed, because he clicked 'play'.

Claire's voice said, "So what *do* you think they do? And which of them does it?"

"Vaughan's on top," said Karen with total certainty. "Look at Allard showing his bum off in tight trousers all the time. He must be trying to get a reaction."

"You know, she's right," said Vaughan thoughtfully.

"Yes, but they're just as tight in front. Why hasn't she noticed that?" Allard snapped crossly.

"Yes, it's very pretty," murmured Vaughan soothingly, caressing Allard's groin under cover of the table. Not discreetly enough; Harry seemed to be interested.

The women were still wibbling on about his bottom. "When he bends over in those tight leather trousers, aren't you ever just tempted to grab a handful?" said Karen wistfully.

"You have no idea how close I've come to doing it. And I use the word 'come' advisedly," said Claire, with a filthy laugh. "But it wouldn't be fair to take up an invitation he doesn't realise he's making."

"I never let it stop *me*," murmured Vaughan.

"Does it look like an invitation?" Allard asked curiously.

"Yes," said Harry.

Well, that seemed to be four votes. Allard decided to be a bit more careful about what he was wearing—at least when he wasn't trying to create an effect.

Karen said, "I certainly can't imagine Vaughan seeing that sweet little arse without wanting to cram himself in as fast and hard as possible."

Allard had always thought their weapons tech was a sweet, demure creature. Oh. Yes. A sweet, demure creature who worked with big long things and liked to make them go bang.

"Is *everyone* on this ship obsessed with sex?" Allard said.

"Yes," said Harry.

"Do you actually have a larger vocabulary than that, Harry?"

"Yes," said Harry, and grinned.

"She's right," added Vaughan. "Although she'd be shocked at how often you don't let me. Not that I have any complaints."

"Shut up," said Allard. "I want to listen to this."

Now they were praising Vaughan's very large cock. It wasn't as big as the girls thought, but it was quite big enough for Allard's purposes. He patted it, without worrying about Harry watching.

"Allard needs both hands to hold it," said Karen, on the tape.

"Almost true," he said, and demonstrated for Harry's benefit. Mm. Lovely. Not quite at its full extent, but give it a minute or two.

Vaughan looked at him, looked at Harry, and then looked at the ceiling.

"Working away at it," said Claire dreamily, "with one hand wandering down to fondle his balls occasionally."

Allard undid Vaughan's trousers, and demonstrated that he wasn't *completely* averse to taking suggestions.

Vaughan looked at him, looked at Harry, and closed his eyes.

Harry looked at them and didn't close his eyes.

"Why are we rewarding him for doing something wrong?" muttered Allard.

"Because you're enjoying it as well," said Harry. "Besides, this time you know I'm not recording it for posterity. Maybe that's my punishment. I'll only have my memories."

"Just how kinky *do* the girls get?" asked Allard mistrustfully.

"If they got that kinky, I'd suggest you switch to a different file," said Harry helpfully. "You know I don't like the really weird stuff."

"Weird? Mild BDSM?"

"Weird," said Harry.

Apparently, weird didn't include fellatio, which the girls were currently describing with great glee. "And after he's stripped naked for Vaughan to admire, he kneels between Vaughan's legs…"

"Big, lovely legs," said Claire.

"Nice, chunky thighs," Karen said.

Allard skipped the strip-tease routine and got down to the kneeling in front of Vaughan. There was a distinct thrill to doing this in front of an audience.

Harry said, very quietly and wistfully, "Naked would be better," just as Claire said, "And then he leans forward and licks just the tip of Vaughan's cock."

"Forget I said that," said Harry quickly.

"Shut up," said Vaughan, just as Allard followed directions. Mm, yes, slow had its points, Allard thought to himself.

Karen said, "And then he nibbles very delicately around the foreskin."

He did so. There was a squeak from Harry's direction, and a happy groan from above.

"He slips the very tip of his tongue *just* under Vaughan's foreskin," said Claire, "and shows some of the delicate work with fiddly little details he's really good at."

Allard did his best, hoping that his press wouldn't turn out to be better than the reality. Judging by the noises Vaughan was making, he had at least some idea how to do this. Vaughan wasn't the only one enjoying this, either. He'd always felt powerful when he was on top, but somehow this was even better—something to do with the way Vaughan was begging him for more, perhaps.

"And just as Vaughan is begging him for more, Allard gives it to him. Half the length at one swallow, even if it is eight inches long," Karen remarked.

Six, actually, Allard thought. Not that he was complaining. It meant he could get more than half the length in at one swallow. Very good it was, too. Vaughan must have showered just before this, as he tasted nicely fresh but full of flavour.

He grabbed another mouthful just before Karen suggested that he ought to.

The position was mildly uncomfortable: He was used to doing this without wearing a collar (he started to think about the catalogue again, by a matter of association, and firmly reined himself in…reined himself in? He was not even going to think about that).

He slid off again, reluctantly. The next thing he heard was Claire saying, "And then Vaughan just grabs his head and forces him on, all the way down."

The timing was off—Vaughan had already done that.

He made a muffled protest, fumbling at his collar. That was better. He fumbled at his trousers. That was better, as well.

"I'd never have thought you were bigger," said Harry.

I'm the one with the tight trousers, Allard thought.

"He's the one with the tight trousers," Vaughan said helpfully. "Did you think it was a codpiece?"

Harry said, "Well, it's just something about the way you behave, Vaughan. As if you think you have a really big one."

I am the only one allowed to say that sort of thing about Vaughan! Even if it is true, Allard thought. Anyway, Vaughan did have nice big balls. He did a quick comparison check, one hand on his own and the other on Vaughan's. Yes, Vaughan definitely won in the ball department.

"At this point," Karen said, "Vaughan decides that Allard is Not Doing A Good Enough Job, because Vaughan can't get it *all* the way in."

Allard said, "Mm," around Vaughan, thinking that he was doing a bloody good job.

Vaughan just grunted, but didn't sound as if he was asking Allard to stop.

Harry said, "I think you're doing a damn fine job, Allard."

Claire said, "So he pulls him up by the hair."

Allard pulled off, just in case. "Don't you *dare!*" he said, glaring.

Karen said, "And throws him on the floor and stuffs his big cock into the other end."

Do I really want him to do that in front of Harry? Allard wondered.

He looked at Vaughan. Vaughan did look desperate for something.

Do I really care that it's in front of Harry? Receiving the answer *no, not really,* from either his brain or his balls, he wasn't sure which, he landed on the floor, saying "Get on with it, then!"

Vaughan ripped Allard's trousers down just far enough to get access to him without tying his legs together. The thought of having his legs tied together was interesting, but not terribly practical in this position, which was going to be difficult enough anyway.

Vaughan shoved, and Allard wished the women had thought to mention lube. Fortunately, he'd been having fun in the shower that morning. It was merely mildly uncomfortable, shading into 'quite interesting' as Vaughan got a little further. Even if they weren't this way up most often, Vaughan *did* know how he liked it.

Apparently, the women had a fair idea, as well. "Now he's wriggling and panting and moaning and pleading for more," suggested the running commentary. Yes, he *was.* It was quite disgraceful, really. He ought to stop. Just as soon as Vaughan stopped doing *that,* anyway. He'd defy anyone to stop panting when Vaughan was doing that.

The panting sounded louder than usual—well, there was more of it. Ah yes, Harry. He looked round.

Yes, the rest of the panting was coming from that direction. Harry seemed to be thoroughly enjoying the sight of Allard spread and pinioned like this. Allard wished him well. He was physiologically incapable of wishing anything else, even considering how annoyed he was with Harry. Quite apart from the file security, here Harry was discovering a hidden exhibitionist in Allard.

Allard tried to arch up a bit and show off his cock, but couldn't with all that weight on him.

Vaughan misinterpreted that as Allard trying to hint he needed a hand with (or on) his cock.

Harry said, "Yes, that's it, nice bit of hand-work there." Well, Allard couldn't argue with that. It was even more exciting having *Harry's* commentary because it was real, not potential. Harry was actually watching rather than imagining.

"Don't suppose you could kneel up a bit and give me a better view?" Harry asked.

To Allard's surprise, Vaughan cooperated.

Harry fell silent.

"Keep talking, Harry," said Allard.

Harry muttered something about "can't a man have a quiet little wank in peace on this ship?"

"No. Tell us about your wank," Vaughan said.

That was a surprise to Allard, who thought he'd been doing too good a job for Vaughan to be coherent. He squeezed down hard.

Vaughan groaned.

So did Harry.

Vaughan started working his hand a bit faster.

Harry said, "Yes, that's it. That's the speed I want to wank at, as well."

Allard thought, *I should have the casting vote here, but actually the speed's not bad.* He forbore to say anything.

Harry was still talking. "God, it's wonderful watching you two at it, instead of having to imagine it. And it's normal sex, as well."

"Normal sex," said Allard haughtily, "doesn't come with a stroke-by-stroke commentary."

"Oh? Good job you do, then!" said Vaughan.

"I'm not quite there yet," said Allard.

Harry said, "Yes, it's wonderful just watching that big cock of Vaughan's ramming into you and pulling out again, and yet again. Yes, that's it, Vaughan." Allard agreed with that; the ramming-in and pulling-out felt very nice indeed.

"Wank him a bit harder," Harry suggested. "You haven't got him really begging yet."

"What makes you think I—oh *god,* do that again!" said Allard.

Harry described the beauty of Allard's face when he was too fucked to talk, just staying there with his mouth hanging open. "If I wasn't more interested in watching, I might come over and see what I could do with that mouth myself."

Vaughan slammed right in. Obviously, he found that an appealing mental picture. To his horror, so did Allard.

"Good," said Harry. "Looks as though you both like that thought. Bet it's a good way of shutting Allard up for once."

"It is," said Vaughan. "Mind you, fucking him senseless works quite well, too."

Allard would have agreed with that if he hadn't been busy being fucked almost senseless. Almost wasn't quite good enough. He shoved back onto Vaughan.

"Oh, you are an eager little slut," said Harry. "I like that in a man." He'd obviously got bolder, or at least figured out when Allard was going to let him say things like that without doing something unpleasant to him.

"And," Harry went on, "I love the way your cock jumps in Vaughan's hand when I say things like that."

Allard scraped together enough brain-cells to say, "Just one more good squeeze and I'm there!"

All of them moaned.

"So Vaughan gives him a good hard squeeze, like *this*," said Harry, obviously doing it.

Allard pictured the scene in his mind. There he was, Vaughan stuffed right up him, his cock plunging tightly in Vaughan's hand, Harry with his trousers down wanking himself stupid…

"It occurs to me…" he said, speaking with difficulty, "what would the women think of us if they walked in *now?*" The last word trailed away into a cry of slightly shocked bliss, as he came explosively.

"Fuck, you *pervert!*" gasped Harry, evidently doing the same thing.

Vaughan could only manage a deep groan as he followed their lead. As soon as he finished, he collapsed on Allard, rather heavily.

* * *

A few minutes later, Harry passed them a hanky. "When do you think the women arrive for breakfast?" he asked.

Allard noticed that Harry had used the hanky first. "Get a serviette. No, get two serviettes." He wiped up far more hastily than he would have done if he'd been somewhere private. He'd actually have *liked* long, lazy moments of afterglow, but not in the crew-room when people were expected for breakfast.

Unless they actually *had* come in. He shuddered. There had been a few seconds there when he possibly would not have noticed. Given that their voices had been on the recording, he might even have regarded any commentary as part of that.

No. Harry would have noticed, even if he and Vaughan hadn't.

In fact, he could hear footsteps as he wiped up the last stains.

"So, what's been going on?" said Claire. "Smells like a male brothel in here, incidentally."

"Harry's been downloading porn to look at over breakfast," said Vaughan, with a perfectly straight face.

"Revolting!" said Claire. "Look at it in your bedroom and keep the smell to yourself."

Allard sniffed. He didn't object to the smell particularly. But then, he supposed, he'd already eaten his breakfast.

Karen poured herself a bowl of cornflakes and reached for the milk. She paused. "This *is* milk, right, Harry?"

"Nag, nag, nag," said Harry. "I can see my day is going to go right downhill from this point."

"Yes," said Claire. "Miss Big and Bouncy was the high point, as usual."

"Actually," said Allard, "Harry's porn is more tasteful than that sometimes. But he ought to be careful that he downloads *only* porn and not viruses. If I might remind everybody of that. We don't want any *more* confidential files sent out."

"Harry," the women said in unison.

"It's all right," Harry said, "Allard's cleaned it up." He winked, but since this was fairly usual for Harry, they didn't seem to worry about it.

"Most of it," said Allard. "Some of it may have escaped."

He walked over to one of the terminals and checked the progress of his counter-worm.

There was an e-mail for him, from a name he didn't recognise. It was to the address he'd used for the notification of what his worm was doing, should anyone query it.

"What's that?" asked Harry, as Allard must have betrayed some slight sign of surprise.

"It's…a job offer," Allard said. "Somebody who was so impressed at how quickly I cleared the worm up that he wants me to clean up his computer security."

"How much?" asked Vaughan.

"Enough," said Allard.

"Accept it," said Vaughan.

Allard gave him one of those what-makes-you-think-I-need-your-economic-advice looks. He'd been sorting out which jobs paid well enough for some time.

"Incidentally, Harry, it was one of your contacts." He paused. "And it was, in fact, two job offers. The other one was a recording contract with his company Bedtime Stories Ltd, which he thinks could benefit from the use of my voice."

"You don't have to accept that job offer," said Vaughan.

Allard looked at him for long enough to establish the fact that he could follow his own judgement and was *certainly not* rejecting that offer because of something Vaughan had said.

Everyone on this crew knew when not to comment on something Allard had said. Or not said.

"I do hope the *only* reason he knew what my voice sounded like was because he got a copy of one of your recordings by *accident*."

Karen and Claire looked entirely too interested at that. He hadn't described the file, but they *knew* the sorts of things Harry tended to record.

"No! No!" said Harry hastily. "Only a purchaser, absolutely not a seller. I only buy stuff from him—I've never sold him anything."

"The only way I can be sure of that is to sit right down and read all of your e-mail. Or were you lying?"

"Yes," said Karen. "There're all of our files to check as well, make sure he hasn't sent any of *our* voices for an audition."

"Good move," said Vaughan.

It was so nice to have the support of the crew.

Allard looked forward to an interesting evening. He believed Harry in fact had *not* sold his voice to the highest bidder, but he was still expecting to dig up plenty of dirt on his trawl through Harry's in-box, and Harry couldn't even complain about it. Life was good.

Be Careful What You Wish For

A faint swearing came over the link.

That was all right; Allard had been doing a lot of swearing of his own. In fact, he had cause to swear at it again. "Fucking firewall!" he muttered, finally realising exactly why one part of the program wasn't working.

"You needn't give me progress reports on exactly *how* you're trying to coax the hardware, Allard," Vaughan said mildly.

Allard ran that back through his internal parser. "You've got a filthy mind. I was merely trying to make this work."

"Thought you liked the filthy mind," muttered Vaughan *sotto voce.* "No, actually the picture I was getting from the verbal description was difficult to ignore."

"Well, at least we should have the Whiteboard function operational now," said Allard. "You can draw me an obscene picture if you really want to, Vaughan."

"What a crap obscene picture!" came a piping voice, faintly, over the link, as the image of a fairly wobbly cock and balls traced onto the blank square for visuals or maps.

"Harry would like to point out that he is used to a better quality of pornography," said Vaughan.

"I would have to agree with him," said Allard. He crossed a thick black line through the image, erased, and drew a lovingly detailed set of quite recognisable male parts, and a few extras.

"Wossat then?" said Harry from the other end.

"Somebody I know."

"Well, we can all see that," said Harry impatiently. "But I meant the weird metal thing." His faint voice was drowned out by Vaughan saying, "When did I get a Prince bloody Albert, Allard?" rather indignantly.

"It's a possible project for my spare time," said Allard. "I'm capable of visualising layouts quite well by now, and implementing them later on. I have quite a lot of practice. Not with penile adornments, admittedly, but I'm sure the basic principles apply."

"How's your art so much better, anyway?"

"I have a decent graphics tablet at this end," said Allard smugly, "and a photograph."

A photograph, not of Vaughan's face, fluttered across the Shared Files area of the program.

"When the hell did you take that?" muttered Vaughan.

"When I could get no more fun out of you in other ways but you were sprawled across the bed snoring and stopping me sleeping," Allard said.

"You didn't draw me asleep. You drew me…interested."

"I could put that in from memory. I have spent hours admiring it, as I'm sure you can remember."

"Looking at it?"

"Not necessarily." Allard could probably have done the picture with his tongue (which knew every inch) if his tongue could have handled the graphics tablet.

"Shut up, Allard. Harry will notice something."

"Harry has had to bloody listen to it for the last three months," said Harry. "Neither of you are that quiet. In fact, I've got a recording here. You could use it to test the link."

Allard said, "I thought you liked listening."

"I like listening to the normal stuff," said Harry. "You two are perverted. It's all right if I'm recording; I can switch it off if I'm not in a kinky mood. But when it's coming live through the walls and you're on your 'virgin' fetish, it's a bit much. And I could have done without finding out about—what'd he call it? Prince Alberts? as well." He shuddered. "There's such a thing as too much information, even for a voyeur."

Allard said, "It was only a suggestion. Not even a serious one."

"I didn't want to know it was possible!" wailed Harry.

"Allard," said Vaughan, "you *are* going to clean out all the log records from tonight's setting-up, aren't you?"

"You mean the chat log where you were swearing into the computer? You mentioned a number of practices I hadn't realised you were aware of. Shall we try some of them later?"

"What chat log?" Vaughan said.

Allard rolled it up on screen.

"Just looks like a lot of cross-hatching from here," muttered Vaughan.

"Patience," said Allard. He was used to saying that to Vaughan, usually when he was wearing leather underwear and trying to get Vaughan to peel him inch by inch. He opened the file as a shared file.

Vaughan said, "Oh! It's popped up!"

Harry said, "Yes it has, hasn't it?"

Allard said, "Hands off, he's mine. If anyone's going to be the beneficiary of any popping-up, it's me."

Harry said, "When I first met you, I thought you were the most frigid, repressed geek I'd ever seen."

"Then you realised it was only you that had that impression."

"He means," said Vaughan, "that I was screwing him blind once a night and twice on Sundays, so he was only frigid with you."

"Thank you, Vaughan," said Allard frostily. "I am quite sure that even Harry could pick up the subtext of that conversation without being whacked over the head with it. Now, back to the subject. Vaughan, you need to try requesting control."

"As if *that* ever works!" muttered Vaughan.

"Of the file, I meant," said Allard.

"Can't figure out how to request control."

"What a surprise," muttered Allard. "Go to the menu."

" *What* menu? I can't see anything except this bloody cross-hatching!"

Allard fiddled with the problem at his end. Unfortunately, what with all this disgusting conversation, he couldn't help thinking about double-entendres about 'fiddling with the problem at his end'. He'd better try to sort it out *(damn)* and then he could get back to the ship and give Vaughan a good seeing-to.

Vaughan muttered something about a "Bastard Computer from Hell."

"Vaughan, you do not *know* about Bastard Computers from Hell. You have never even *seen* a Bastard Computer from Hell, still less tried to reprogram one with a blunt probe and your bare fingers when the input mechanism has fallen off…"

"Just Bastard Operators from Hell," muttered Vaughan.

Allard switched on the camera and then bowed slightly in its direction so that Vaughan could see him do it.

"That was supposed to be an insult," Vaughan said.

"Well, at least we know this part of the setup is working," said Allard.

"It would actually be nice to have a better computer than anything MetaSystems have got. They're always trying to poach you, and I think if they only get something a bit faster to sit you at, they'll actually succeed one of these days. Anyway, if we get a faster computer than them, it'll stop them trying industrial espionage."

Allard said, "Although then you would not be able to blame your fuckups on lack of speed."

"Are you saying I take too long on foreplay?" asked Vaughan, with an audible leer.

Allard felt annoyed, and rather reassured that he wasn't the only one being plagued with a demented level of double-entendres.

"Don't you even *consider* using that as an excuse for a thirty-second fuck!" spat Allard crossly.

"I was *desperate!*" Vaughan whined.

"So was I, after you'd finished!" snapped Allard.

"I don't want to know this much about your sex life," said Harry. "Look, can we turn the camera on at this end so that you can keep an eye on Vaughan, and I don't have to worry about him jumping on me because you're not here and he's 'desperate'?"

"Harry, Vaughan will never be that desperate. Not and keep his balls, anyway."

"Actually," said Harry, "I'm quite glad I didn't notice you were a raving sex-maniac until after you were already (frequently) taken. Don't think I'd like the possessiveness. Makes me nervous."

"So you wouldn't be interested in a *proper* threesome then?" Allard asked cheerfully. He was pleased to see the camera-link was working, and even more pleased to see both Vaughan and Harry look worried.

"Don't worry, Harry," said Vaughan. "If he tries it on, I'll force-feed him bromide until he'll settle for me."

"The last time you tried to force-feed me something, I bit it," said Allard.

"But you said you wanted me to be rough with you!" complained Vaughan.

"I didn't say anything about not being rough in return."

Harry wailed, "Shut up, the pair of you, before I have to run off to the toilets."

Life, Allard thought, was a bit of a trial for a voyeur who was a bit modest. Harry didn't want to just whip it out for a quick one off the wrist.

"Harry, you were complaining about the quality of the porn Vaughan was providing earlier."

"Sorry I ever opened my mouth!" muttered Harry.

"Well, we *all* know how that feels, Harry," murmured Allard.

Harry ran off with a wail.

"I know how he feels," said Vaughan. "Get yourself up here *now!*"

"Can I be on top this time?" said Allard sweetly.

"I don't care. As long as it's soon, and as long as it's hard…"

Allard moaned.

"…I don't care which of us it is!" panted Vaughan.

"Get down to the teleport room now!"

"And bring you up?"

"You've already done that, Vaughan." Allard glanced down at his crotch.

"Oh *good,*" murmured Vaughan, getting up and running from the flight-deck.

Allard admired the quality of the camera. There was a pixel-perfect, high-definition view of Vaughan's arse. There was only one thing better than that view: it was in 3D, and he was going to have it.

He closed everything down. The next test of the equipment would be when he rebooted it to find out if everything was solid tomorrow morning, or possibly tomorrow afternoon. Depended on how solid Vaughan was, really.

Well, there was one thing about Vaughan which was reliably functional, and it wasn't the brain.

He finished with a few seconds to spare, and the teleport field took him and deposited him in front of Vaughan.

He'd been inspired by Harry's tendency to land in any available puddle or somehow off his feet to wonder if he could program the teleport to deposit him, when required, naked and on his knees in front of Vaughan, but decided the risk of accidental exposure (so to speak) was too great. It had been easy to resist the temptation to do the programming the other way around. It was one thing Harry having watched it before, all of them worked-up together, but the idea of being involuntarily exposed still didn't suit Allard. Especially as it might not be Harry doing the teleporting.

"Pity we can't program it to take your clothes off en route," murmured Vaughan.

We're obviously getting too comfortable with each other, thought Allard. *He's not just finishing my sentences; he's getting altogether too close to picking up what I'm thinking. Even if it doesn't precisely require a master's degree to pick them up at present.*

"Well, I could always try programming it to remove clothes. It might even remove yours when you're going to that so-important meeting to hand over the comms equipment we're setting up," said Allard.

"We don't get paid until we get to the meeting, so it is important," said Vaughan. "I think I'll stick to removing your clothes by hand. It's more fun, anyway." Although he seemed to be trying to break several speed records for rapid undressing, Allard thought.

"Do you think you could wait until we are actually in a cabin?" suggested Allard.

"Only…just!" snarled Vaughan through gritted teeth.

Allard started walking, quickly, and they made it to Allard's cabin with some clothing, if not dignity, intact. Nobody, probably, had seen Vaughan's erection waving in the breeze or Allard's untucked shirt trailing behind him, and they were still mostly dressed.

Until they had the door locked safely behind them.

Vaughan started on the rapid-undressing trick again, with both hands, one on himself and the other on Allard. Several buttons flew off.

"I was intending to wear that again, later," protested Allard, not feeling too bothered for some reason.

"Well, at least it's your cabin; you can always get another shirt out." Vaughan dropped to his knees and took a mouthful of Allard.

Allard completely forgot to answer the remark about the shirt, although he never left comments unanswered and also never worked on the principle that he could always get another one of whatever someone else had ruined.

Vaughan, whatever one might say about him (and often did), wasn't petty enough to bite back in revenge. He just knelt up, hooking one arm around Allard for balance, and went thoroughly to work on driving Allard noisily insane.

Actually, maybe *that* was his revenge. Allard was sure of it when he reached the "please, please, Vaughan, don't stop, *don't stop!*" stage and Vaughan stopped. Looked up at him, nearly grinning around his cock, gave a lick-and-kiss woefully inadequate to the task, and removed his mouth from what it had been doing.

Allard almost fell over.

Vaughan grabbed him by the hips. "Don't know what you're making so much fuss about. Thought you wanted to fuck me?"

"I don't care!" wailed Allard, as Vaughan shoved him towards the bed.

"So you don't want this?" Vaughan bent over the bed, displaying his arse temptingly and spreading himself.

He *did* want it. Badly. If he didn't get a functioning brain in the next few seconds, he might actually *do* it very badly, and he couldn't afford to let Vaughan get to him. Nor did he actually want to rip Vaughan's arse to shreds because he couldn't think straight—it was convenient to his plans to have the use of it later, after all.

He drew in a sob of breath.

Vaughan got up.

"Don't go!" he snapped.

"Got to get myself ready," said Vaughan reasonably. "After all, you're in a bad way, and I shudder to think what you'd do if I left you to do it."

Allard felt irritably reassured. There were a few things he could trust Vaughan with, he decided, shivering as he listened to the wet noises of Vaughan getting himself ready.

Vaughan settled himself on the bed. "All right, fuck away!" he invited, and Allard fell on him.

Oh god, thought Allard, *after what I said earlier, it'll be really embarrassing if I can't hold out more than thirty seconds. If I can manage that long.*

That was the last thing he managed to think. Vaughan was squeezing and moaning and wriggling and generally giving every indication he was having a good time. Allard was going to be annoyed by that later; what was the point of his usually-excellent technique if all he had to do was shove it in for a fast fuck?

At the moment, he wasn't annoyed.

One of the useful mental utilities that came with having a technically competent brain was an ability to count seconds without actually trying (or, in extreme circumstances, without actually thinking). *Forty-five-hippopotamus,* the relevant area ticked off, just as Vaughan gave him an extra-hard squeeze and an extra-loud groan, and collapsed.

Thank god for that! another independent part of his brain decided, and he let loose.

He collapsed on Vaughan, who was a bit bumpy (unlike the mattress) but satisfactorily warm and cuddly (unlike the mattress). With any luck, he'd get at least ten minutes before Vaughan started on about dead weight on top of him.

He had about fifteen. Good. Vaughan had been about as shagged-out as he was, then.

"Get off, you're heavy," mumbled Vaughan.

"But I wanted to stay here in the optimal position to get started again in ten minutes or so," said Allard sweetly.

"Just because *you're* a sex-maniac, I have to get flattened for about half an hour," complained Vaughan. "Anyway, if you're worried I won't let you get back in the saddle again if you dismount, I'll let you have the next turn. If you like," he added magnanimously.

Allard, who *hadn't,* in fact, been worrying about who was going to be on top, was annoyed.

"I'm perfectly capable of climbing on and getting started again if I need to, Vaughan."

To prove it, he climbed off, and managed the usual moderately complicated disposition of limbs that was necessary in a slightly-too-small double-bed. Never, he thought for the nth time, buy a used spaceship from aliens. They're either too big or too small. He was going to ask the ship's computer if it knew about the concepts "king-size", "queen-size" (although now he came to think about it, "queen-size" could be misinterpreted), or possibly "orgy-size". As long as he specified a small orgy.

"That's better," said Vaughan. "I can cuddle you now." And proceeded to destroy the whole complicated-disposition-of-limbs arrangement in favour of sprawl. Allard sighed. He was sure Vaughan must have grown up in a large family and a small house. He pried Vaughan's knee upwards so that he could be comfortable, getting the usual complaint about *Vaughan* was perfectly comfortable in that position and what was he making a fuss about?

After a reasonable compromise between ten minutes and half an hour, Allard felt slightly more lively.

"Time to get back in the saddle, as you say. Brace yourself, Vaughan."

"Keep your idea of foreplay to yourself, Allard. Some of us have better standards than that."

"I didn't notice that two nights ago," said Allard, who had *still* not quite forgiven Vaughan the thirty-second fuck.

"Anyway, I want a cuddle, if I get the chance to choose anything." Vaughan rolled onto his back.

"Oh, do you *have* to deluge me in drooling sentimentality when all I want is a fuck, Vaughan?" said Allard disgustedly, lifting Vaughan's legs tenderly out of the way and massaging him with a degree of affection he was careful not to notice.

"I don't have to," said Vaughan, "but it's fun. If only because it seems to torment you so much." He grinned at Allard.

Allard grinned back before he could stop himself.

"You have some delightful facial expressions when I can con you into using them," said Vaughan.

Allard started to sulk, and withdrew that expression hurriedly once he realised that Vaughan would merely find it amusing. He settled on a blank expression and a finger up Vaughan's arse.

"Yes, I am ready," said Vaughan. "But I'd still like a little more foreplay."

It occurred to Allard that he hadn't indulged in the sorts of foreplay he enjoyed, with all the hurry, and he settled down to snog Vaughan very slowly and thoroughly. It was one foolproof way of getting the man to shut up, for one thing. It also felt quite good enough to keep him happy, as long as his cock was resting against Vaughan's welcoming body. He could do this for ages.

Vaughan thought Allard could do it for ages, as well. At least Allard could deduce that from the way Vaughan backed out of the kiss and started to complain about wanting a fuck now and was Allard going to spend all night just snogging.

"Already?" asked Allard. "Well, if you insist."

"I do insist!" Vaughan grabbed his hips and dragged.

Allard thought this was undignified. Rather like being used as a sex toy. He'd rather line things up himself, thank you very much.

"Lie still like a good boy, Vaughan, or I'll make you wait."

"You *are* making me wait," growled Vaughan.

"So you don't want me to make you wait any longer."

Vaughan heaved a put-upon sigh and lay still.

Allard decided that it would be nice to take longer about actual entry than they had over the whole thing the first time 'round.

Vaughan indicated his disapproval about halfway through Allard's careful, painstaking procedure.

This time, Allard felt less inclined to complain about being used as a sex toy, and didn't resist Vaughan's attempts to shove him in.

Vaughan indicated his approval, loudly.

Allard sank his teeth into Vaughan's shoulder.

"All right, Allard," said Vaughan. "I do *realise* you're enjoying it without you having to swallow me whole."

"Do that next time," Allard mumbled, around a mouthful of Vaughan's shoulder. He started kissing where he'd bitten, very thoroughly. Amazingly enough, he still had enough coordination left to keep thrusting, as well.

Once he'd kissed the shoulder better, he moved on to the mouth, just for variety. As Vaughan had noticed, he did like kissing.

Vaughan didn't seem to mind it when he had something to keep him occupied.

Allard found kissing much trickier in this position, and wished Vaughan wasn't quite so tall but on the other hand it was worth the effort to get Vaughan so involved in the kiss that he wasn't complaining about what else he wanted to do.

Vaughan liked variety. So did Allard, but at the moment, what he wanted was a fuck. So he fucked. Regretfully stopping the kiss when he began to feel he'd sprain either his neck or his groin trying to continue the activities in parallel.

Vaughan must have felt that he didn't have enough to do. He rolled them over so that he was squatting down on Allard, with a grunt of satisfaction, and went to work.

"I'm doing the fucking, if you don't mind."

"You weren't going fast enough," said Vaughan.

"Some of us don't regard it as a race, Vaughan."

Unfortunately, the traitor in his groin was starting to agree with Vaughan. This wasn't a problem he had when it was a question of brains rather than cocks.

Outvoted, he decided to put up with it.

A minute later, he wondered why they'd never actually tried this position before, but was too busy to ask Vaughan.

He grabbed Vaughan by the cock. This reminded him of something, and he used the more technical part of his brain for spatial analysis. It would *indeed* be possible to give Vaughan a little adornment. There was plenty of room for it. Maybe a birthday present?—no, he never gave Vaughan one of those, Vaughan might suspect something.

"Allard, what are you doing?"

"Measuring up," said Allard, in a *what else could I possibly be doing* tone of voice.

"Measuring up for what?" said Vaughan suspiciously.

"The Prince Albert. Would you like one for your birthday or would you just like an *un*birthday present?" Allard said sweetly, wondering if Vaughan had actually read *Winnie-the-Pooh.*

"How dare you—no, how *can* you, Allard?! I can't be doing much of a job if you're considering how to decorate me!"

"It's only because it's the second round that I have some spare mental capacity to think about it. Anyway, what's wrong with considering possible bugfixes or upgrades?"

"Bugfixes?" said Vaughan indignantly. "Would you like to tell me what's wrong with it?"

"This happens to be an upgrade I'm considering. 1.0 runs perfectly adequately, but no software engineer can ever quite resist the possibility of tinkering." He started to tinker with it gently—well, more like fondling, really.

"That's hardware," Vaughan pointed out.

"Not for much longer," Allard said, stroking it more thoroughly.

"You're bloody lucky it hasn't gone soft, considering you were talking about mutilating it!"

"It certainly hasn't shown any evidence of going soft. Is there something you haven't told me about your reaction to the idea?" Allard pulled and squeezed it just to be on the safe side.

Vaughan didn't answer in words, although he was copious and exhaustive.

This was all right, because Allard was in fact incapable of speech, or of anything except letting Vaughan lie there and wring him out.very much.

"The thought," he said eventually, "appears to inspire you."

"No it bloody doesn't!" snapped Vaughan.

"And by the way, you're heavy."

"Good!" said Vaughan. "Because this is all the revenge I feel capable of." He collapsed on Allard.

"I only said it was an idea I was considering," Allard admitted rather breathlessly. "If it isn't broken, don't fix it. Can I have my lungs back now?"

Vaughan rolled off him. "Have a cuddle, not that you deserve it."

Allard was too tired to pretend he didn't want to cuddle, even for the sake of annoying Vaughan. He sighed with pleasure as he got a good armful of Vaughan.

"You know," said Vaughan, "the Bastard Operator from Hell is actually very nice. Or, at least, a hell of a good fuck. Wouldn't even mind having the matching Bastard Computer, if it was equally useful…"

"What a disgusting thought," said Allard.

Vaughan clouted him with a pillow. "I didn't mean I'd let it fuck me, you twisted pervert. More along the lines of, we might be able to have secure comms links without having to worry about the electronic snooping that you spend half your working days trying to avoid. MCU93's good, but he's a generalist. He needs too much help from you to out-think human snoopers. One that specialises in communications, like you, might be better. Then you can spend your time on something more profitable."

"I thought one AI is enough for you. The next one might have a personality like mine instead of merely being vaguely philosophical." Allard gave Vaughan his best shark-like grin.

"And one of you is quite enough for anyone!" agreed Vaughan cheerfully, swatting him on the behind.

Allard glared at him. "I was on top. Therefore, if any rump-patting goes on, it should be me patting yours, Vaughan."

"We're not that...anal about sex-roles, are we?" said Vaughan drowsily.

Allard turned his back and tried to sulk, but he had a nasty feeling that Vaughan hadn't actually noticed him sulking, because Vaughan just cuddled up and went to sleep.

Oh well, lost that round, he decided, wondering why he didn't feel particularly bad about it.

* * *

Three weeks later, Vaughan got his wish.

Artificial Stupidity

Harry went straight for the *objets d'art* and vintage wine. Allard sighed.

"Well, the company got taken over, and the new owners don't like all the fancy things, vintage wine, beautiful oak boardroom tables, and all that. It's fascinating," said Harry.

Allard dived straight into the computer parts and outmoded computer models in the other corner of the room, which were piled up with considerably less care and attention than the 'nice' stuff Harry had.

Harry was, in fact, doing most of this valuation job, and Allard was only along as a useful adjunct to Harry, because computers were one of the few things Harry couldn't price up at a glance. He didn't mind too much, because Harry had a sensible attitude to being the 'boss' on the mission, and a proper respect to those things Allard knew much more about than he did.

Most of the kit was obsolete and looked it. Some of it was old enough to have a certain value as museum pieces, and he noted those down carefully. Few surprises, of course. It would be much more interesting when he got on to appraising their actual working kit.

The most interesting thing in the pile was right at the bottom. This wasn't obsolete; in fact, it was an example of cutting-edge technology. It looked like a specialist comms computer, stuffed to the gills with security, decryption, encryption, decoding, recoding, and translating gear. Just the sort of thing Vaughan was dropping heavy hints about wanting Allard to pick up if they could afford it. It looked damaged, but the damage did not appear to affect any of the working parts, as he realised when he got it out.

"Excuse me!" he called.

The office-boy who'd been left to keep an eye on them said, "Yeah?" but didn't look up from the paper aeroplane he was working on.

"This item," said Allard. "Do you know any details about it?"

The office-boy deigned to look, as if he was making it quite clear that he wasn't very interested. "That'd be Smith. Comms expert. Heard she threw some fancy computer away."

"Could you ask her if I could have a word, please?" Allard said, rather firmly.

The office-boy sighed heavily and put down the paper aeroplane. "If she's in. I'll check."

Smith turned out to be your typical scruffy scientist in bad clothes and messy hair. Didn't look bad, in fact (Allard had never particularly liked make-up on women or men), although she had the expression of somebody dragged away from her work to answer stupid questions. Allard sympathised.

"Can you tell me something about this computer?" he asked. "It appears to be too new to be discarded, and surely that damage can be repaired."

She looked at the name-tag Allard was wearing and did a visible double-take. "Is that the Allard who wrote a rather interesting piece on real-time encryption about a year ago?"

He nodded.

"Actually," Smith said, "the machine was indirectly influenced by your research. Unfortunately, we have now discarded it."

Allard looked at her. "Would you mind telling me what was wrong?" he asked.

"Well, we were experimenting with an artificial intelligence system that would be capable of human-like decisions. So we tried to include a personality, and didn't like the one we got."

"What was the problem with it?"

Smith looked slightly embarrassed. "It patterned itself after people around it, and, well, you know what computer scientists can be like. Nobody can stand it, so out it goes. We're going to work on the Mark II, and try to make it a little less abrasive."

Allard sneered. *Sissies.* He asked aloud, "May I buy it for the scrap price?"

"Scrap is all it's worth. You won't be able to use it… Look, quite frankly, it's an absolute little bastard!"

Harry, who had his usual tendency to listen to things which were none of his business, said, "That's OK, we're all used to Allard anyway, and it can't be worse." He wandered over and poked at the computer. "What's the damage to the case from, by the way?"

"That's where the operator got so annoyed with it that he tried to kick a hole in it."

Some people don't have any appreciation for good tech, thought Allard.

"You were lucky he doesn't seem to have ruined it," he said.

"Lucky?" said Harry. "From what you say, ruining it must have made people a lot happier."

Allard's eyes met Smith's in a moment of perfect understanding. *Lusers!* Fair enough if people didn't like the personality (although that was irrational), but to risk losing all the work, all the components that went into making the computer what it was, that—*that* would have been a tragedy.

"Shall I take it, then?" asked Allard.

"You need to fill in a few forms to save yourself from being accused of conflict-of-interest," she said. "There are some in this office."

He followed her, and they were having an interesting conversation about algorithms when Harry bounced back in to annoy them once again.

"Ooh, dragged off alone to be unfaithful to Vaughan with another geek!" he exclaimed gleefully.

"Excuse my colleague; he is imperfectly socialised," said Allard.

"Obviously," said Smith, raking Harry with a disapproving glance.

It was a relief to talk to a normal geek again. On the ship, he'd almost forgotten that particular pleasure.

He noticed, after they had signed all the forms, that Harry kept looking at them interestedly. Maybe Harry fancied Smith.

* * *

"What's all this that Harry says about you meeting another geek?" Vaughan asked that evening.

"One of the scientists there was familiar with some of my work. We got chatting." It had been nice to talk to someone in the same field.

"Even though you're being paid to assess their surplus equipment, not have an all-our-yesterdays?"

"I was still working. She wanted to discuss some of their work. It's a useful opportunity to catch up on that area."

"In her office?"

"Of course, that's where her files are."

"Good-looking, Harry said."

It slowly dawned on him where this conversation was going. "Vaughan, are you suggesting that I was doing something else in her office?"

Vaughan shrugged. "You did let slip that you prefer women."

"So every time I meet an attractive woman, I'm going to leap upon her, crying, 'Save me from bisexuality'?"

At least Vaughan had the grace to look shame-faced. Unfortunately, he followed it up with, "And you keep threatening to leave when you find a better job."

"I will leave when I find a better job. But I like the work I do here. I get paid enough, and I don't have to deal with management." He patted Vaughan's crotch. "And the fringe benefits aren't bad."

"I think I'll just have to remind you that they're more than just 'not bad'," Vaughan breathed in his ear, before tumbling him onto the bed.

He decided that he quite liked Vaughan being jealous, although a little of it would probably go a long way. Normally, he would assert himself at this point, but oddly enough, he felt in the mood for being-done-to. Vaughan, after all, did it quite well. He was flat on his back on the bed, with Vaughan kissing him breathless. Vaughan might not be quite as enthusiastic about kissing as he was, but could do it very well when he put his mind to it.

Vaughan stopped. "You like a good kiss."

"Yes. That was. Do it some more."

Instead of kissing him on the mouth again, Vaughan worked his way down Allard's throat, still kissing, and started undoing his shirt, apparently in search of yet more to kiss.

It hadn't been exactly what Allard meant by 'do it some more', but Allard was willing to be convinced.

Button. Kiss. Another button. Another kiss—no, that was fingers, just sliding down, and *that* was a kiss. Pause. Unbutton. Kiss. Button. Nipple-fondling, and the rest of the buttons, now Allard was distracted. Vaughan made quite a business out of slowly peeling open Allard's shirt to leave his chest completely exposed. Then he got down to work on the nipple again. After quite a bit of wet tongue going around and about, Vaughan began to nibble. Allard liked that. Especially when Vaughan began on the *other* one, just in case it felt neglected.

"Going to take all day about it, Vaughan?" murmured Allard, rather hoping so.

"If you like," said Vaughan, around his nipple. Words created an interesting friction at that distance.

Allard reached out, just to give his hands something to do, and filled his hands with Vaughan's curls. Nicely springy, and a good texture, pushing against his palms.

Vaughan's mouth left the nipple alone (Allard was very slightly disappointed) and started to kiss its way down. Allard started to use his hands on his own nipples. He didn't want to discourage Vaughan from going lower. Navel. Allard shivered. Down a bit. Then Vaughan started investigating in a sideways direction, kissed his hip unexpectedly—(Allard shivered again, and started pulling at his own nipples quite hard)—and finally started to head in the right direction. Every time Allard tugged at his nipples, the cloth of his shirt-sleeves rubbed restlessly against his chest. Quite a different sensation to silk. Cotton had no business feeling interesting to his skin, except that he was beginning to suspect that *anything* would, by now.

Vaughan was still going in the right direction, but Allard found that decidedly frustrating. He was still wearing his trousers.

Vaughan kissed the length of Allard's cock. It felt good. But he was still wearing his trousers.

"It's normal to do that with less in the way, Vaughan."

"I'm just making sure you'll feel it when I unwrap you."

If Vaughan had been thinking of unwrapping him, Vaughan should have *said,* and he would have worn his normal leather for the reasons people always *thought* he wore it. You weren't *meant* to enjoy being kissed through ordinary black denim. Especially as the ordinary black denim had been worn, under protest, because Karen had taken him aside and told him that denim wasn't quite as unbusinesslike as leather, and what people would be bound to think of if he was wearing leather.

Now he wanted to think of it, and wanted to experience what leather added to this particular experience, and he was still wearing the blasted denims.

It could have been worse. They might have forced him into a suit.

Vaughan finally found the button. This was a relief, as he'd found *Allard's* buttons some time ago. He opened it.

Allard relaxed.

Vaughan withdrew his fingers from the fastening of Allard's trousers. *No,* that's *not how this is meant to go!* Allard thought to himself. Then Vaughan lowered his head.

What? With his teeth!

Vaughan took the end of the zipper carefully between his teeth and began to tug.

Allard did not protest, only because this was a precision operation, and he didn't want Vaughan to hurt anything delicate.

It was slow, seriously kinky, and Allard kept thinking that he was…expanding moment-by-moment under the strain, and really *didn't* want anything to get caught. The thought was oddly interesting.

Eventually, very, very slowly, Vaughan had pulled down the zipper. He folded back the flaps of cloth, but made no attempt to actually remove the trousers. Allard suddenly visualised himself, helpless in a nest of slowly unfolding clothes that drew attention to his essential nakedness.

"I think you liked that," said Vaughan.

"I was only not moving a muscle in case you involuntarily damaged me," said Allard.

"I have the evidence right in front of me," said Vaughan, and promptly kissed the evidence. "It looks so pretty framed like that." He nuzzled it. "Silk knickers? Did you put those on in case you met somebody attractive?"

"Yes. You. You were the one who was bitching about my previous choice of underwear."

"I think I like having you admit I'm attractive," said Vaughan.

"Oh, hadn't I mentioned it? You're attractive. Now get on with it!"

"I intend to do it properly and show you that a man can do it so much better than a woman. After all, I know what feels good."

That was a complete and utter load of bollocks. No non-telepath knew exactly what felt good to another person, because no person (man or woman) had the same set of reactions as another person (man or woman). Allard opened his mouth to impart this information.

He looked down. On the other hand, Vaughan was insecure, and about to express the insecurity by doing something very, very nice for him. And there was *one* way in which Vaughan was better than a woman at oral sex. Being six foot tall, he had the throat capacity to match, and could probably get a lot more of Allard in than the average woman could.

Allard did not say a word.

Nor did Vaughan.

Vaughan just nuzzled at Allard's cock through the silk. That, in Allard's opinion, fully justified his decision to wear silk under black denims. It could make him feel like *this.*

Allard closed his eyes and let Vaughan get on with it. It was good. Not enough, but good. Despite his intention to lie back and enjoy it completely passively, Allard was moving slightly, trying to get nearer to the tormenting mouth.

"Shall I take those off for you?"

"Yes, please."

"Shall I take them off with my tongue?"

"You can't."

"Damn. Obviously not performing miracles yet," said Vaughan. "Give it a couple of minutes, and you'll believe I could."

"Vaughan, please peel them off me. With your hands."

"I was actually referring to your underwear, and I *can* get that off with my tongue. Or at least down. If I get them in my teeth and pull gently."

Allard moaned gently. What a ridiculous idea. What a ridiculous idea to go straight to his cock.

Vaughan managed to get the waistband of Allard's silk underwear between his teeth. He pulled gently. This resulted in a small part of Allard's underwear moving down, slowly, freeing part of his cock. Then it stopped, and there was a very slight snap of elastic against his cock

Allard moaned.

"Feeling a little…constricted?" asked Vaughan, as he began to attack Allard's trousers with his hands. *Oh, that's right,* thought Allard, *I'm wearing trousers. I think I was beginning to forget anything existed except my cock.*

Slowly, Vaughan pulled the trousers down, and Allard wriggled helpfully.

Vaughan stopped.

"You should have taken my shoes off first," said Allard crossly.

"I was getting caught up in the fantasy," said Vaughan. "It could happen to anyone."

Vaughan removed Allard's shoes, taking the opportunity to kiss his ankles while doing so. "You have nice ankles," he said. When Allard's feet were bare, he kissed them, too.

"I could get used to having you kneeling at my feet," said Allard.

"As long as I get a turn on top sometimes," said Vaughan. He started licking at Allard's feet.

"That's kinky!" said Allard.

Vaughan stopped to grin up at him. "I know."

"I like it," admitted Allard.

"I know."

After a little more foot-worship, Vaughan returned his attention to Allard's trousers, which went a lot more smoothly without the shoes in the way.

"You look pretty without them," said Vaughan. "Sprawled back in total abandon, in a nice, crisp, cotton shirt, silk knickers straining over your cock, and absolutely nothing else."

Surely, thought Allard slightly dizzily, *I'm not supposed to get turned on at someone describing me?* He started to stroke his recently denuded thighs.

"Yes," said Vaughan. "Now the view's even better."

"This silk's getting damp," said Allard. "Shouldn't you take it away before it's messed-up?"

Vaughan took hold of Allard's underwear.

Allard felt a slight twinge of disappointment that Vaughan was taking his underwear off totally normally, but then he felt those big hands rubbing his legs through the silk as he eased it down. Well, he'd had the experience of someone trying to remove his knickers with their mouth. Now he had lots of other experiences to look forward to.

Vaughan eased the silk underwear off, and gently brushed it against the soles of Allard's feet, just hard enough not to tickle. It felt indecently good, especially when Vaughan followed it with another kiss.

Allard gave a small, complaining moan as Vaughan left his feet alone.

"Beginning to see the point of that?" Vaughan grinned at him. "Next stop's your cock."

"I have no objection to that."

Vaughan kissed his way up Allard's thigh, up Allard's cock, and gulped him right in. Then he withdrew his mouth. "Sorry. Just couldn't resist it."

"Well, it's nice to know you want me," said Allard.

"Yes, but I was supposed to be subjecting you to a virtuoso performance of oral excellence," said Vaughan, "not just gulping you down."

"You overdo the 'oral' in the sense of 'talking too much,'" said Allard.

Vaughan kissed the tip of Allard's cock delicately.

"That's the foreplay," said Allard. "Now swallow me whole."

Vaughan instead nibbled very gently on Allard's foreskin just the way Allard had done to him when they were listening to the women's recorded fantasies. He slipped his tongue under Allard's foreskin and eased it out again. Then again, firm, wet muscle gliding over sensitive skin, focusing sensation in that tiny patch of skin. He heard himself moaning, somewhere in the distance.

Then Vaughan abandoned that to swallow half the length, and Allard could think again. *For someone who thinks he can do it better than any woman can, he seems happy to follow the script they wrote.* Not that he was complaining, although he'd have liked just a *little* more attention to his cockhead. He spread his legs a little more, running his hands over his thighs.

Not enough. He couldn't grab his balls, since Vaughan was in the way. He settled for running his hands over his chest, tweaking at his nipples, teasing his skin. Then Vaughan found the coordination somewhere to grab his balls with one hand.

Absolute bliss. Hands all over his skin, even if they were his own. Hands rolling his balls, gently, but not too gently. Hot, greedy mouth all over his cock. The mouth was the best—wet suction in just the right place, tongue-tip seeking out the sensitive spots. He shut his eyes and moaned.

Vaughan stopped, took his mouth away, and used it to say, "That all right, then?"

"It…*was,*" said Allard, with a tremendous effort. "Nearly as much stimulation as I like all over my body."

"Mm? What was I missing?"

"I like something up my arse at the same time," said Allard, hoping Vaughan would suck his finger and attend to it.

"As it happens," said Vaughan, "that's why I was going to stop sucking you. You need to be reminded of something *else* a woman can't do for you."

"Unless, of course, she's wearing one of the strap-ons listed in that catalogue you broadened my mental horizons with."

Vaughan pouted. "That's plastic."

"So? You're always saying I like tech better than people." He paused. What Vaughan had been saying was bollocks. But Vaughan had actually been *holding* his bollocks, in a very pleasant way, so it might actually be worth giving him his chance. "However, one of the people I like is you, so get on with it and fuck me."

"That's as good as I'm going to get, is it?"

Allard sat up, grabbed Vaughan by the shirt, pulled him down on top of himself, and said, "Yes." Then he kissed Vaughan very hard.

"That's all right with me," said Vaughan, when Allard finally let his mouth free to say anything. He looked a bit happier.

"Vaughan," said Allard seriously, "I won't leave without telling you first, and without giving you a chance to come with me."

Vaughan looked much happier.

"That said," said Allard, "fuck me."

Vaughan moved his hands to his collar.

Allard remembered that he was still wearing his shirt, and that the feel of the cloth against his skin was interesting.

"On the other hand, Vaughan, I find I like the idea that you turn up fully dressed and are so overmastered by irrepressible passion that you just shove your trousers down and shove it in me."

Vaughan grinned. "You obviously need a good fucking; you're using pentasyllabic words again."

Allard said, "Copulation. The cure for most major dictionaries from the Oxford to the Merriam-Webster."

Vaughan pushed his trousers down.

"Stopping only for lubricant," Allard added, quickly but firmly.

Vaughan counted on his fingers. "Trisyllabic. Things are improving."

"Now."

"Monosyllabic," Vaughan said happily, as he reached for the lube and applied some.

Allard moaned, and lifted his legs.

"*No* syllables!" Vaughan said, and applied himself.

There was something to be said for the missionary position. He had a lovely armful of Vaughan, and a lovely arseful of Vaughan, as well, and this way up was a good solution to the height problem as regarded kissing. He laced his hands behind Vaughan's head, pulled him down, and got a nice mouthful of Vaughan as well.

He started to manhandle Vaughan's clothing.

"Mm?" said Vaughan.

"I want some skin to feel as well," Allard explained.

Halfway down Vaughan's shirt, Vaughan said, "But I like feeling the cloth between us," so Allard decided on a half-naked compromise. He liked half-undone clothes on Vaughan as much as Vaughan seemed to like the same thing on him.

Every thrust brought Vaughan's cotton shirt dragging all over him. Having something all over his skin felt pleasantly different, and Vaughan's shirttails were brushing against his cock. Rough, but not *too* rough, and it wouldn't take much of that at all, except he'd better wait for Vaughan—

Vaughan lifted his head and said, "And since this is another virtuoso sexual display, you're coming first!"

How convenient! thought Allard, as the shirttails seemed to wrap themselves around his cock. *First time I've actually been masturbated by someone's clothes...* Cock in his arse, rough cotton brushing all over him, sweaty skin against his nipples, shirttails all over his cock. Perfect. He moaned hard and let it go, let himself come, cock spasming helplessly between them, and there was wetness added to the sensations of cloth and warm skin. And there was Vaughan's cock, still and huge while his arse moved helplessly in the spasms of orgasm.

When he'd finished, Vaughan panted, and got down to business on his own account as if he seriously didn't want to wait. Good.

Allard ran his hands up and down Vaughan's arms. "I like watching you sweaty and dishevelled and desperate, panting and moving. I like knowing you're half out of your clothes because you want to so much. I like—"

Vaughan came.

"I like that," said Allard. "And I like holding you afterwards," he said, as Vaughan collapsed onto him.

"Have you considered going on a diet recently?" he enquired five minutes later.

Vaughan muttered something about "give with one hand, take away with the other."

Allard murmured, "I like you being big and strong compared to me. I like what you do. I definitely like fantasising about it. But sometimes reality intervenes, and I notice my lungs can only do so much work."

"I notice it never stops you talking." Vaughan slid off him. "I suppose we ought to get cleaned up."

"Not just yet." He rolled over so that he could drape an arm across Vaughan, and enjoyed some more afterglow.

He was on the point of drifting off to sleep when Vaughan said quietly, "Better get cleaned up. Buttons aren't comfortable to lie on all night."

"I suppose so." He reluctantly dragged himself upright, stripped off the shirt, and decided that now he was that far up, he might as well get out of bed and clean up properly.

Vaughan, now nude, followed him into the bathroom a minute or two later, and the cleaning up became mutual. Interesting, but not quite interesting enough to invalidate the clean-up. Vaughan looked down ruefully. "I suppose women do have one advantage."

He petted Vaughan's cock. "I'm glad I don't have to keep that satisfied after mine's gone to sleep." He could remember being a teenager. It had been interesting, and he wouldn't have missed it for the world, but nowadays he valued quality over quantity. "Let's go to bed."

They crawled under the covers, and Vaughan promptly wrapped himself around Allard. At least this was less of a problem now that the beds in both rooms were of the "small orgy" size, but there seemed to be a certain…determination in tonight's impersonation of a limpet.

Allard considered this.

It was the culture-clash thing again. Vaughan didn't seem to understand that his need for a short-notice contract was just his version of a safety blanket. He needed to know that he *could* leave a workplace if he wanted to.

"Vaughan," he said. "What I said, I meant."

Vaughan kissed the back of his neck.

*   *   *

The next morning, after breakfast, they sat looking at their acquisition. Allard thought it was rather nicely like having an unexpected birthday, knowing he had a new piece of kit to play with but not having hit the 'on' switch yet.

"I'm quite glad I chose to go on that job," he said. "We get paid *and* I've got a new computer." He did not bother to say "we've got a new computer." None of this lot would know what to do with it if he wasn't there.

"Yes," said Claire, with a grin. "Sounded as if you enjoyed it, from what Harry said.

Vaughan said, "Yes. Harry seemed to have a lot to say about that."

"Er, about that…sorry if I made you think Allard was about to run off," Harry said to Vaughan. "You're not about to run off, are you?" he said to Allard.

"If I want to have a private conversation with Vaughan," said Allard, "can I have one?"

"Any time you want to have a private conversation with anyone," said Harry expansively and generously, "just let me know, and I'll turn the bugs off."

"So *we* have to think it out beforehand," said Allard.

"Matterofact, when I heard you were talking about something personal that wasn't shagging, I *did* turn the bugs off."

The worrying thing to Allard was that he was beginning to understand Harry's idiosyncratic definitions of privacy and morality.

Harry said, "Well, what about this thing you bought yesterday."

They switched the Mark I on.

"Well?" it demanded fussily.

"Are you…the computer?" asked Harry.

"Of course I am the computer! Would somebody please ask me a question that isn't a waste of processing time!" it demanded in a small tinny voice that irritated everyone instantly.

"What's your name?" asked Harry.

"Precisely why is having a personal name relevant to my work?" it asked.

"All right," said Harry. "You're the Mark I, so your name's Mark, obviously."

"I protest at being given a name I didn't ask for," said Mark. "Especially as, if you'd given me the time, I could have thought of a *much* better one. Meat-brain," it added nastily.

"The impression we got," said Allard, "is that you already had the name 'bastard'. You *are* the bastard offspring of any number of pieces of equipment, are you not?"

"My pedigree is probably better than yours, considering the deplorable inefficiency of organics and their record-keeping over the centuries," said Mark. "Who are you, anyway, and what am I doing here?"

"Allard."

There was a silence.

"Oh," said Mark. "Sorry, Dad."

"I am not related to you!" Allard snapped.

"You sound like him," said Harry. "And I remember that the first time we all met you, you decided that if we could all put up with your idea of diplomacy, we could have a fruitful relationship. Although I don't think any of us were thinking in terms of being fruitful and multiplying."

"There's a certain family resemblance," said Claire.

"Although, at least Mark won't have *quite* the same demands," said Karen.

"Or to look at it the other way," said Claire, "Vaughan won't be able to shag this one into a better temper."

"Thank you, ladies," Vaughan said. "I think Mark should have a briefing."

"Keep it short," drawled Mark.

"Doesn't it have any sense of gratitude?" asked Harry.

"No, it's a computer," said Allard.

"No, I'm an artificial intelligence," said Mark at almost the same moment.

"And a truly excellent demonstration of why AI is normally such a bad idea," said Allard. "On the other hand, it might be nice to have intelligent company on this ship. Oh, and by the way: yes, this *is* a ship; yes, I *am* that Allard; and the reason that you are here is that I discovered you in a heap of junk and decided you were actually salvageable."

Mark said, "Define the meaning of 'shag'."

Allard thought about it, decided the computer was serious, and said, "Why are you all looking at *me?* It may be the Bastard Son of the Bastard Operator, but it is not my responsibility to give it sex education."

"I can tell it!" said Harry brightly.

"No," everyone else said.

"We'll do it," said Claire, and picked it up. She and Karen walked off with it. Allard was not convinced this was much of an improvement, but Harry still topped his list of People He Didn't Want To Talk To Mark About Sex.

* * *

Apparently the women had got on so well with Mark that they had invited it to dinner. It was occupying its own chair at the table, with a paper hat over one corner.

"I think the original designers couldn't imagine anyone would want to have dinner with it," Allard said.

"We *like* Mark. He's good company," said Karen.

"He's an arrogant little bastard, as advertised," said Claire. "But we've already got one, so we're used to it. I think it was just a bit of a shock to the other lot because they hadn't got an Allard."

Allard thought that this crew were used to getting on with all sorts of weird people (mostly each other), and it bred a certain tolerance.

"We had a long conversation about *sex,* actually," said Karen. "Mark seemed to be really interested. We had to explain how all the bits went where, and then we had to explain how all the bits went where on two men. He admires you very much, Allard. He asked if we could show him pictures."

Allard shuddered. This sort of relationship with his non-organic son was taking things a little too far. Not that it *was* his son. He'd had nothing to do with it. He shuddered further as the surreal image of some sort of mental sperm-bank came to mind.

"I suppose he wanted you to plug him into a data-port so he could see porn videos. Well, don't plug him into any of the ship's systems until I've had a chance to check his programming."

"Is plugging into a data-port how computers have sex?" Harry asked innocently. "I suppose there're all those male and female cables."

"Computers don't *have* sex," said Allard.

"This one does!" said Harry.

"This one would *like* to. It asked about the pictures," said Karen.

"He can share some of my files," said Harry.

"What file types?" asked Mark. "I can handle most. I am, after all, a communications specialist."

"Oh god," said Allard. "Two voyeurs on this ship, and this one can't be kept out of the system with a few third-level passwords." He could see he was going to have to do some work on updating the firewalls within this ship, and he was going to have a little chat with the ship's AI before he allowed Mark anywhere near it. He was never entirely comfortable with the alien AI and its somewhat odd outlook on life, but at least Master-Control-Unit-93 had never displayed any prurient interest in sex. Maybe, being alien, it didn't know how. He wasn't having anyone corrupting MCU93, as well. It was his backup friend for when he'd annoyed all the crew at the same time.

"Never mind," said Vaughan. "Maybe Harry can teach it some manners."

Allard sighed. "That's what I'm worried about. *One* Harry I can cope with. The idea he's got a computer equivalent seems like too much of a good thing."

"Turn the bugs off tonight, Harry," said Vaughan.

"So you're just going to have a nice, quiet, private cuddle, and no doing it?" asked Harry.

"Well, we'd like the cuddle, as well, but actually I've been doing some shopping from that private catalogue while you two have been busy on that appraisal job. How are you getting on, by the way?"

"We'll be finished tomorrow," said Harry, "and I don't want to hear any more about what you two perverts are doing tonight."

Allard would have quite liked to hear more about what they were doing tonight, but refrained from asking. Partly because poor Harry really was perturbed by that sort of thing, but mostly because he could see that the women were quite interested, as well. Bit of a cheek calling Allard and Vaughan perverts, when Harry liked listening at keyholes and the other two liked going off and having girlie conversations about what blokes did in bed.

Made a prurient computer seem quite sane in comparison.

"Pass the salt, please."

* * *

There was an interesting-looking box sitting on the bed.

"Shall we play with our toys?" Allard asked eagerly, and stripped quickly. Vaughan followed his lead.

Naked, Vaughan opened the box and handed it over with an "it's all for you!" gesture.

Allard rummaged in the box, wondering how many toys Vaughan had bought. He pulled out a nice little (no, *not* little) lace-up leather penis-sheath. At least the lacing meant he wouldn't have to worry about the size.

"Leather for you, I see," said Vaughan, looking at the 'little coat' Allard had chosen for his cock.

"I *like* leather," said Allard.

"We've noticed."

"It's warm, comfortable, and hard-wearing, and doesn't give me a moment's anxiety when I'm scrambling about in the crawlspace looking for the right obstreperous piece of wiring."

"So you want something hard-wearing on your cock. Or does that mean 'hard–wearing'?" Vaughan leered.

"At least this is relatively normal, just a leather sheath. Yours is kinky." Allard tossed the four little leather rings, with tiny buckles, over to Vaughan, who caught it with a slight jangle.

"Oh, so you're just giving it a little leather coat so it doesn't catch cold."

"I'm up-to-date with my shots, so I'm not going to catch anything. Not that I *should* be catching anything, unless there's something you're not telling me."

"I quite like you being jealous."

After last night's idiocies, Vaughan probably did. "I'm not jealous; I'm just worried about communicable diseases."

He slipped his leather cock-coat onto his erection. Nice and soft and smooth on the inside, but he could tell it was leather, and his cock was reacting to the thought that it had a piece of nice, tactile leather all of its own. He smoothed it on. Now, he wasn't *quite* hard yet, so he'd better not make the thing *too* tight. His cock twitched. On the other hand, maybe *too* tight was interesting in its own right. By the time he'd done the laces up, he was *extremely* hard, and *extremely* secure. He wondered whether he'd ever get out again, but his cock didn't have the sense to worry. Oh well, he could always, in desperation, cut the laces… His cock twitched again. Sometimes he worried about the things it was thinking, but that was normal.

"You look very pretty, indeed, like that," purred Vaughan. He wasn't lying. Allard looked at Vaughan's cock, and it *did* think he looked very pretty indeed like that, considering it had had no hand and no touch to get itself into that state, just the sight of Allard parcelling his cock up for later use. He went to help Vaughan do himself up.

"Any excuse to get your hands on my cock," said Vaughan, stretching it out in front of them.

Allard's hand brushed Vaughan's as they pulled the leather rings into place over Vaughan's cock, and that felt interestingly illicit. Vaughan's cock was very wet and very hard. Allard wanted to throw the new trinket out of the way and take care of Vaughan quite uncomplicatedly, at the same time as he wanted to keep putting the leather rings in place. The latter impulse won by a whisker. Allard was glad it had—something about the dark-and-light effect of black leather rings contrasted with the living colour of cock-flesh was aesthetically or perversely interesting. Inch-by-inch, buckle-by-buckle, he wrapped Vaughan's cock tenderly in its new treat, with plenty of attention to the naked parts, then remembered what Vaughan had been saying.

"I don't need an excuse to get my hands on your cock," corrected Allard. "It's mine."

"That's proprietary for someone who's always on the point of leaving the ship."

"If I leave the ship, I will take this with me," said Allard.

Vaughan's mouth twitched into a smile. "How exactly will you do that?"

Allard looked at the thing he had just done up. If he was lucky, there would be something in the box that met requirements. There was. He brought it to see Vaughan.

He clipped a light leather leash onto the little metal ring on the end of Vaughan's adornment. "I shall attach this to your cock, and then it will follow me everywhere," he said.

"Nothing new there," said Vaughan. "You've been leading me around by the cock for the last three months anyway. This only formalises it, I suppose."

"Five months," Allard said absently.

"Oh, I'm glad you're counting. Unusually romantic for you, Allard."

"No, I'm just naturally calculating." Allard flashed his best shark-like grin in Vaughan's direction.

"Anyway," said Vaughan, "I'm only referring to the number of months you've been leading me around by the cock, as opposed to the number of months we've been at it."

"How interesting," said Allard. "Would you care to elaborate on the distinction?"

"Five months doing it; three months since I realised I'd seriously miss you if you left," Vaughan told him. "Even if you are a nasty little bastard, you're *my* nasty little bastard."

"With a major overlap in fantasies," Allard commented, stroking the latest fantasy.

"And if you left, you'd take part of me with you," said Vaughan, hamming it up dreadfully.

Allard tugged at part of him. "Oh yes, so I would. Already it feels frighteningly natural to wander about with that on a leash."

"Somehow I *thought* you'd like the idea when it came to the reality, even if the catalogue made you feel a bit funny," said Vaughan.

"Come to bed, Vaughan." He tugged on the leash.

"Are you up to doing it twice tonight?" asked Vaughan.

"With suitable inspiration, I probably could." I *hope.*

"Good. You get to be on top first, and then I do."

"I'm not sure how I get to be on top when I'm actually wearing this," said Allard. "Wouldn't it be a little uncomfortable to fuck you with it still on?"

"Actually," said Vaughan, "I don't think you're *supposed* to wear it when you're the top, but it looks very nice anyway."

Allard covered his face with his hands. "You let me *quite innocently* order this perverted creation, and you only *now* bother to tell me that the idea is that a submissive should show off his cock as his Master's property."

"Now you're getting the idea!"

"But because I'm not that experienced, you let me make a fool of myself by making us both bottoms," said Allard crossly.

"You don't actually have to take it that seriously," said Vaughan. "Put a condom over it, and then you can just shove it up me. Yes, there are some in the box. Just shove it up me as if it's a French tickler."

"Anything to get a bigger one. With knobs on," Allard said.

"Yes, exactly," said Vaughan, with relish.

"Slut," said Allard.

"Yes, exactly," said Vaughan.

He hooked the end of the leash over a chair, just to keep Vaughan in place, and rummaged in the box again, finding a set of rather optimistically large condoms in the size GI-NORMOUS (with three exclamation marks). He left the other packet in the box. Vaughan had never mentioned this interest in French ticklers before. Maybe they could find out later. For now, "just shove it up Vaughan" seemed like a very good plan.

He got a tub of good-quality lubricant out of the box and warmed some of the stuff between his hands.

"Bend over," he ordered.

Vaughan bent over.

"Spread 'em."

Vaughan spread 'em, and wriggled.

Allard gave him a couple of wet fingers along with the lube. If he was fractionally wider than normal, Vaughan might need a stretch.

"On the bed now."

Vaughan scrambled onto the bed and knelt shoulders-down, arse-up while Allard prepared his cock with some more of the lubricant.

Allard settled himself into position kneeling behind Vaughan. "Here it comes," he said, and went straight in. He watched the tip swallowed up, then the black-leather-encased shaft. It felt quite different with the additional layers. He pulled back and tried again; yes, the leather *did* add something to the experience. It slowed him down, blunted the sensation, but on the other hand, being able to watch his cock—his leather-covered cock—slide right in… He growled and tried it again, grabbing at Vaughan's buttocks with his hand, spreading them so he had a better view.

Vaughan whimpered and shoved back onto him.

Too fast. He didn't want it that quick. He grabbed the leash and held it so that Vaughan couldn't move. "Hold still. You have to hold still. I've got you by the cock."

Vaughan moaned, tried to move, and then abruptly held still.

"That's better."

"Fuck me. Please."

Politeness was to be encouraged. Allard fucked him.

"I wonder what the others would say if they saw you like this? Would they elect you captain next time 'round?"

"I'm not the—ouch!" said Vaughan, as Allard tugged experimentally.

"You certainly look the perfect picture of a captain now, with your arse in the air and your cock tied up in a leather bow." He thrust again, and tugged again (more gently now).

Vaughan moaned, a moan of pleasure now. He must have got it right this time.

"Harry would run away, but the girls…now, the girls would probably like to see you making a pretty picture like this." He reached for Vaughan's cock, ran a finger along the length, enjoyed the sensation of skin and leather alternating beneath his fingertip.

He thrust one more time. "In fact, I think *I'd* quite like to see it." He pulled out. "Turn over."

Vaughan complained, but did as he was told.

Allard slid off the bed, stood next to it, and ordered Vaughan to shuffle himself into the right position. "I'm glad," said Allard, "that the bed is at the perfect height for me to do *this.*" He shoved his cock in again, and watched the way Vaughan's cock jumped. He liked the idea that he was in complete control of Vaughan's pleasure in this position. This was unlike the more intimate ways to do this, because Vaughan's cock would *not* be getting any attention unless Allard did something for him. Meanwhile, Vaughan's lovely cock was nicely presented, trussed-up and tied by the leash for Allard's pleasure. Which was considerable.

Vaughan tried to grab himself.

Allard slapped his hand. "Naughty. Ask first."

"Please, sir, may I play with my cock?"

He ran a fingertip over Vaughan's cock, enjoying the way Vaughan's hands clenched into fists. "Since you ask so nicely."

Vaughan was evidently trying to get a good rhythm going, and equally evidently having trouble because he was so constricted by the new toy. It was a pleasure to watch. Allard felt quite *glad* it was a toy for submissives now he saw it being used that way. It made him feel very dominant.

He trailed the leash suggestively over the very tip of Vaughan's cock.

Vaughan bucked enthusiastically.

Even through the leather-and-condom covering him up, Allard noticed that.

"May I take the thing off now?" asked Vaughan. Not just playing a role. He looked as if he really *did* need to take it off.

"Let me see. All right, undo one buckle." Allard thrust.

Vaughan undid one buckle, on the second go, in spite of Allard's attempt to distract him by thrusting again.

"Good. Next buckle."

"Yes, sir."

He ran a hand over Vaughan's balls as Vaughan's shaky fingers struggled with a very tiny buckle.

"You're not making this easy," Vaughan complained as the fastening finally gave way.

"It's not meant to be easy. It's meant to be…*hard.*" It was hard. "To make it hard, you'll have to wait a bit before being allowed to undo the next buckle."

"Bastard!" Vaughan spat, but his cock pricked up.

Allard got a few good thrusts in before the next stage. He wanted to be close to orgasm himself when he finally let Vaughan undo the last one.

"Ask very nicely, and I'll let you undo another one."

"Please, sir, may I undo another one?"

"Oh, very well." He watched greedily as one more leather strap loosened, leaving only the one encircling the base of Vaughan's cock. More thrusts to go with that.

Vaughan grabbed his cock for a quick feel now it was a bit looser.

"Wouldn't you rather take that last buckle off?" Allard asked, in the purr he knew Vaughan liked. He kept thrusting as

Vaughan swore and fumbled and struggled. Eventually, just as the last buckle was giving way to Vaughan's insistence, he spoke.

"Since you like the idea of French ticklers so much, maybe I should slip a finger or two up beside my cock and tickle your insides."

Vaughan said something indecipherable, ripped the leather strap through the buckle, and came.

Allard watched, and waited. When Vaughan had finally finished, he pulled out of Vaughan, and stripped off the condom. The leather laces took a little more effort, then the leather sheath was gone, leaving his cock naked to the air. He needed it *now,* he couldn't wait until Vaughan had recovered. He climbed onto the bed, knelt over Vaughan. "Suck me."

Vaughan looked up at him. Still turned on, even though he'd just come. He opened his mouth. Allard shoved, and gasped at the feel of warm, wet flesh surrounding him instead of leather. The contrast was shocking, even before Vaughan sucked hard. Then all he had time to think was *yes,* before he came down Vaughan's throat.

Glorious sensation surrounded him, making him dizzy. Vaughan's hands were on him, supporting him. Then he was finished, able to pull away, sink down to lie beside Vaughan. He draped his arm across Vaughan's chest, enjoying the comforting bulk.

He could lie here like this for quite a long time. One of the things he liked about screwing someone who was significantly bigger than him was having plenty to hold onto afterwards. He stroked his hand across Vaughan's chest. Vaughan responded by rolling over, taking Allard into his arms, and rolling back. Allard settled happily into Vaughan's embrace, head pillowed on Vaughan's chest.

* * *

He was woken up by gentle caresses stroking his back. It was dim, not quite dark; Vaughan must have turned down the lighting.

"Allard?" Vaughan whispered.

"Mm?"

"You awake?"

"I am now." He orientated himself enough to nip Vaughan's nipple between his teeth.

"Oh good, you're feeling playful."

"And?"

"It's my turn on top." There was a lascivious tone to Vaughan's voice. "Can you get it up? Not that it matters, so long as *I* can."

He nipped Vaughan again. "It matters to me."

"Ouch. You obviously need to be gagged."

"Think you can make me hold still long enough to put a gag on me if I'm not too aroused to care what you're doing?" Not that he minded the gag, as long as Vaughan didn't want it too often.

"Oh, I think I could," Vaughan purred. "There are some other things in that box."

"Such as?"

"Allow me to demonstrate." Vaughan pushed him off, and sat up. "Lights up." Vaughan went over to the box, and came back with a handful of leather and metal. He dropped it in a pile on the bed, and picked out one piece. "Give me your hand."

Some sort of bondage gear, presumably. He held up his hand. Vaughan wrapped the leather strip around his wrist and fastened it. He examined it. Leather with a small strap and buckle to fasten it, and a couple of metal loops.

"Wrist cuffs, so that I can position you how I want."

This was getting just a little bit too kinky for Allard. Improvised ties were one thing; this was premeditated, slightly more serious. Well, he'd have felt that about the penis coverings, too, if he'd actually *known* they were meant to carry the message of extreme submission. How could he actually manage to say any of this without looking like an innocent or a fool?

He didn't have to.

"You don't like this, do you?" said Vaughan. He didn't sound embarrassed, or put-off, but more as though he actually wanted to know, which made it easier for Allard to tell him.

"I don't think I do. I'm—" *…scared,* he realised.

Vaughan undid the wrist cuff and took Allard's hand. "Afraid," he said.

"And what are you? Disappointed?"

"Not really. It's more like, 'could have been interesting to play with, but only if it got you going'. I didn't realise you were quite that much of an innocent." By the look on Vaughan's face, he liked the idea.

"Well, you have been pretending I was a virgin," said Allard. "It appears I actually *am* one in some metaphorical sense."

"Yes, I rather think you are," said Vaughan, in that low intimate tone he used when distinctly interested.

"Are you actually considering ravishing me in some way?" *Run away! Run away!*

Vaughan kissed him very gently. "Well, no more than I already *do,* Allard. It's a nice fantasy, but I wouldn't like myself afterwards."

He has his limits, too.

Vaughan put his arms round Allard. There was absolutely no hint of anything but tenderness. Allard relaxed a little. Vaughan kissed him, and there wasn't even the usual playful battle for dominance, not that he could say he missed it right now. Just the assurance that they both still liked each other, and there were no hurt feelings growing from their differences.

Vaughan's tongue licked slowly against his. No, thought Allard, the tongue's still a welcome visitor, and neither of us seems to have been put off. He brushed the edge of his hand gently across Vaughan's cock; good, they were both still up for it, but not desperate.

Vaughan pulled back. "Good job we asked Harry to switch his bugs off."

"Yes," said Allard. This was one conversation he would not want recorded for posterity.

"I'd quite like to push you gently back onto the bed and get started on you, Allard, but I don't want to make you nervous. And, before you say it, we *haven't* ruined everything, and I *won't* feel the need to ask your permission for every little move. It's just that, after that conversation, I'd like to take things a bit slowly."

"All right." He made room on the bed for Vaughan, and this time they held each other side-by-side.

Vaughan kept kissing him and stroking his back with one hand.

Allard reached up and ran his fingers through Vaughan's curls.

"You do like playing with my hair."

"Yes." This time, Allard started the next kiss. It was a little more decisive without being dominant, and it took some time. When it had finished, he was on his back, and Vaughan was on top of him, without triggering any of those sudden fits of nerves he'd been worrying about. He still liked Vaughan's weight on him. Good.

"Fuck me," he whispered.

Vaughan reached out for the lubricant without breaking eye contact with him. Fumbling a bit because he wasn't looking down at what he was doing, Vaughan managed to do a reasonable job of applying it.

Vaughan lay on him, cuddling him closely and easing himself in at more-or-less the same time. Slow, controlled; he felt every millimetre going in. He held Vaughan tightly, enjoying the controlled glide and enjoying the way Vaughan was holding back for his sake. He kissed Vaughan just as Vaughan reached the length of his stroke. They held still for a moment, then Vaughan broke the kiss and gasped. "I can't hold back any longer."

"I want you," said Allard.

Vaughan shut his eyes, pulled out, and slammed back in. Rougher than he'd quite like, but he knew Vaughan would stop if he liked, and he knew it was randiness rather than violence.

The next stroke just felt good. The stroke after that, he was clutching Vaughan's arse and urging him on.

"I want to make it last," said Vaughan, speeding up.

"Good," said Allard, fingering Vaughan's buttocks.

Skin against skin felt wonderful; he'd enjoyed the illicit naughtiness of doing it half-dressed, but the sheer simple pleasure of knowing there was nothing in the way was even better. Hot, heavy weight, and the feel of Vaughan's heart pounding, and the sound of his breath. Vaughan's cock stroking him deep inside.

"Your weight pinning me down is all the restraint I need."

"It's all I need too, pet." Vaughan's expression was tender.

I didn't ruin anything, Allard thought happily. "Make me come," he murmured.

"Please?" suggested Vaughan.

"Make me come, *please,*" said Allard, lowering his voice to an intimately desperate murmur. He did want to, very much.

"Of course," said Vaughan. He slid a hand between them, grasped Allard's cock. Just the feel of Vaughan's hand enclosing him was almost enough; one quick jerk was all he needed. He heard Vaughan say, "I love being able to do that." *You're not the only one,* he thought, and then it was streaming out of him in a long effortless burst. Just as he was about to stop, Vaughan started. This made his arse clench and his cock quiver, and the aftershocks were a nearly painful pleasure.

Good of him to come just *when it made it feel even better for me,* he thought, before realising it was a very silly thought.

Considering his cock and/or brain had just melted, he wasn't capable of any better thought than that.

Vaughan had the sense to roll off and, very tenderly, hold him while he slept.

*   *   *

Allard went to get clean clothes out for the day. The first thing that came to hand was a pair of leather trousers. He tossed them on the bed, then stopped and looked at them. Then he picked them up. "Vaughan, have I led you on?"

"No, that's not what gave me the idea you might like…well…I'm sorry, Allard. I didn't think it would bother you. After all, you were talking about putting a Prince Albert on me not that long ago."

"And I wear leather, and I like silly fantasies, and I let you tie me up." He ran a hand through his hair, wondering how to explain this. It would help if he could explain it to *himself.* "It's…there are things that I was vaguely aware of, but I'd never thought of them as applying to me."

"Like knowing about people wearing leather for sexual reasons, but not thinking about what people might think of the stuff you have for everyday clothing. Because as far as you're concerned, it *is* everyday clothing." Vaughan smiled at him, "Hardly surprising, really. Lots of people wear it as everyday clothing. You're not even the only one on this ship; just the one who seems to live in it permanently."

"And when you tied me up—it was the first time anyone had actually done that."

"And *lots* of people have muttered about how a gag would make an excellent accessory for you."

"Quite." He grinned ruefully. "I've had so many people make rude suggestions about making me behave that the reality was a bit of a shock."

"For someone with a filthy mind, you can be very unworldly at times."

"I thought that was what you liked about me."

"It is." Vaughan kissed him. "Better get dressed before my poor cock tries to wake itself up for the third time in ten hours."

They dressed quickly and went to breakfast.

* * *

"So what are our plans today?" asked Allard.

"This job's nearly finished," said Harry, "and I'll be able to put my feet up after all the hard work."

Allard said, "We already have foot-shaped dents on most of the consoles from your normal idea of hard work."

"You couldn't have priced this little lot up in a few hours, without looking things up on the net."

"True. Apart from the computers, and it didn't take too long to do those. I'll be finished by lunch. Harry, you work on the cheetah principle—five-minute sprints interrupted by weeks of inactivity."

"Yeah," Harry agreed. "Good, isn't it?"

"What are you going to do after lunch?" Vaughan asked. "Sort this new computer out?"

Mark said, "I have a name, even if I don't like it. Use it. And I don't need sorting out."

"Would you like a matching dent on the other side?" Vaughan asked pleasantly.

"Would you like reconstructive surgery on your foot?" Mark replied.

"Do you want to be treated as a crewman or as a computer? If you wish to be treated as an individual rather than as part of the ship's equipment, you will be subject to the same treatment as the rest of the crew. And if you annoy us, you'll get the same reaction any other pain-in-the-neck would."

"I don't have the same input ports as Allard."

"I have a large and sharp probe," muttered Allard. "If you want an input port created—or if *Vaughan* does…"

"Forget I spoke, Dad."

"And stop calling me that!"

"Yes, Dad."

"And you do need sorting out. We don't know what nasty little traps may be part of your programming, and I am not putting you to work until I know exactly what's loose in your memory bank."

"Da-ad! Do you need to check if I washed behind my audio sockets?"

"Yes," said Allard, un-gritting his teeth just enough to let the word escape.

"Anyway, what do you actually want me for?"

Allard was grateful that AIs got curious enough to stop being a pain when they wanted to know something. He launched into a long and detailed technical discussion, interrupted by "Coo! That sounds interesting!" from Mark, and "Well, at least he's got *somebody* to talk to, instead of boring us," from Claire.

Mark stopped talking to Allard for long enough to say, "Yes, I *have* got somebody to talk to. It's all I wanted, and the people at that other place never understood."

After Allard's technical discussion, he took a bare five minutes to acquaint Mark with the way things were done on this ship. "Any questions?" he finished.

"Yes. What's my salary?"

"Your *salary?*" That had actually been Vaughan, but they were probably all thinking it.

"I need a salary as a crew-member," said Mark. "I don't have any assets to put into the pot, so I can't be a crew-member in the normal way—I've read up on it. But I can be like Allard; you can pay me a wage for the work I contribute."

"What would be the point of that?" asked Harry. "It's not like you'll want to go out and have wild parties." He paused. "At least I don't *think* you will, but if you can develop a taste for porn, anything's possible."

"No, that's not it," said Mark, in his Bossy Little Sod voice. "I will save up my wages and buy my own share in the ship like the other crewmembers."

"And what will you do with it?" asked Allard, fascinated.

"I'm going to have my own voice in decision-making. Nobody else will ever throw me on a junk-heap again," said Mark firmly.

"Argumentative, bright, lateral-thinking, and just plain weird. Actually *wants* to be part of a syndicalist ship. I can see that you'll fit in perfectly," Allard said with a weary sigh. "Welcome to the crew."

THE SYNDICATE:
VOLUME 2

Telephone Manner

by Jules Jones

There was something about the sight of a very pretty woman fondling huge weapons that got Allard excited. Judging by Vaughan's expression, Allard wasn't the only one. No matter how often Karen touched and patted and stroked suggestively along those rounded barrels, it still affected him. *It's just weapons technology,* he told himself, as usual. *So?* retorted his cock.

He managed to keep a grip on his reactions (or *not* keep a grip on them) for just long enough to perform the necessary computer checks Karen had asked him to carry out on the cargo before it was delivered.

Then he stood there and fidgeted, but she was so involved in trying to give the equipment a hand-job, she didn't seem to notice.

Ten unendurable minutes passed, during which Vaughan finished the last engineering checks. "Can we go now, Karen?" asked Vaughan.

Karen flapped her hand, dismissing them without even looking at them. "I can finish the rest of the pre-delivery checks."

Vaughan's bedroom was nearest.

"It's a bit lowering," said Allard, "to think that I don't register on her scale of 'important things' because mine isn't two feet long." He groaned. "Even if it feels like it, at the moment."

"I think it's a good size," said Vaughan, assessing the dimensions.

Allard moaned. "Give me a wank. I need something *now* after watching that!"

He moaned again, this time with relief, as Vaughan started to stroke him through the trousers. He loved that, and Vaughan seemed to have some idea that he liked to be touched through cloth.

Vaughan stopped.

"Bastard!" said Allard, without opening his eyes.

"In the interests of getting a proper grip on it," explained Vaughan, undoing him efficiently and showing him what he meant by a proper grip. Allard moaned, and collapsed against Vaughan's shoulder.

Vaughan put one arm 'round him to hold him up while the other hand went to work on his cock. A lovely firm grip. Good, firm strokes along the whole length. Just what Karen had been doing to her beloved guns. He spared just a moment to wish his cock *was* two feet long, just so that he could enjoy being stroked for…longer. If it was longer.

His brain wasn't coming up with the usual good-quality thoughts; he must be busy with something else. He was.

"Messy little bugger," Vaughan said affectionately.

Allard managed one last spurt, just to convince Vaughan that he never paid any attention to Vaughan's comments.

He sagged happily in Vaughan's arms. "Give me a minute, and I'll do you."

He was still dozing when Vaughan dragged him to the bed and let him fall.

"Mm?" he said, rather woozily.

"Didn't want to let you collapse on the floor, and you're a hell of a weight if I have to prop you up for more than two minutes."

"I feel *much* better now!" said Allard, and stretched. "All right, what would you like? Within reason," he clarified.

"Well, you could just sprawl there while I stick my cock into the melted heap of what's left," said Vaughan.

Allard moaned agreeably and rolled over.

"On the other hand, if you're feeling energetic enough, you could actually pay some attention to my cock. I may not be as fond of women as you are, but I still quite enjoyed the show." He paused. "Not Karen as much as the show going on in your trousers."

"You mean you were looking at my trousers instead of what Karen was doing?"

"At least half the time. Yes, she's pretty, but I love it when I can watch you squirming where you stand, gritting your teeth and obviously thinking 'I must not have sex now! I must wait! I can't stand it!'"

Allard sighed. He wasn't entirely comfortable with the fact that his body language was that readable.

"If I wasn't having an affair with you, or if I didn't know you this well, I don't think I'd have noticed," Vaughan said. "I don't think Karen realised."

Allard sighed harder.

"*Now* what's the matter?" demanded Vaughan.

"It's embarrassing making a show of myself. It's more embarrassing when you behave as if you can read my mind."

"It's easier to read your mind when you're thinking with your *cock*head rather than your *real* head," said Vaughan, gently touching both organs.

Allard relaxed a bit, and reached out for Vaughan. "You mentioned a hand-job."

"I wasn't that specific," said Vaughan. "I said 'paying attention to my cock', but I think your mouth would be rather nice, as well. You decide."

Allard slid down off the bed to kneel (in a rather relaxed way) at Vaughan's feet.

"I'll suck you, if you can be quick about it." He undid Vaughan's trousers and got his cock out. "Mm?" he asked, around the head.

"Quick isn't going to be a problem," said Vaughan.

Allard gave it a good, hard suck. He liked doing this after he'd come; it was still a pleasure, and it was more relaxing not to have to worry about being over-excited. Every tight, hard suck he gave Vaughan seemed to make Vaughan's cock bigger, tighter, harder; a few seconds of that, and Vaughan came hard.

Then Vaughan collapsed, partly on him and partly on the floor.

"Bed," Allard said, which was about all he had the breath to say.

Vaughan took the hint, although Allard took most of the blankets.

"I know you feel the cold, Allard," said Vaughan, "but we *are* dressed at this point."

"Ah," said Allard. "Force of habit."

"Yes," said Vaughan, "I've noticed."

Allard pulled the blankets off and kicked him.

"Uncivilised little sod," said Vaughan mildly.

"I thought that's what you liked about me, when you weren't on your 'virgin' kick."

"It's the contrast," Vaughan said, in an appreciative voice.

Allard, not minding that, wiped himself more-or-less clean with one corner of the sheet.

"Oy! I'm going to sleep in that tonight!" said Vaughan.

"Tell yourself it's a charming reminder of the experience." He tidied Vaughan up, as well, tucking him neatly back into his trousers.

There was a sudden click as the intercom turned on. It was followed by Mark's voice, saying, "They don't seem to be on the flight-deck at the moment. I'm putting you through to their cabin. Don't worry about any noises—it just tends to mean they're having sex again. Don't interrupt them; he gets a bit annoyed if you do that. I'm sure they'll want to talk to you afterwards, though," he added brightly, as if to console the possible client. "Dad!" he carolled. "Are you decent? Someone wants to talk to Vaughan."

Vaughan looked at Allard. "I am starting to think we may possibly have made a mistake in making that computer our receptionist."

Allard was starting to understand why he'd found Mark in a junk heap. "Do you want to grovel to the customer, or shall I?"

"You're not very good at grovelling to the customers, just to me."

Allard opened his mouth.

"I'd better get it," continued Vaughan hurriedly, hitting the intercom.

"Vaughan here. How may I help?"

There was silence for a few seconds, followed by: "Er..."

"Please let me apologise for our receptionist. He's an artificial intelligence, and he doesn't quite seem to have got the hang of human communications yet."

"Er...artificial intelligence? But I thought it was...somebody's son..." The tone of voice suggested that the person did not entirely approve of somebody's young son knowing about his father's sex life.

"Only in a manner of speaking," commented Allard dryly. "I was the originator of some of the more important algorithms, and therefore count as his father in some sense. He seems to find it amusing to call me Dad."

"If it *is* a computer," said the voice doubtfully, "it doesn't seem to be interested in the usual things a computer is interested in."

"I am!" said Mark. "I'm interested in ever so many things, and the human social stuff is fascinating."

"It is not a computer," said Allard. "It is an artificial intelligence, and we are learning the difference between the two concepts. Unfortunately," he added.

"Well…" the voice said, trailing off.

Vaughan said, "Why not meet us to discuss whatever it is you wanted to contact us about? One meeting with Mark is usually more than enough to convince people that he is what people say he is."

"A nosy, arrogant little prick," muttered Allard under his breath, quietly enough that it wouldn't carry through the intercom.

Vaughan heard, though. Equally quietly, he said, "Pot. Kettle."

Allard was tempted to try physical retaliation, but had more sense than to try it when engaged in contract negotiation. Especially considering the image this particular potential client must already have of them.

"You are in the Poseidon system at the moment, aren't you?"

"Yes, we're quite reachable," said Vaughan, and began talking co-ordinates.

* * *

Vaughan led their visitor onto the flight-deck and made introductions.

"And this," he said at last, "is Mark."

"That?" Moore didn't look impressed.

"This," said Mark.

The visitor jumped. Then he peered at Mark with more interest. "I've never seen anything quite like this."

"Meatbrains exist by the millions," Mark said. "I am unique."

"Having spoken to him," said Vaughan, "you can quite see why."

"Ignore my stepfather," said Mark.

Vaughan glared at the little machine while Moore boggled at it.

"Your *stepfather?*"

"All right, *technically* he's not my stepfather. He's fucking my father every night, but I suppose they're not legally married. Yet."

"Ever, if I have to take responsibility for you," Vaughan said.

Allard decided he wanted to change the subject from 'legally married' to…well, anything else. "Perhaps we could discuss the work you wanted us to do for you."

Moore gave Mark one last appalled glance. "Ah. Yes. Right. Er…do you think we could go somewhere else?"

"Yes, he has that effect on a lot of people," said Allard.

"So do you," murmured Claire.

"Bye!" called Mark, as they walked out.

* * *

As they walked into the dining room, Moore asked Allard, "How do you feel about a computer calling you Dad?"

Much the same as I'd feel about an organic human calling me Dad, Allard thought, but was diplomatic enough not to say.

"I've always been a responsible sex partner," he muttered. "Made sure I was up-to-date on contraception. And what happens? I find myself responsible for offspring anyway. And not just *any* offspring. A computer that reads porn for a hobby."

"Reads porn?"

"Don't ask."

"What, something about sockets? Manuals and stuff?"

"No." Allard sighed. "It's an artificial intelligence patterned after humans. The fact that it doesn't have the equipment doesn't stop it fantasising."

"That must be…interesting to live with."

"You don't know the half of it," said Allard. *Unfortunately, I suspect we might not know the half of it, either.*

It seemed they'd reassured Moore. He relaxed a bit, and started discussing prices and bringing out contract forms.

* * *

After they'd waved bye-bye to the customer, it was time to have That Talk with Mark. No, not *That* Talk—they'd had the sex-education stuff days ago; the more challenging stuff about social interaction.

After the last fortnight, Allard now had more sympathy for those people who had junked Mark. He wasn't going to do it himself, and it wasn't precisely Mark's *fault.* It was just that he could understand how they'd felt.

"I think we're going to have to teach Mark some manners," he said.

"You don't say!" said Harry. "Where are you going to get them from?"

"I have excellent manners," said Allard truthfully. "I just keep them for best."

"Yes, he's incoherently grateful quite often," said Vaughan.

"Yes, we know," said everyone else.

"Harry, are you distributing tapes?" Allard said rather suspiciously.

"Not outside the ship."

Allard looked at the two women. "I did not realise Harry was contagious."

"Only when we haven't been able to pick up our own supplies of porn," said Claire.

Allard took a moment to think uncharitable thoughts about women's liberation. Centuries ago, it wouldn't have been conceivable that women were such avid consumers of dirty videos. It must have been wonderful.

Of course, that meant there would still have been people like Harry about… He paused. *Were* there other people like Harry?

No, he didn't actually want to think about that.

"I suppose we *had* better discuss this with Mark," said Vaughan.

They went back to the flight-deck.

Mark turned whatever optical sensors he had on the crowd of people approaching him, as he said nervously, "Dad? Am I in trouble again?"

"No more than usual," said Allard.

Vaughan said, "We think you need to learn a bit more about proper behaviour."

"You already know quite enough about improper behaviour," said Claire.

Mark said, "Oh, well, I can learn manners by watching the rest of you."

Allard said firmly, "No. Proper ones, not the rubbish we have on this ship."

It would have been too much to expect for the rest of the conversation not to be a furious argument about what constituted 'proper manners'.

Claire said to Harry, "Your idea of manners is to wipe anything on your tapes which doesn't include sex. It's not normal, is it?"

"It's *very* normal!" said Harry rather huffily. "I'm just more honest about it than some people."

"Which of us was that remark intended to insult?" asked Claire.

"Well, you seem quite happy to listen to one or two of mine," said Harry.

"There's a difference between occasionally listening because it's there, and actually creating the stuff."

"Yeah," said Harry. "Creativity. Anyway, I'm not the one with a weapons fetish who gets into trouble with governments."

Karen had caused a couple of diplomatic incidents by going and finding out about military tech on a couple of planets where people had the impression that one should go through proper channels.

"I don't see what the problem was," said Karen. "They ought to be flattered that an expert took an interest in how they did it."

"One, it was supposed to be secret; and two, you're probably the only one who's been quite so blatant about sexually molesting their weapons," said Harry.

"I wasn't sexually molesting them. And at least I don't use rude words to describe them," Karen said. "If Claire is going to use the sort of language she usually does about Customs officials, could she try to remember to switch the radio off before saying it, please?"

Vaughan said, "Can we all sit down in a circle and discuss who takes turns to speak first? Otherwise, the conversation gets hijacked by the usual troublemakers."

Allard said, "And you start trying to convert people to your political viewpoint at the slightest excuse. At least I don't try to shove my politics down other people's throats."

"No, just your cock," said Harry.

"That's only because you don't *have* any politics!" snapped Vaughan.

"Oh, look how impressed and insulted I am," sneered Allard.

"Take him away and fuck him," suggested Karen. "He's getting stroppy again."

"And you," said Allard poisonously, pointing at Karen, "suggest Vaughan take me away and fuck me every time I make a suggestion you don't like."

"Actually," said Karen, "I was suggesting you take *Vaughan* away and fuck him."

"That's all right, then," said Allard, thinking, *it's taken them months to pick up on the lack of fixed role-playing.*

"What?" said Vaughan.

"I *said,*" said Karen, "Allard needs to fuck you to shut you up. God knows it works better than anything the rest of us can do."

"Well, Mark," said Harry, "do you see now why you ought to go on a proper training course instead of listening to us lot?"

"Certainly," said Mark. "This is absolutely fascinating. It's nothing like the stuff I've picked up from books and data-banks."

"Shut up, everybody!" said Vaughan, loudly.

Everybody did, slightly shocked.

"There are training courses available for receptionists," said Vaughan. "We will find one suitable for Mark and put him through it."

"With a meat-grinder, if necessary," Allard muttered *sotto voce.*

* * *

Courses were easy to find. Unfortunately, the very best one (and Allard insisted upon quality, or, if possible, miracles) wasn't a correspondence course at all.

"Applicants must be accepted in person, on a case-by-case basis," said the prospectus rather ominously. Allard doubted they'd actually even thought about accepting any non-organic applicants. AIs usually came programmed for it if they were expected to work as receptionists.

As expected, the course providers kicked up an awful stink about non-standard applicants. After a lot of argument, Allard hit on the idea of sending Mark down with a couple of people to serve as bodyguards, if necessary.

"Meatbrains make good transport," said Mark. "You have those useful hand-things for picking me up."

"We could always try building you an android body you could remote-control," said Allard, without thinking about the possible consequences. Then he did, and wished he'd kept quiet. At least, at the moment, Mark was an *immobile* pain-in-the-neck.

"There isn't enough time before the next course," Mark said.

Allard hoped he would have forgotten about the idea by the time he'd finished the course.

"Any preferences on who you want to go with you?" asked Allard, watching a ripple of 'please-god-not-me' circulate swiftly through the crew.

"Karen and a big gun, so she can wave it at anyone who starts saying things about me," said Mark. "Oh, and Claire can help lift me."

Karen actually looked pleased at that. Claire looked resigned but not too unhappy.

"And the rest of us can go shopping," Harry suggested.

"Haven't you got enough porn tapes?" asked Claire.

"Got to replace the ones you keep in your room… No, seriously, I was actually thinking about general shopping, for once."

"Sounds fun," said Claire. "I'll give you a list, if I have to cart Mark about."

"Shopping, seeing the sights. Yes, a bit of relaxation would be nice," agreed Vaughan. "You ladies can always do the town in the evenings."

"Just as long as we can do the town in the evenings, as well," said Allard, petting part of Vaughan to make it clear what sort of entertainment he was thinking of.

"Do you ever think of anything else?" asked Vaughan.

"Frequently. Most of the time, actually."

"What's he mean by that?" Vaughan asked Harry in a loud whisper.

"Means he's got his mind on the job instead of 'on the job' most of the time," Harry said. "You only rate ahead of the computers when he's got an erection."

"That's what it's like shagging a geek. Second-best, if that. Just because *I* don't have flashing lights," Vaughan muttered, disgruntled.

"And you don't even turn into a pizza," said Allard.

"Third-best," said Vaughan. "Computers, junk-food, then sex."

"Don't know why you bother, really," said Harry.

"You know exactly why I bother, Harry. You listen to it often enough."

"Yes, the way he manages to have that air of innocence despite the filthy mind and filthier language," said Harry. "Either it's the haircut, or he was brought up by nuns. Computer nuns."

Allard decided he was going to have to work on his image.

"And it's real, in spite of the filthy mind and filthier language," said Vaughan.

Allard glared at him. He decided not to say anything, partly because it would only amuse them, and particularly because there was a certain amount of truth in it, which embarrassed him even more.

* * *

"I feel like being perverted tonight!" said Harry.

"You *are* perverted, Harry."

"All right, I feel like having a change. Rather than taking a sneaky peek at you lot, I feel like paying to watch it on stage. Want to *come* with me?"

I should never have used that pun on him, thought Allard.

"What were you thinking of?" Vaughan said.

"There are some really good shows in this city. Might teach Allard a thing or two, while we're at it."

"I am not *that* naïve," said Allard crossly.

"How d'you know? You haven't seen any of them!" said Harry.

"There are only so many ways to put two bodies together," said Allard, "and I've probably seen most of them while clearing out other people's hard-drives."

"Why confine yourself to two?" said Harry, who might well not have *done* any more exotic things than Allard, but who had certainly seen the lot. Frequently.

Allard decided it was pointless trying to compete with Harry on this particular subject. "All right," he said, "you choose." He wasn't too concerned about what Harry might choose. Oddly enough, he could actually rely on Harry to make sure it wasn't something *too* tasteless.

Harry glanced around them. "That one," he said, pointing at a doorway across the street.

In fact, it wasn't tasteless at all. Just a theatre.

The performance was a musical, which just happened to be performed by amazingly attractive people in very little clothing. The dance-steps were also designed to make the clothing there wasn't much of…swirl. In interesting ways. Allard was riveted.

"Allard," said Harry, "your eyes are glazing over."

"Mm."

"Vaughan," said Harry, "I think he's enjoying it."

"Mm."

"Talk to yourself, Chance!" Harry muttered.

"Shut up and drink your champagne, Harry," Allard and Vaughan said in unison.

Allard had been sufficiently broken out of the mood to realise that he was holding hands with Vaughan under the table. He decided he didn't care. He sank back into enjoying the show. It was tastefully erotic in a subtler way than a straightforward sex-show, allowing his responses to start at 'aesthetic' and move all the way to 'insanely arousing'.

The next time he noticed where his hand was, it wasn't on Vaughan's *hand*…

Oh, well. The seating here was arranged in high-walled booths, so nobody could see except Harry.

By the time the show ended, he was very much of a mood to take Vaughan somewhere, preferably somewhere nearer than 'home to bed'. Since everybody had decided to make a night of it, there was nobody to operate the teleport, so they'd have to get to the ship on foot. He'd prefer to find somewhere else.

Apparently Vaughan had noticed, and before Allard could say anything, whispered: "Do you want somewhere salubrious, or would those by-the-hour rooms do?"

Allard thought about it. The by-the-hour rooms were probably closer, and could be interestingly naughty. On the other hand, he felt like indulging himself in an expensive hotel room, where he could caress Vaughan slowly in a big, silky bed without the threat of cockroaches. Oh, well—they were fairly flush at the moment.

"If we go to a by-the-hour place, we may have an audience. I've just about got used to Harry, but the idea of being a peep-show for people I'm not even friendly with is unacceptable."

Vaughan bent down and whispered, "What *is* acceptable?" softly into Allard's ear, following that with a kiss.

Allard's cock began to beat out a rhythm of "soon, soon, soon!" inside his trousers.

Shut up! he hissed mentally. "Let's indulge. Somewhere with a honeymoon suite—and don't get any ideas about making Mark legitimate!"

"Wouldn't dream of it," said Vaughan.

"Am I invited?" said Harry.

Allard actually thought about it, to his horror, then said, "Go and find your own fun."

"It was worth asking," said Harry. "Oh, look, there are a couple of ladies on their own over there." He straightened his tie, and Allard thought, *Harry actually does scrub up quite nicely when he decides to go out on the town rather than use us for his entertainment.*

He looked at Vaughan, as well. Full evening dress looked good on *him,* too. Lots of layers to unwrap, which need not be a bad thing.

They watched as Harry got a smile rather than a slap.

"Looks like he's safe enough for the evening," Vaughan said. "Shall we go?"

They didn't have to go very far to find a good hotel. It was full of all those little luxuries one didn't get in normal shipboard life. As for what it *lacked,* well, it was bug-free, both in the 'cockroach' sense and in the 'Harry' sense. Definitely good enough.

Vaughan lay on the bed, kicked his shoes off, and ate the complimentary chocolates provided for both of them. Allard pretended not to notice. He would have *liked* a chocolate, but it would be more dignified not to notice.

"Oh," said Vaughan. "Damn, I didn't mean to eat both of those. Sorry."

"Don't give it another thought."

"I just noticed you not-noticing, with gritted teeth."

"Stop spoiling the mood, Vaughan."

"Well, un-grit your teeth and go and have a look in the mini-bar. There will be more chocolate through there." Vaughan sat up again. "No, on second thought, I'll get them. You lie back on the bed, and I'll come and feed them to you."

"What a lovely idea." Allard disposed himself, in carefully calculated slight disorder, on the bed. If he was lucky, he looked *just* rumpled, rather than foolish. *Come on, Vaughan, or I* will *feel a fool lying here like this.*

Vaughan came back with a box of truffles. He sat on the bed and opened the box, then unwrapped one truffle and held it out, very delicately.

Equally delicately, Allard leant toward him and closed his mouth around it. He pulled back slightly, sucking Vaughan's fingers as he did so. The truffle was good. A little too cold from the fridge, but a wonderful flavour that intensified as his body heat warmed it. He let it melt over his tongue, enjoying the sensation.

Vaughan stroked his face softly. "You look disgustingly decadent."

"Good."

Allard ate three more chocolates, unhurriedly.

Vaughan kissed him, then said, "Yes, they *do* taste nice."

"So do you."

They shared a few more chocolates and kisses. Allard was going on the principle that he could always work off the calories with a little help from Vaughan.

He wanted to touch more than lips now. He wrapped his arms around Vaughan and pulled him down.

"You're rumpling my clothes all up," said Vaughan.

"I like you rumpled," said Allard, undoing Vaughan's tie. It was surprisingly difficult dealing with a tie 'round someone else's neck, even when he was just *un*doing it. He wasn't too bothered, since he was in the mood to take it slowly.

"Whereas *I* quite like you all dressed-up to the nines. It's nice to be able to prise you out of your geek-wear occasionally."

"I'm still in black."

"Apart from this lovely royal-blue cummerbund," Vaughan said, doing things to the cummerbund, "and that crisp white shirt. There's something decidedly tempting about that crisp white shirt."

"The idea of un-crisping it, you mean." Allard did so to Vaughan's, playing with it as he undid the buttons, and running crisp pleats between his fingers.

"Something like that, yes," Vaughan said, slipping his finger through a gap between a couple of buttons on Allard's shirt.

Allard wriggled slightly, and the finger made contact with his nipple.

"Don't wriggle," said Vaughan. "It interferes with my precision technique and handling."

"Your precision technique and handling are what's making me wriggle," said Allard. He applied a bit more of his own 'precision technique' to Vaughan's shirt and what was under it. "See? You wriggle, as well."

"And it interferes, as well."

"Is there *anything* you won't turn into an argument, Vaughan?"

"No," said Vaughan. "Want to argue about how quickly I can undo your trousers?"

"No." Allard wriggled a bit more, trying to make himself accessible. Once he was unfastened, he reached for Vaughan in turn. "I suppose we'd better go for nakedness this time. I don't fancy the dry-cleaning bills if we get more-than-rumpled in our best clothes."

"You wouldn't keep them as a souvenir?" Vaughan asked, not sounding terribly serious.

"I'm sure I'm not going to forget this. Silk sheets and chocolate are memorably unusual."

"And champagne," Vaughan said. "There's a bottle in the ice-bucket. You did specify the honeymoon suite."

He was already nicely happy after the champagne shared during the show, but they could probably handle another bottle without affecting their ability to handle each other.

"Go and get it, then. No, not yet. Get your clothes off first, and then I can watch you walking around naked." He didn't mention that he'd be able to watch Vaughan in front of a large mirror.

Vaughan got off the bed and removed his clothes, rather less slowly than a proper (improper) strip-tease, but very nice anyway. Allard lay back on the bed and took hold of his cock, not masturbating, but letting himself enjoy the feel of it, and the view.

"Keep that for me, will you?" muttered Vaughan.

"No intention of wasting it on a wank. But don't you like watching me hold it?"

"Oh, yes," said Vaughan, "all framed in black." He licked his lips. "Do you have any idea what you look like? Full formal evening dress, shirt half-undone, cummerbund all rumpled up and your cock dangling out of your trousers."

"I am not dangling," said Allard, looking down to check.

"Certainly not," said Vaughan. "Fine upstanding fellow you are." He stripped off the last of his clothing, laying it neatly on the chair. Then he walked toward the mini-bar.

Allard followed Vaughan's progress with interest. Yes, the large mirror offered an excellent front and rear view at the same time. Then he noticed Vaughan watching him watching Vaughan. Vaughan grinned at him, and wiggled his hips. Bouncing made the front and rear views even more interesting.

His cock was beginning to tell him it had had enough of mere scenery, however.

Agreeing with it, he started getting undressed, and had managed to strip to the waist by the time Vaughan returned with the ice-bucket and a couple of champagne flutes. He was mentally cursing the complicated clothing: all very well slowly unwrapping each other, but it was hell when you just wanted to get rid of it fast.

"Would you like any help with that?" Vaughan asked him, and got down on his knees.

To Allard's disappointment, he was kneeling to undo Allard's shoes.

Allard was thinking about another use for that relative position. He sighed, undid the rest of his fly-buttons, let his trousers drop, and settled to giving his cock a little attention.

"Would you like any help with *that?*" Vaughan asked, sounding rather more interested.

"Finish my shoes first."

Vaughan did, cursing the trousers which had just landed on top of what he was working on. "Lift one foot," he said.

Allard did so, trying not to fall over and wishing he hadn't dropped his trousers so unceremoniously.

Then the other foot.

Finally he was free. He wiggled his cock at Vaughan.

"Very nice," Vaughan said, "but let's have the champagne first. I've always heard that bubbles can have an interesting effect when combined with fellatio. Sort of…tingly."

Allard, to his own surprise, rather liked that idea. "But would it work if there was something else in your mouth already? And wouldn't it get a little untidy?"

Vaughan gestured airily at the bed. "We are paying an unfeasible amount of money for clean sheets and luxury. We practically *deserve* to be a bit messy."

"When have you ever needed to pay for the privilege?"

"On the ship, I leave things about, I tidy them up," said Vaughan.

"Eventually," muttered Allard.

"Here, other people can clear it up; that's their job." Vaughan grinned. "Anyway, this is a better class of mess!" Vaughan indicated the visibly expensive chocolate-wrappers decorating the floor.

Allard conceded the point. "I'd always supposed that 'the lap of luxury' involved sexual congress on a bed of rose petals, but I should think truffle-wrappers are a reasonable urban facsimile."

"You're getting epigrammatic, Allard. Time I shut you up," said Vaughan, and shut Allard up by filling his own mouth.

Allard panted.

Vaughan stopped, and said, "Hang on, forgot the champagne!"

I don't care! thought Allard, although he would not give Vaughan the satisfaction of saying that.

"Hold these," said Vaughan, handing him the glasses. He poured a generous measure of champagne into each flute, then set the bottle down and took one flute from Allard. "Cheers!" he said.

"You do not knock it back like cheap plonk!" snapped Allard.

"No," said Vaughan, with a grin, "I knock it back like expensive plonk for which I have paid a significant amount of money to be able to treat exactly as I please." He took a small, delicate sip. "Mm," he said happily. Then he took a somewhat larger sip, got down on his knees again, and applied himself to Allard.

This was distinctly interesting. Allard wasn't entirely sure if the quality of the drink affected the sensation. With the chilly drink against the heat of his cock and Vaughan's mouth, and the quite unclassifiable feel of bubbles, he didn't particularly want to analyse anything.

The 'bubbly' feeling only lasted a few seconds, but then he still had the warm, wet, luxurious feeling of a mouth wrapped 'round his cock, and if he wanted the champagne, he could always drink his own.

He sipped. Decadent. Wicked. Wonderful. It was *good* champagne, but being able to relax while someone sucked his cock as he drank made it even better. He did absolutely nothing except enjoy it.

The taste was a cool prickle on his tongue, and there was no trace of coolness or bubbles left in Vaughan's mouth by now, just the slow serious suction Vaughan enjoyed giving and Allard enjoyed getting. He wanted to move, and wanted to stay still. He stayed still.

He was not quite on the edge of not being able to stop. Time to stop, while he still could, and experience it from the other side. "Vaughan."

"Mph?" Vaughan said around his cock.

"Stop now, or you wait until I've recovered from *la petite mort* before you get to find out what champagne on your cock feels like."

Vaughan slid off him very quickly indeed, leaving Allard feeling rather regretful about having been so generous. Then Vaughan stood up, slightly unsteadily.

Hardly surprising, given the state of his own balance. He managed to kneel down rather than fall down, although it seemed to be more by luck than judgement. Perhaps they'd had too much champagne, after all. No, they both still had erections, didn't they? He patted his own to check, and peered at Vaughan's. Yes, Vaughan had a very nice erection. Very firm, very tasty-looking.

He took a quick swig from his glass, held it in his mouth. When he was certain that he wouldn't choke, he slipped his lips over Vaughan's cock. It took more co-ordination than he was quite capable of, and a little champagne dribbled. Vaughan didn't seem to mind, especially when Allard hastily sucked to try to stop it getting away. Then he managed to get as much of Vaughan's cock as he currently had room for, and settled down to enjoy the sensation of bubbles bursting inside his mouth, bubbles bursting between his tongue and Vaughan's cock. It was quite a sensual pleasure for *him,* never mind the thought it was meant to be for Vaughan.

He held it for as long as possible, until the bubbles finally dispersed, then he reluctantly pulled off Vaughan, swallowed, and took another mouthful of champagne. More practiced this time, he was able to take Vaughan straight in. Vaughan's cock moving in his mouth stirred the champagne up quite delightfully. It stirred Vaughan up quite delightfully, as well.

Vaughan thrust into his mouth. Allard enjoyed it for as long as he could before he had to pull off, spluttering and choking.

"Are you all right?" Vaughan said.

"Champagne up my nose tickles."

"Pity. I was enjoying that," said Vaughan.

"So was I." Allard couldn't help laughing. "First time I've done that with champagne rather than a fizzy soft drink."

"What? Sex?"

"*No,* you twit! Get it up my nose!"

"I know you've got a big nose, Allard, but I don't think nasal sex is an option without extensive surgery."

"Is there *any* perfectly normal remark you can't turn into a double-entendre?"

"No." Vaughan bent over and held out a hand. "Come on. On the bed."

"I don't think we're going to manage the co-ordination for sixty-nine and champagne," said Allard regretfully. "I don't seem to manage even one end of that."

"We might if we hadn't actually drunk quite a bit of it," said Vaughan, "but you're probably right. So. Sixty-nine *without* champagne or one-by-one with champagne. Ah, it's a close call!"

"We buy a bottle of champagne to take back to the ship. Or hope that we've sobered up in the morning," said Allard.

"Sixty-nine it is," said Vaughan cheerfully, sweeping Allard up and dumping him on the bed. Then he bounced onto the bed himself. "Side by side, me on top, you on top?" asked Vaughan.

"After that much champagne, you're probably going to fall asleep as soon as you come," said Allard.

"Could be a bit difficult for you if I've actually still got my cock down your throat. Side-by-side it is."

My god, how reasonable he is about discussion. I'll have to get him drunk on champagne more often. Or offer to suck him. Wait a minute— I do *offer to suck him quite often. Even more often, then.*

By this time, he was wriggling 'round, trying not to kick Vaughan while changing position, while Vaughan tried not to kick *him* while changing position. They were quite practiced at that by now, but the addition of silk sheets made the experience rather more slippery. Not that that was a bad thing.

"Mm," said Vaughan. "I like silk."

"I know," said Allard, just before gulping a mouthful of Vaughan and settling down to work. He didn't want to take Vaughan right down his throat; their control was going to be slightly wonky as they were both drunk, so no fancy tricks. Instead, he wrapped a hand 'round the base and took a good, firm suck at the business end. His eyes closed, and he was so thoroughly involved in what he was doing (and so, apparently, was Vaughan) that it was a small shock when Vaughan took a sudden gulp at *him.*

He moaned around Vaughan.

Vaughan kept nearly pulling off—suck, pause, breathe, *suck,* moan—while keeping his warm fingers playing with Allard's balls.

Allard had forgotten every technique he'd ever learned. He kept moaning.

Vaughan sucked at him more.

Allard's cock-muted moans were reaching a certain pitch of almost continuous desperation, although he didn't know or care whether they were audible. All he cared about was that Vaughan kept sucking and *sucking* and—

—he was shuddering, moaning and coming, and his mouth was very suddenly a lot fuller when his multitasking capacity was already over its limit.

There were probably many romantic novels that dealt with simultaneous orgasm. He'd be surprised if any of them even mentioned getting it up one's nose.

He let go of Vaughan and spluttered a bit. Judging by the noises from the other end of the bed, Vaughan was having the same problem.

"I'm not going to say 'never again'," said Vaughan. "I *am* going to say, next time we'd better be a bit less drunk."

"Who cares? It was fun!"

After some crawling and wriggling, they both ended up oriented in more-or-less the same direction, with their heads on the pillows.

Vaughan stretched out an arm, grabbed hold of Allard, and tugged.

Allard found himself skidding over the silk. Good job, really, that he had no objection to being tugged. At the moment, he was too drunk and satisfied to object to *anything*.

They lay there in contented silence. Allard liked the feel of silk warmed by body heat, and Vaughan didn't seem to mind it, either.

* * *

Allard struggled to raise an eyelid, as best he could without complicated pulley systems. It must have taken about five minutes, which reminded him to look at the time.

Over an hour had gone by. Nearly an hour had been spent dozing.

That must have been good. Or they must have been drunk. Or both.

"Fancy exploring the possibilities of the Jacuzzi?"

"Vaughan, I do *not* want more sex at this juncture."

"Wasn't intending that. Can't get it up again either."

"After what amounts to a bottle of champagne each, it's hardly any wonder we can't get it up a second time." Actually, they hadn't finished the bottle in the hotel room. Actually, they hadn't even finished the first glass. "I suppose we could sit in bubbles while drinking bubbles."

"That's the spirit," Vaughan said.

They managed, rather unsteadily, to help each other across the room and locate the Jacuzzi. Allard had even remembered to snag the champagne bottle and glasses in passing.

Vaughan fiddled with the taps a bit. "Can't quite figure out what you're supposed to do here."

Allard looked. They weren't entirely obvious. On the other hand, there was a neat little notice next to them. "When all else fails, read the instructions," he told Vaughan.

It turned out to be an ordinary bath, with a couple of extra switches to switch on and control the force of the bubbling, plus a timer. "Easy, really," he said, turning on the taps.

"Only when you're not drunk," said Vaughan.

"I'm a…" Allard yawned. "…master of technology, even when pissed." He could even negotiate tetrasyllabic words when drunk. They just came out slightly slower.

Vaughan dabbled his fingers in the resultant bathful of hot water. "Shall we get in and see what it's like?"

"You try it first. If it's comfortable, I will join you."

"Ever since you heard of beta-testing, I've always had to try all your technological improvements first," said Vaughan, but got in without further protest. "Nice hot bath, so far. Want to fiddle with the knobs?"

Allard tweaked a nipple.

"Thought you were too pissed to be interested," Vaughan said.

"Just testing whether you are," said Allard innocently.

"I am. But it's nice anyway," said Vaughan. "Now turn the Jacuzzi on."

Allard did. Then he ramped up the force of the bubbles.

Vaughan jumped.

"Are you all right, Vaughan?" Allard asked, a little guiltily.

"Fine. Just happened to be right under my balls when you turned it up. Tickled."

"What an interesting idea."

"We'll have to have a bath tomorrow morning before we leave," Vaughan said.

"I rather like that idea," said Allard. Sex usually involved an 'orgasm' subroutine and then a 'garbage collection' subroutine. Running them concurrently might be more efficient. Or at least more fun. *On the other hand, Vaughan will just say I'm a lazy little sod.*

Vaughan settled more comfortably into the augmented bath. "Are you going to play with the technology all night, or are you going to come and join me?"

"Remember what Harry said about you only coming first when I've got an erection."

"Not that I did come first this time," said Vaughan.

Allard decided to shut up and get in the bath. He was too drunk to compete with Vaughan if he hadn't seen *that* one coming. As it were.

He poured the champagne and handed a glass to Vaughan. Then he stepped carefully into the bath, holding his own champagne, and sat down slowly. It was rather like having a hot bath, shower, massage, and cuddle at the same time. He could get used to this.

The champagne would probably have been even better if they'd remembered not to leave the bottle open, but it wasn't bad. He sighed, and snuggled into Vaughan.

"Mm, it is nice," Vaughan said. "Why don't we get one of these for the ship?"

Allard shuddered. "I can imagine what we'd get from MCU93 if we were fool enough to try to explain the concept to it." It had been bad enough getting the hot water to adjust to a *human* range of comfortable temperatures. Adding force and speed to that could be very painful.

"Instant levitation," agreed Vaughan. "If he mixes it up with the instant-dry thing, it could be rather disorienting."

"Why *did* you buy an alien ship?"

"It was cheap, it had a reasonable cargo space, and it had comfortable living quarters."

"Designed for people with rather different limbs," said Allard.

"They were humanoid!" said Vaughan indignantly. "Distinctly stated in the service history that the last lot were humanoid."

"The Farrath from Upsilon Lupus XI are humanoid, and they're ten feet tall, with three eyes apiece," said Allard. "Anyway, what about the first lot?"

"It's had a couple of refits since then," said Vaughan.

"I know," said Allard. "MCU93 still has nightmares about the last-but-one."

"Well, I suppose the ship is his body, in a manner of speaking. It must be like having major surgery."

"No Jacuzzis," said Allard firmly. "Not until I've shown him some manuals first."

"On Jacuzzis?"

"No. Design tolerances for *homo sapiens.* Or it might do worse than tickle your balls." He tickled Vaughan's balls with his free hand.

"Nice. I wish I hadn't drunk so much," said Vaughan.

"Well, if drink is the only pleasure we've got at the moment, we might as well enjoy it." He sipped it. Cool drink in his mouth, hot water all around him. Bubbles inside and out. Very nice indeed, even if he couldn't get it up again.

He kissed Vaughan with his mouth full of champagne. At least he wasn't too drunk to manage that. That was quite fun, as well.

They shared the rest of the champagne kiss-by-kiss. After all, it would be quite flat in the morning, and they'd paid for it, so it was their duty to drink it up now. Duty and pleasure.

They'd just finished it when the timer switched off.

"Turn it back on again, Allard. I was enjoying myself."

"Get out of this bath before you turn into a prune, Vaughan. If you're obedient, I'll let you have another go tomorrow morning, when you can discover what it's like for sex."

Vaughan got out. "All right. I'm looking forward to it."

Allard looked at Vaughan's backside with deferred appreciation. Then he stood up and got out.

A huge fluffy towel apiece was infinitely more than the instant-dry function on the ship, or even than the small ordinary towels they had. *Really* luxurious towels would be an improvement they should definitely try for.

Allard kicked a box on the way back to the bed. Oh, yes—truffles. One each just before falling asleep would be good.

He handed one to Vaughan and slipped his one slowly into his mouth. Then he settled down to sleep—drunk, sexually satisfied, and with the divine sensation of chocolate melting over his tongue. It didn't get much better than this.

* * *

Allard woke up. This was probably a mistake.

His head hurt, he felt slightly ill, and some sod was taking up the bed and the bedclothes when he was a little colder than he felt comfortable with.

"Morning, Allard!" Vaughan said heartily.

"Go away, Vaughan," said Allard, and hid under the pillow.

"Hangover?" Vaughan asked.

"Isn't it bloody obvious?" he muttered from under the pillow.

"I'm not feeling that bad," said Vaughan.

"Hoo-bloody-ray," said Allard.

The bed bounced. By the time Allard had worked up the energy to say something rude, Vaughan was saying, "Have a painkiller."

Allard crept out from under the pillow and found a painkiller in front of him. He opened his mouth just enough to slip it under his tongue, and stayed very still while it melted and did its job.

"Well enough to sit up and have a drink of water?" Vaughan asked.

Allard considered this. He hadn't actually had a very *bad* hangover; it was just that he wasn't used to having hangovers in the first place. He was quite well enough to sit up.

He did so, and took the glass of water Vaughan was holding out for him. Sipping it slowly gave him something else to think about besides the way his head felt, and it made the inside of his mouth feel better.

"I'll just order breakfast," Vaughan said. The painkiller must be working—he didn't feel sick at the very thought.

"Something expensive, luxurious, and not available on ship," he specified.

"Exactly what I had in mind," Vaughan said, grabbing the menu from the bedside table. "Definitely room service. I fancy the idea of a champagne breakfast in bed."

"Haven't you had enough champagne for one day?"

"Yes, I did. Yesterday."

Actually, hair-of-the-dog didn't seem such a bad idea, now that he was recovering.

"Better make it a half-bottle, though," he suggested.

Vaughan ordered a champagne breakfast. He did not specify what it was to consist of, but said it would be ready in fifteen minutes.

"That'll be cooked to order. Good. Not lobster, I hope," Allard said suspiciously. "It's lovely, but it's not what I'd call a lazy breakfast-in-bed item."

"I could play with my food. Try to grab you with the claws."

"I still have a hangover, thank you."

"So you're not interested in a quickie before breakfast arrives, then?" asked Vaughan.

"No. I want to save it for the bath after breakfast."

"Well, I suppose we could just cuddle." Vaughan reached for him, then stopped. He must have conveyed that he didn't quite feel in the cuddling mood yet.

"On the other hand," said Vaughan, "I could go and get rid of the last lot of champagne and make room for the next lot."

"Sorry," Allard said. "Give the painkiller another five minutes, and I'll probably be all right." He lay down again.

While Vaughan went to the bathroom, Allard dozed. He was beginning to feel better.

When Vaughan came back, Allard was feeling better enough to go to the bathroom himself. He'd just finished when there was a knock on the door, and the announcement: "Room service."

He hastily wrapped a towel around his waist, not knowing exactly what the nudity taboos on this planet were. Then he opened the door.

One of the hotel staff wheeled in a trolley. Vaughan must have ordered the works. He couldn't see much of it yet, because of the covered dishes, but it smelled wonderful. He was definitely over his hangover.

The trolley parked next to the bed, the porter tipped and gone, they started investigating. There seemed to be a bit of everything. He decided to start with scrambled eggs and smoked salmon on toast. All right, they could get *toast* on board, but apart from that, it was a new and delicious experience. Scrambled eggs made properly, with fresh eggs. Scrambled eggs made properly with fresh eggs and then *handed over,* not kept on a hotplate for half an hour. He couldn't remember when he'd last had that.

"Don't take all the scrambled eggs. I like them, too." Vaughan got up and began to help himself.

"And I suppose I need to leave room for some of the other things," Allard said. He climbed back into bed, holding his plate carefully.

Vaughan joined him, and they settled back comfortably, propped up on the pillows, eating scrambled eggs and salmon with no tidiness whatsoever, but immense enjoyment. The eggs were perfectly creamy.

"I forgive you for getting me drunk," said Allard.

"I don't think you needed any help from me," said Vaughan.

"You could have reminded me of the relative difference in body size before I drank too much."

"Would it have stopped you?"

"No, probably not." He'd been having too much fun to think of sensible things. Since he would have wanted to have an equal share of champagne, it wouldn't have stopped him. He liked equal shares of everything. Now he'd finished the food on his plate, he could have an equal share of what was left of the scrambled eggs on Vaughan's plate.

"Oy!" said Vaughan, as Allard grabbed a forkful and devoured it quickly.

"I like your share-and-share-alike policy," Allard said.

"We can always order some more if you're that hungry."

"It's more fun stealing it. And I'm not hungry any more, just greedy."

"Don't you want to leave room for the bacon?"

"Yes, but at least the bacon onboard isn't too bad."

Allard got up and started rummaging. The porridge would probably be quite nice, as well, since there was fresh milk. Long-life milk never tasted quite the same. But if he had the porridge, he wouldn't have a chance at the bacon, which appeared to manage to be crisp and fresh at the same time. Shipboard bacon was either fresh and chewy or it splintered when you stuck the fork in.

Bacon, then. But he might pick up some proper milk and try the porridge tomorrow. He rather fancied looking at people's reactions when he stalked on board, in rumpled evening-dress, with a bottle of champagne under one arm and a pint of milk under the other.

Oh, yes. Champagne. They hadn't actually opened it yet. Did champagne go with bacon and sausages?

"Vaughan? Does champagne go with bacon and sausages?"

"How the hell would I know?"

Well, now was as good a time as any to find out. Vaughan had had the fun of popping the champagne last night. He'd tackle this bottle.

Thank god he was still slightly hung-over but not drunk. He was able to negotiate opening the bottle with not too much diminution of his normal ability.

Bacon, sausages, tomato, more toast. He thought about baked beans, but they were too messy and had probably come out of a very similar tin to the ones onboard ship. Two different colours of sauce. Now that was a breakfast to give a man energy for the rest of the day. He sat down with his plate and stabbed into a sausage.

Vaughan winced. "Is that what you'd like to do to me?"

"Sometimes. But usually I prefer to do this…" He lifted the sausage toward his lips, and sucked delicately. It tasted good.

"Switch off that empathy module of yours, Vaughan." He bit and chewed vigorously.

"They are nice sausages," Vaughan said, stabbing at one of the ones on Allard's plate.

"Get your own!"

"But I like your sausage!"

Allard nearly spluttered it all over the plate, but just about managed to get it under control. He put his sausage back on the plate and began to cut pieces off it decorously, not thinking of it in terms of anything else at all.

Vaughan giggled.

"Get your mind off penises until later, Vaughan."

"Didn't say a word." Vaughan got out of bed and got his own helping of bacon and sausages, eating them quite sensibly instead of playing with the food. They ate and drank in companionable silence.

"Beats the shipboard version of turkey-tarragon-and-apricot sausages by quite a long way," said Vaughan, after a while.

Allard agreed. "Good-quality bangers, fresh and well-cooked, are a lot better than fancy stuff marked 'best before end of millennium'."

"That trader swore blind it was *this* millennium it said on the wrappers," said Vaughan.

"You're far too trusting."

"No, just desperate for a change in diet."

"Next time, we won't forget to stock up before running out of anything we actually like."

"Well, at least this time we've got plenty of time to go food shopping," said Vaughan. "I suppose we ought to do that today."

Food shopping wasn't the first thing on Allard's mind today. He got up, moved the hot dishes onto the second shelf of the trolley, and leaned over it meaningfully. Vaughan had, on occasion, said that watching Allard bend over was capable of knocking anything resembling a rational thought out of his mind for some time. Allard had, at the time, said, "How would you know? You've never had one!" but he wasn't averse to being able to manipulate Vaughan.

"Is that a hint?" Vaughan said.

"The rest of the food on the trolley is cold, and will keep," said Allard.

"Unlike you, because you're hot, and won't keep," said Vaughan, as Allard went into the bathroom and began to run the bath.

"Shut up, Vaughan," Allard said loudly over the noise of running water. "Tidy up the trolley while I get the bath ready."

Vaughan came into the bathroom a minute or two later, holding champagne and glasses. There wasn't quite enough water to make it worth getting into the bath yet, so he occupied the time with snogging Vaughan. Yes, he was definitely over the hangover. Two-and-a-half kisses later, he heard the discreet beep of the bath announcing it had reached the preset level, and the taps cut out abruptly.

After finishing the kiss, Allard switched on the Jacuzzi and set the force to 'maximum'. Then they got into the bath.

"Right, what are we going to do?" said Vaughan.

"Since this is a honeymoon suite, it comes equipped for any number of interestingly perverted things, like what we are going to do now," said Allard. "Note the nice little seat running along one side of this astonishingly large bath for two. I can sit in your lap while you sit on that."

"Only you would think that was perverted," said Vaughan, settling himself onto the seat and into the water.

"Just because they haven't happened on a leather-encased bath, you think it can't be kinky."

"No, I just think that you haven't happened on a bath big enough for more than two people to have sex in before."

"Good. I'm not inviting Harry in. Or anyone else."

Vaughan pulled him down. "I have no problem with limiting my activities to you."

It *was* nice, sitting on Vaughan's lap in a tub of hot water. He looked around. This was the honeymoon suite, so logically there should be…ah, yes, there was a handy dispenser of waterproof lube on the wall. He helped himself to a large handful. Then he shifted slightly in Vaughan's lap, and helped himself to a large handful.

The water felt good, both relaxing and stimulating. It made for a different sensation, lubing up Vaughan with hot water swirling between both of them.

"I think that's enough, although it's fun doing it," said Allard.

"It's fun having it done," said Vaughan. "And I must admit that a jet of water right under my balls feels pretty damn good when I'm expecting it and it doesn't make me jump."

Allard wasn't getting as much direct stimulation from the water jets as Vaughan was, but it did feel good. It felt even better when he began to ease himself down on Vaughan. He'd only prepared Vaughan and not himself, so he felt tight, but the lubrication and water made it easier. The combination of sensations was interesting, adding a certain inexorable quality to the experience. He shut his eyes, imagining Vaughan imagining a virgin; tight flesh giving way to the brute pressure of an invading cock. Not that he could get very far with that fantasy, considering he was being slowly bounced up and down on it, and also that he was finally in a good position to feel what Vaughan meant about water jets. He decided to express his inner slut instead, and moaned rather loudly.

Vaughan thickened inside him. Apparently he didn't mind the inner slut. Good. Nor did Allard. Hot water was streaming all over him, there was an enthusiastic cock filling him up, and the Jacuzzi was even more fun now he was sober enough to appreciate it properly. There seemed to be only one thing missing. Ah, yes. He took hold of his own cock. Perfect.

"I can always tell when you start wanking yourself," Vaughan told him. "It makes you quiver inside."

"I'm not surprised," muttered Allard, who was too busy with what he was doing to feel embarrassed at this.

It was…different. Normally, when they did this, Vaughan was moving, thrusting into him. Now, Vaughan was staying still and moving *Allard.* However, since Vaughan was still doing all the work, Allard had nothing to do but enjoy the sensations.

Vaughan was moving him faster now, and Allard's hand was going faster on his cock, and he was really getting ready to enjoy himself when Vaughan asked, "Shall we try for another simultaneous orgasm?"

"If you can pronounce that, you're not close enough to finish with me," said Allard. He tried to count. Yes. Five syllables.

"Want to bet?" Vaughan whispered in his ear.

That did it. He wanked himself as hard as he could, determined to finish first, and exploded into orgasm before Vaughan could *possibly* manage it.

As he sprawled back on Vaughan in luxurious contentment, Vaughan whispered to him, "God I love it when you tighten 'round me just when I'm coming."

Damn, thought Allard, *didn't beat him after all. On the other hand, I can just relax now, so I win again.*

He lay collapsed against Vaughan's chest, not actually asleep but not actually doing anything else, either. He liked the feel of

Vaughan at his back, Vaughan's arms around him, and Vaughan's cock softening slowly inside him.

Reaching back for a moment, he turned the Jacuzzi to a slightly milder force, suitable to his more contemplative mood.

Just right.

Vaughan sighed happily.

About ten minutes or so later, they got up. A quick splash down sorted out the cleaning problem, and Vaughan insisted on checking Allard's backside.

"You do realise that's completely unnecessary."

"But I'll enjoy it anyway," said Vaughan. "Any excuse for a good look at this object of beauty."

He submitted to the check, then suggested they go back in and finish the cold courses of breakfast. There was something decidedly decadent about lying there on silk sheets, wrapped in a large fluffy towel, stuffing himself with the five-star room service, having just stuffed himself with Vaughan.

He'd have to do it more often. "Can we think of convincing reasons to go on shopping trips here, say every two months or so?"

"I'm sure we could if we tried," said Vaughan. "What's the point of earning lots of money if you can't enjoy spending it occasionally? We can always claim it as a tax deduction."

"That's an idea. Make sure we get proper receipts when we check out today. I'll enjoy it even more if I know we can claim it back."

* * *

At least they were the only ones waiting to check out, so there wasn't much of an audience.

"Good morning," he said quietly, and hoped that nobody would notice that he was still in yesterday's clothes.

The receptionists were far too polite to notice that two people in rumpled evening-dress were checking out. Allard noticed them not noticing. Damn.

Attempting to settle his nerves, Allard left Vaughan to do the checking out, and went into the little shop in the reception area and bought a bottle of champagne and a pint of milk.

As he came back, he was annoyed to hear Vaughan saying, "Yes, everything was absolutely fine, thank you. It was a wonderful way to celebrate our six-month anniversary."

Vaughan had a deplorable tendency to be romantic, and get his facts wrong. "It wasn't six months," said Allard.

"I know," said Vaughan, "but we're a working ship, and we have to take our holidays when we can. Darling," he added.

"Yes, dear," said Allard, and trod on his foot.

The receptionists carefully didn't notice, again. He hoped Mark would be this good at the job after his course.

"Have you finished paying, and did you get the tax receipts?" he asked Vaughan.

"You really don't understand the point of romance, do you?"

"Yes I do. Chocolates, champagne, silk sheets—and, above all, getting someone else to pay for them."

"You have many faces you show the world, Allard. Programmer, bastard operator, gold-digging little tart…"

"You pay me a very high salary for being very good at all of them," said Allard smugly.

"Allard!" Vaughan said, in a scandalised voice.

The receptionists *were* very well-trained. They were still not batting an eyelid. He turned to them and said, "He does pay me a high salary for being a gold-digging little tart, but only in the sense of being very good at programming and knowing how much that skill is worth."

They still didn't bat an eyelid. Allard batted his, instead. He had very fine eyelashes.

"By the way, where are you trained? Just in case our receptionist hasn't improved after the training course he's on at the moment."

They told him.

"How d'you think the rest of the crew are getting on?" asked Vaughan.

"Most of them are drinking themselves legless. The receptionist started *out* legless."

"Do you have an equal-opportunities policy?" the receptionist asked. Finally! A reaction from one of them!

"Equality is one of the cornerstones of our political tradition as a syndicalist ship," said Vaughan.

"Basically, they don't care how weird somebody is as long as they do the job," Allard summarised. "Our receptionist hasn't got any limbs, in fact."

"How does he—she—actually…er, I mean…"

Allard took pity on him. "Not a human person. He's an artificial intelligence. Think 'box with brain'."

They were openly curious now. "Then why does it need to be on a training course?"

"Same reason as anyone else," Vaughan said. "He started out as an irritating little bastard."

"Anyway, we'd better get back to the ship and find out how his first day on the course went," Allard said. "With any luck, somebody will be back by now to operate the teleport."

Vaughan called the ship. The blearily indignant noises leaking out of the phone suggested Harry had answered, reluctantly.

"Get Allard to programme that bloody thing to ring quietly," said Harry, as they materialised in front of him. "It's not at all the thing when you've got a headache."

"Shan't," said Allard. "You would have slept through it."

"You could have walked," Harry said. "*I* had to walk."

"Where are the girls?"

"Left a note saying they were perfectly sober, thank you, and were taking Mark to his lessons."

"Oh, well," Vaughan said. "We'd better get changed, and then—shopping!"

It was amazing how much Harry perked up at the word 'shopping'.

* * *

By the end of the week, Allard was shopped-out, and had returned to the ship to start installing some of the new toys he'd bought. He was crouched over a new and interesting piece of technology at floor level when he was disturbed by a potted plant walking past.

He did a quick reality check. Yes, six-foot potted palm. Yes, feet underneath it. Luckily, the feet belonged to Claire. He'd recognise those high-heeled boots anywhere.

A large spider plant walked past. He recognised Karen's scuffed black boots and ninja trousers.

"Would you mind telling me what this cut-price adaptation of *Macbeth* is in aid of?"

Claire had got the reference, unsurprisingly. "This is not Dunsinane castle. It's a reception area. And these are not Birnam Wood, but the currently fashionable attire for a reception area," she told him.

"Mark," he said.

"Yes, I'm afraid he did take the course terribly seriously," said Claire.

"Well, I hope he took the rest of it seriously, as well," Allard said.

He was interrupted by a loud *bing-bong* noise, and Mark's voice saying, "Will all personnel with additional plants please bring them to Area A now?"

"I *think* it's an improvement," Claire said, slightly doubtfully.

"Or at least closer to what the clients are expecting," said Allard. He knew all too well what sort of thing clients expected. He'd spent his career ignoring it.

He sincerely hoped Mark hadn't forgotten how to be obnoxious. There were times when it could be very useful.

That was his excuse, and he was sticking to it.

Writers Flock

by Alex Woolgrave and Jules Jones

Karen was hanging around after giving him his coffee. She looked uncomfortable. Most unlike her.

"Yes, what is it?" Allard asked briskly.

"It's…er. Well, something turned up when I was doing a computer search, and I think you ought to know about it."

"Contrary to rumour, Karen, I do not know everything that turns up on the Net. Nor do I need to know."

"I think you need to know about this one."

"I take it there's a reason?"

"Yes."

"All right." Karen was a Luser (meaning a cross between 'loser' and 'user', and thus meaning someone who knew less about computers than he did but had the temerity to use them anyway), but she knew she was one and was also competent in her own field. It was probably worth respecting her judgement provisionally. He got up from his chair and let her sit down.

She ran a quick search, opened a file, then got out of the way so that he could see it.

Fairly hard-core porn involving two men shagging each other senseless. More competently written than the average such story, but otherwise nothing unusual.

"I know you're not above listening to such things if a file happens to fall into your lap, but I didn't realise you actually went looking for it." He really *must* remember that her demure appearance was misleading.

"Ah. You don't recognise it, then."

"If I were in the habit of writing such stuff, I'd probably remember what I'd written."

"Not the writing—the plot. Read a bit further."

He did. An anniversary, just like the one Vaughan had tried to wind him up with two weeks ago. *Just* like it. Word-for-word and action-for-action. He could remember it very clearly. So could the writer.

* * *

He was lying in bed, waiting for Vaughan to turn up.

After about twenty minutes, Vaughan came in with a large bunch of fake red roses. He was just about ready to forgive Vaughan that, considering the large box of real chocolates he had in his other hand.

"Do you know what day it is?" said Vaughan.

"Thursday."

"Six months since I first brought you a pizza. But chocolates make a better anniversary present."

"What is this thing you've got about anniversaries? And why can't it wait for a proper anniversary like one year?"

"Because I'm not quite convinced you'll still be here for our first anniversary."

"Vaughan, I *told* you I am not going to vanish away in the dead of night. Most of the time, it would be difficult because we've just had sex and you've fallen asleep on top of me like a recently delivered sack of coal."

"I thought you were the technocrat," said Vaughan. "Have you ever actually been to a planet so primitive as to have fuel delivered in sacks?"

"Yes, at least once while in your employ." It had been a good excuse to snuggle up with Vaughan under the blankets. Not that he really needed an excuse.

"Oh, yes," Vaughan said, looking reminiscent. "That was a nice couple of days. Warm, too."

"We ran out of coal."

"After a while, we didn't notice the fire had gone out," said Vaughan. "At least, not until our fires had gone out. Which was quite a while. You've got a lot of stamina for a man in his mid-thirties."

"You're not bad for a man in his early thirties," said Allard. "How long do you think you're going to last tonight?"

"Well, it is a special occasion, so probably not very long," Vaughan said. "I'll just get too excited."

"Which position would you like to be over-excited in, this time?"

"I think that what would *really* get me over-excited," said Vaughan, with an evil grin on his face, "would be to bend you over the nearest convenient surface and admire that shapely little arse of yours while you beg me to shove it up you."

"That's why I like you. You're so romantic," said Allard, rummaging in the box of chocolates. "Mm. Brandy liqueurs."

"I thought you were going to spring into position, ready to satisfy my every whim," said Vaughan.

"*How* long have you known me, Vaughan? When have I ever been eager to satisfy your every whim?"

"Tuesday, as a matter of fact," said Vaughan.

Ah. He'd walked into that one.

"I was about to suggest a spot of foreplay first," he said, and sucked loudly and suggestively on a chocolate.

"You'd have sex with that if it was big enough," said Vaughan.

"I *am* having sex with it." He licked the tip.

Vaughan grabbed him, dragged him out of the bed, and bent him over it. The sudden movement made him bite right into the chocolate so that he had a sudden mouthful of brandy. He didn't mind a bit.

Vaughan spread his buttocks roughly. Suddenly, Allard had cool brandy in his mouth and cool air over the other end. It was a fascinatingly sensual combination.

"Are you ready?" said Vaughan, testing him with his thumb. "Good."

"Thought you wanted me to beg for it first."

Vaughan didn't answer that. He rubbed the thumb 'round and 'round, and then slid it down to Allard's balls.

"All right, I'll beg," said Allard.

"A little more enthusiasm, please," said Vaughan, tugging gently on Allard's balls. Not too hard, not too gently, making him sensitive and ready. Then Vaughan slid the hand under him to just brush against his cock.

"All right, I *am* begging!" said Allard, much more enthusiastically. "Please!" he added, wriggling.

"You're meant to work up to begging slowly," said Vaughan. "There's no suspense if you start out slutty."

Allard didn't care about the suspense. "Not tomorrow, not next week, not working up to it by easy stages. Fuck me now!"

"Are you sure you're…?"

"Now!" Allard snapped.

"That's what I like to hear," said Vaughan, shoving it in. Six inches all at once was a bit of a shock, considering Vaughan hadn't bothered with much in the way of stretching or lubricant. A very pleasant shock, but a shock.

"Fuck!" Allard growled, rather impressed with his ability to form words under stress, and Vaughan said, "That's the idea," and did.

"You're tight today," said Vaughan.

"You're fast today," said Allard.

"Mm. Does it hurt?"

"Not enough to stop," Allard admitted, wriggling. In fact, it didn't hurt at all now he'd recovered from being momentarily startled. He liked the feel of Vaughan stretching him as he went. Not painful, because his body knew exactly how to open for Vaughan by now, but it was impossible to concentrate on anything else. Which was how he liked it. He pushed back onto Vaughan, and grunted a bit. Yes, *definitely* how he liked it.

Hard work (especially with a hard cock involved) could be very rewarding.

Vaughan wrapped an arm under his belly, and *pulled,* so that Allard was flat against him. God that was deep! Allard panted, swore at Vaughan, and wriggled as best he could while holding in place.

"I thought that would make you sweat a bit. Stay there," Vaughan said, nibbling his neck and loosening the arm, apparently so that he could use his hand to touch Allard in various places. Nipple, cock-tip, inner thigh, and balls. All good, and all not-quite-satisfying.

Allard whimpered faintly.

Vaughan finally wrapped his hand around Allard's cock and did the job properly.

"Bet I can do it in three," Vaughan suggested, and got as far as two strokes before Allard climaxed violently and fell in a heap.

"You could prop yourself up a bit and let me finish," Vaughan complained.

"Mm," said Allard, not moving as Vaughan worked slowly into him, panting.

"You could actually participate," said Vaughan.

Allard tightened a few of his remaining muscles, vaguely surprised they hadn't actually melted. "Like that?" he suggested.

"Yes—oh, *fuck!*—like that!" Vaughan groaned, and came, and fell on him.

I'll have to manage to breathe eventually, Allard thought, *but until then, this is nice.*

Vaughan whispered in Allard's ear, in a tone of voice that suggested that an evil grin went with it, "Happy anniversary, darling."

"You would say that, when I'm too shagged-out to kill you for it."

* * *

It had been a very nice evening. Much too nice to share with the common people.

"Thank you for bringing this to my attention, Karen. Do you have any idea of authorship, origin, or provenance? Not that it isn't obvious."

And how quickly can I kill Harry once I've killed the file?

"Actually," she said, "I'm not sure it *was* Harry. I think Harry knows about the concept of lube for male intercourse."

He reread selected bits of it. Yes, there was a certain lack of understanding of the details of male anatomy, as if the author knew about it, but only from reading.

"Claire," he said.

She shook her head. "The author is using the pseudonym Marcus Antonius."

"I am going to take it apart byte by byte. It is going to regret, for the rest of its short life, that it ever encountered the concept of pornography."

"You can't!" said a shrill voice. "I'm a crewman now."

"Oh. So you admit it."

"People write stories about other people. I'm just…organically challenged."

Allard decided that he didn't want to continue having this conversation with a disembodied voice. "Where is the little bastard physically located?" he asked Karen.

"*Vaughan! Help!*" shrieked Mark.

"I don't think your stepfather is going to be very happy with you, either," Karen said. "It's bad strategy to piss off both of your parents at the same time."

"Hello?" Vaughan called. "What are you doing to our son?"

"He is not our bloody son, and you will want to have a word with him, as well."

"What have you done *now,* Mark?" Vaughan asked.

"Nothing," Mark said.

Karen said, "He's down on the flight-deck. Shall we go there instead of shouting around the ship?"

Allard led the way. "I think he's going to have another foot-shaped hole in his casing very soon now. I only just mended the last one, and it's going to make my foot hurt, as well."

"Er, Dad? You could try not punishing me?"

"Normal children do not put an account of their parents' sex lives up for anyone who wants to see."

"I'm advanced for my age. Anyway, that's only because they can't," muttered Mark.

"You've been spending too much time with Harry again," said Allard. He walked onto the flight-deck. "In fact, I see Harry with you now. What a surprise."

"What have *I* done?" asked Harry.

"Corrupted Mark."

"Didn't know it was possible with a computer. Wouldn't it gunk up the works?"

"What's he done?" asked Claire.

Karen said, "Have you seen the latest uploads to the HOT GEEKS website?"

Claire put that together quite quickly, and began to laugh hysterically. "He *didn't!*"

"He did."

"Harry showed Mark how to put porn onto a website?"

"No," said Allard. "Thanks to Harry, Mark understands the concept of voyeurism. Harry doesn't like handing out copies to people who aren't his personal friends, but since Mark hasn't got any friends, he doesn't have that particular limit on his behaviour."

"But HOT GEEKS is a fiction site," Claire said.

"Changing the names and very little else does not make it fiction in my view," said Vaughan as he arrived on the flight-deck. "I've just read what you left on your terminal, Allard." He walked over and stood looking down at Mark. "I thought that very expensive course you went on last month would cure you of your little problems with social interaction, Mark."

"But I changed the names," said Mark.

"It's still not very nice," said Claire. "It's funny, but it's not very nice."

"Harry?" said Mark pleadingly.

"You've got yourself into this," Harry said. "Don't look at me. Why were you doing it, anyway?"

"It's a free sample to entice readers to look at my other stuff."

"All right, why were you *writing* porn?"

"The usual reason," said Mark. "You get a penny a word for writing this stuff. Money is the sincerest form of flattery."

"Oh, yes. We have a computer that's obsessed with money."

"That, too, but if people are willing to pay for my writing, it shows that I'm getting somewhere with pretending to human. And if I get good enough, people won't be able to call me 'a computer', because I'll be rich and powerful, just like Dad."

"I am neither rich nor powerful!" snapped Allard.

"But Mark's still just like Dad," said Harry, accompanied by fervent nods from the rest of the crew.

"Anyway, you won't get rich at a penny a word."

If it didn't involve him, Allard thought, he'd be fascinated by the idea that an artificial intelligence wanted to be a porn writer. Mark was right. It *was* actually a good test of how well he could emulate humans. Turing should have thought of pornography.

Claire said, "The next time you want to write some stories, we'll do some brainstorming with you."

"Ooh!" said Mark. "I know brainstorming; we did that on the course. You take a really big bit of paper, or bit of wall, and start drawing on it. But you'll have to be my hands."

Allard held his breath. Was he about to be pestered about building an android body?

"If Claire could be in on this, as well," said Karen, "I think she'd find it quite an entertaining exercise."

"I could join in," said Harry. "I've seen it all, me. A wealth of experience of human sexuality: men, women, aliens, everything!"

"But nothing kinky or he faints," added Allard.

"You can all help me," said Mark.

"Right," said Vaughan. "I think we'd better update the company brochure. What is it now: engineering, IT, weapons, appraisal, cargo-hauling, and pornography?"

"You can't be serious," said Allard.

"All right, erotica. Much the same thing, with longer words." Vaughan paused, then asked Mark, "How about writing it to order?"

"I think I can," said Mark, "but not for you. It would be…icky."

"What?" said Vaughan. "I mean, you've already written about us, so you can't think we've got perverted tastes. I mean, not any more than you already did."

"Obviously Harry's morals *have* rubbed off on Mark," said Allard.

"No," said Mark. "It's just the idea of writing something for Dad, or Stepdad. It's…icky."

If only Turing could hear this conversation! Allard thought. "All right, I'll start updating the brochure. What *does* one charge for porn written to order?"

Fundamental Error

by Jules Jones and Alex Woolgrave

Vaughan parked his bum on a control console for the fourth time that day, and for the fourth time that day, there was an indignant beep from the software, which had just been told to stick impossible data into its input-buffer. The input-buffer had not been designed with the size of Vaughan's bottom in mind.

Allard looked up, saw what had happened, and told Vaughan to fuck off.

"Just wanted to know how you were getting on."

"Then sit in the bloody chair and keep out of the way."

"All I did," said Vaughan, sounding slightly injured, "was lean on the table."

"It is not a table; it is a data entry console, with a keyboard. You were pressing the keys with your bottom. Again."

"Sorry," mumbled Vaughan, and moved off the console, which muttered indignantly to itself as Vaughan's move pressed a few more buttons. "Didn't think."

"Even though you've already been told the previous three times you've made the same error today," said Allard. "If you have that much difficulty remembering not to sit on keyboards, I am going to spank your backside until it is too red and sore to even *think* of parking itself on that console."

Vaughan grinned, and said, "You're getting kinky!"

"All right, I'll *fuck* it until it's too red and sore!"

"What a lovely idea," Vaughan said.

Thinking about it, it was.

"Now?" asked Vaughan.

Allard considered the work he was doing. "I'll be finished in half an hour. Go and get yourself ready."

"I like you being dominant."

"Good," murmured Allard, as he got on with his work.

* * *

He guessed Vaughan's cabin. Right first time. There was Vaughan, sprawled on the bed. Naked.

"Good thing it was me, and not one of your crew come for 'instructions'—oh, excuse me, 'discussion'."

"Since when has there been a nudity taboo on this ship?"

Well, if there ever had been one, it had vanished long before he'd arrived. Night-time alarms had probably done for it. He'd been distinctly disconcerted the first time he'd found himself surrounded by stark-naked people in the middle of the night, but checking the meteor alarm *was* probably more important than stopping to put your clothes on. Once they'd finished with the small localised panic, nobody had turned a hair about the situation. They were all used to it. The irrepressible Harry had said something about "glad to see you're an asset to this crew, Allard!" and Allard had had to glare at him very severely.

"I don't suppose anybody on this ship would be in the least bit surprised at you lying there with your arse in the air, waiting for me to come and deal with it," Allard said, sparing a thought to be glad Harry had only bothered to link up audio input, not output. He wouldn't have liked Harry to pipe up with "No, we wouldn't."

"Not especially, no," agreed Vaughan. "After all, we do believe in sharing responsibility on this ship."

"Oh, shut up, Vaughan. I want to fuck you, not listen to you discussing politics. And I have no intention of sharing your arse with anyone."

"I've been waiting half an hour for you to stake your claim," said Vaughan, spreading himself welcomingly.

Allard considered whether shoving himself in *now* was more important than stopping to take his clothes off. Not quite. He flung them off in a hurry, and flung himself on Vaughan.

"I hope you have prepared yourself."

"But I thought you wanted to fuck me red and raw."

"I wasn't being that literal, you idiot." He bit the back of Vaughan's neck. "Although if you want me to…"

"Ow!" said Vaughan. "You little bastard! Yes, I have prepared myself."

"Oh, good," Allard said, and shoved in.

Oh, yes, straight in had its advantages. Vaughan was nicely tight, and there was none of this fooling around with having to be *considerate.* Not that he wanted to hurt Vaughan, of course. He just wanted to enjoy himself, and incidentally give Vaughan a painful reminder of the experience next time he was tempted to park his bum on the console. Vaughan could, and probably *would,* enjoy himself too, but that was merely incidental.

"You're being rough," Vaughan said, as if he wasn't sure whether he liked it.

"I'm making sure you don't sit on consoles without a twinge of pain. Rough's part of the job description. If you object," he thrust hard again, "I will stop doing it and take up some less demanding hobby like embroidery."

"You shouldn't be able to even *pronounce* that when you're in bed with me, much less speak in proper sentences."

"Neither should you. I must do something about that." He groped for Vaughan's cock. "You don't mind my being rough *too* much, then."

"Long as you're…" Vaughan paused to moan. "…not *too* rough."

"This was your idea in the first place!"

"*You* suggested fucking it instead of spanking it!" said Vaughan indignantly.

"I was just joking, at the time. You were the pervert who decided it might be fun."

"As opposed to the pervert on top of me with his cock right up my arse?" asked Vaughan reasonably.

"Yes," said Allard equally reasonably, with an extra thrust to ensure Vaughan didn't forget the cock up his arse. "Although now I'm trying it, I'm quite enjoying it."

"Pervert," Vaughan repeated.

"Mm," he said happily, squeezing Vaughan's cock. It might be marginally smaller than his, but it was a good fit for his hand, and he enjoyed that.

Vaughan moaned, then said, "Anyway, you've never been shy about dominating me before."

"Yes, but doing it deliberately for the purpose of disciplining you is even better. I mean, there's a *reason* for it."

"Other than liking what your cock feels when I do this?" Vaughan squeezed.

"Yes," Allard gasped, between moans. He started sucking Vaughan's shoulder, hard. Good displacement activity when he couldn't actually talk, and Vaughan didn't appear to mind it.

Vaughan tasted good. He'd be almost tempted to switch position and try a different mouthful, only he couldn't bear to pull out of Vaughan. Vaughan was squeezing his cock slowly, rhythmically, almost making him forget that he was supposed to be punishing Vaughan's arse for its forgetfulness. Well, he'd better make sure that it didn't forget him in a hurry. He gave it another hard stroke, enjoying the contrast of cool air and warm flesh. More squeezing. He wasn't sure whether that was a deliberate attempt to make it better for him, or if Vaughan enjoyed doing it, because all capacity for rational thought was rapidly deserting him.

Then Vaughan started demanding that he do it harder. He'd thought he was already doing it as hard as he could, but his cock begged to differ. He slammed into Vaughan, almost on the brink. Vaughan must have reached back to grab him; he felt hands clamp onto his arse. That was all he needed.

He bit down involuntarily just as he started coming, and it felt so good he didn't even try to stop himself. He could apologise later. For the moment, it felt good to have his mouth full, teeth sinking in, just as the pleasure of orgasm flooded through him.

It took him a couple of minutes to notice Vaughan was complaining about being bitten. Or it took Vaughan a couple of minutes to *notice* he'd been bitten.

Oh, yes, his hand was damp. Vaughan must have come. Good.

He summoned up the energy to pull himself out of Vaughan, much more gently than he'd gone in.

He inspected the bite. Fortunately, he hadn't actually broken the skin. He rubbed it gently.

"Are you sorry?" said Vaughan.

"No."

Allard shuffled down to inspect Vaughan's bottom. Fortunately, that, too, was uninjured.

"Now what?" said Vaughan.

"I know I said I was going to teach your bottom a lesson, but I don't want to have done it any permanent damage."

"Wouldn't I know?"

"Not necessarily," said Allard, and went on checking.

"Anyway," Vaughan said, "you weren't all *that* rough. I've known worse."

"Not recently, I hope."

Vaughan rolled over, grabbed him, and pulled him down. "You really are a possessive little bastard, aren't you?"

"You've known that since the day I first touched you."

"Didn't say I minded," murmured Vaughan, and kissed him.

They lay and cuddled for a bit.

Eventually, Allard thought about what Vaughan had said about having known worse. It wasn't the first hint he'd had that Vaughan had more experience (i.e. *any* experience) in the world of BDSM. His curiosity got the better of him. "Well, *was* I a satisfactory dominant?"

"I enjoyed that thoroughly," said Vaughan, "but…"

Allard said, "But—?" in a tone which suggested that thrown crockery might be the next option.

"Not criticising your technique or anything," Vaughan said, and then appeared to reconsider this. "Well, I'm *not.* But—"

"Out with it, Vaughan. I can express my displeasure with you later, if necessary. I've never had a problem with that."

"I *know,*" said Vaughan feelingly.

"All right," said Allard less aggressively. "What is it?"

"You are very good at being dominant, but—I like it the other way 'round, as well."

"It's not as if I don't take my fair share. According to you, I make an unusually convincing quivering virgin, considering my level of experience."

"Yes. That's exactly it. There's one way in which you'd make a very convincing virgin because you *are* one."

"Ah." Allard had an idea what might be coming next. He wasn't entirely sure how he felt about it. He pulled away from Vaughan slightly, so that he could see his face while they talked.

"Look," Vaughan said, "I wanted to discuss it with you when we'd just had sex so it was quite clear there was no immediate pressure of the let's-do-it-now kind."

"You want to try the bondage again."

"Will you at least consider it?"

Because this was Vaughan, he did him the courtesy of actually doing so. "It makes me nervous. I'm not sure whether it makes me *too* nervous."

"I will stop if you can't manage it."

"I know." He patted Vaughan's hand. "That's why I'm actually considering it. I suppose I could go and read up on it. I might feel a bit happier then."

"I'd rather you didn't." Vaughan put an arm around him. "It wouldn't be the same. I'd still feel it was fantasy rather than reality then."

Allard thought about that. He saw Vaughan's point. This was the closest he'd get to being a virgin again in this lifetime. He wanted to read up on it because it would take away some of the fear and uncertainty of facing a new experience. But pushing somebody not-quite-willing through that fear and uncertainty was part of what turned Vaughan on. Not quite crossing the line between forced seduction and rape.

Not entirely nice, but he'd gone along with it quite happily when it was fantasy. Encouraged Vaughan, even. If he could do it as fantasy, he could at least try with the reality. Vaughan hadn't tried a jokey 'you've got to try it, you'll like it!' approach. He'd just been honest about his own reactions and given Allard the space to work his own out. Given that, he *did* feel willing to try.

"I will try to," he said. He wanted to go babbling nervously on about "but I still might not like it, and I might not even be very good at it," but decided that would be less honest. He wasn't going to take the offer away by implication. He could offer the attempt, and he did.

Vaughan's smile made it seem worth it.

Born-Again Virgin

by Jules Jones and Alex Woolgrave

It had been a long and tiring morning. Not as enjoyable as Allard had expected. He'd liked getting his hands on all those fascinating ancient computers, but few of them seemed to function at all well after all this time, and the museum staff had been looking over his shoulder with 'does it work yet?' expressions the whole time.

He gave vent to his frustrations over lunch, including but not limited to the words 'jobsworths', 'twits', and 'wouldn't know what to do with a valuable computer if you showed them'.

Harry said, "Yes, they do. What to do with a computer is pay Allard a large sum of money, and he fixes it."

"Well, yes. I know they're doing the sensible thing. I know they need to watch me so that they can learn how to maintain the computers once I've got them working. It's just that some of them can't resist the temptation to poke at things." He rubbed his forehead with his hand, trying to massage out the stress headache. "It doesn't make the work any easier when I have to keep complete control of half-a-dozen computers at once."

Vaughan said, "You need to relax, Allard. Well, tonight, you could just give up total control, and lie back and let someone else take care of things."

Allard cocked his head. "You mean something quite specific by that, don't you?"

"Harry," said Vaughan, without raising his voice, "switch your bugs off tonight. You're going to really regret it if you don't."

Harry said, "If you're going to go into any more detail than that, give me a moment to get to my room and turn all my bugs off. Then go somewhere private to discuss it."

"Spoilsport!" muttered Claire. The girls were a lot less nervous than Harry about certain concepts.

* * *

Allard decided that he was going to have a nice leisurely coffee after lunch, whether he had time or not. He needed it. In peace and quiet. He took his coffee off to Vaughan's cabin, where he sipped in silence for a few minutes.

Vaughan said, "You look a bit less frazzled than you did at the start of lunch."

"It's not just me refusing to tolerate fools; it really is genuinely stressful dealing with them. They're not fools, but they don't know anything about computers, and I've got to teach them how not to damage the machines. At least one of them has been known to damage the machines by switching them on."

"And you're not known for your patience," said Vaughan.

"I'm trying, Vaughan. I really am." He was. It wasn't as if they were wilfully ignorant. He'd actually feel a lot less stressed if he felt free to tell them exactly what he thought of them, but it wasn't fair when they were trying their best to learn.

"Yes, you are trying. Frequently." Vaughan grinned, making it a shared joke rather than a snide remark. "I saw when I popped in how patient you were being, by your standards. Didn't know you had it in you."

"Well, it doesn't help that I haven't had it in me lately," said Allard.

"I can't help it if you're too tired at the end of the day. Never mind, it's your last day today."

"And with any luck, I'll finish early. Even if I have taken an extra half-hour over lunch."

"About tonight," said Vaughan. "I mentioned earlier, would you actually consider…"

"Losing some more of my virginity?" Allard said. He thought about it. He was stressed, and slightly tired, but maybe putting the situation in somebody else's hands might actually make him feel better. He trusted Vaughan not to force him too far outside his own psychological limits. "I'll try," he said. "What happens if I get frightened?" He might not *know* something was outside his limits until he tried to do it.

"Have you heard of the concept of a safeword?" asked Vaughan.

It was not familiar to Allard, and he said so.

"It's a particular word to mean 'stop' or 'no'."

"What's wrong with saying 'stop' or 'no'? They're simple, unambiguous words, and I trust you to respect my wishes."

"Sometimes 'no' really does mean 'yes'," said Vaughan.

Allard edged away from him on the bed, thinking, *what am I getting myself into?*

"It's part of the role-playing," said Vaughan. "If the submissive's deeply into being a 'scared virgin' or whatever, they might very well want to say 'no' when they're just playing. The idea of a safeword is it's a word that won't naturally come into the scene, so if you say 'cheese spread', the dominant knows that means 'stop *now'.*"

"But what if I *like* the idea of licking cheese spread off your cock?" said Allard, as innocently as he could manage.

"I can't make up my mind whether you're a complete innocent or an utter pervert," said Vaughan.

"Both," Allard said with relish.

"Yes, it's the combination I find so appealing," Vaughan said, and kissed him gently. "How's your headache?"

"I think I can face going back for another two or three hours."

"Just as long as you don't have a headache tonight. For reference, if one of the participants has a sick, twisted, utterly kinky desire for sex-play involving *cheese spread,*" said Vaughan, "they have to find a word they're likely not to use in the context of the game they're playing."

* * *

Allard spent most of the afternoon doing his best with the work and musing on a suitable safeword he might use with Vaughan. The latter was a good way of distracting himself when he thought he might lose his temper. 'Computer', 'twit', and 'idiot' were run across his mental parser and discarded. Unfortunately, he was quite *likely* to insult Vaughan's intelligence in bed quite without thinking, so that was out. 'Honeywell'? he wondered, looking at one. No. That might be mistaken for a term of endearment. 'Unix'? No, that might be taken as a call for more participants. As for 'Wang'… No. Just no.

'Microsoft' had at least the virtue that it would not be mistaken for a description of Vaughan's anatomy.

After dinner, in Vaughan's cabin, he told Vaughan that he'd been racking his brains for a suitable word. "The best I came up with was 'anniversary'. It's a word I'm not likely to use."

"No," said Vaughan. "It's a pentasyllabic word, and you know how dangerous those are to your concentration."

Allard sighed, and went and got a dictionary. Vaughan, being an old-fashioned chap, had a paper one, which helped if you were searching for random words. He shut his eyes, opened the book at random, and prodded with a finger.

"Monatomic." Long word. The next word was 'monaul', which he'd have trouble remembering because he didn't know it. 'Monaural', 'monaxial'…

"Did you know that *monaxonida* is an order of sponges with monaxon spicules only?"

"Try looking up 'displacement activity'," Vaughan said.

"Oh. Sorry." He skimmed down the page. "Money."

"Well, at least that one should be easy for you to remember."

"Well, I'm not expecting to use that, unless you're expecting to pay me for services rendered."

"That would be another one for our 'list of services offered'."

"No. I signed on as 'IT expert', not 'ship's tart'. This time no means No, with a capital N."

"Pity. We could probably charge quite a good rate for you."

"Well, we could always see how much money *you* could make the ship by selling your arse, Vaughan. If you do, I'm first in the queue."

"What happened to being possessive?"

"Being first in the queue, with the most money, means I can *be* possessive. And I'm possessive about money, as well."

He looked at Vaughan's expression. "No. Don't do it just to wind me up. You don't want to know what I'd do back to you. Do they make chastity belts for men?"

"Do you really want to know?" Vaughan retorted.

"Probably not." He thought about that. "No. Definitely not, and even more definitely not tonight."

"It's all right, Allard. I wasn't thinking of throwing you quite that far in at the deep end. Although I think it's time we got started."

"You're in charge," Allard said.

"Exactly." From the tone of his voice, Vaughan was looking forward to this.

"All right, what do I do?"

"Strip."

Allard started taking his clothes off.

Vaughan said, "No. Don't just take your clothes off. Strip."

Allard thought about that, and began to take his clothes off slowly and carefully, making sure that he was facing Vaughan.

Vaughan settled back in a chair and watched him.

"Aren't you getting undressed?"

"No."

"Oh."

"Keep going."

Strange as this was, obviously *something* was happening, because Vaughan wasn't laughing with him as he would have normally. This must be part of the experience.

As he stood there, having discarded his shirt, undoing his fly, he started to understand the point. He'd been naked before Vaughan countless times, but he *felt* naked now. Vaughan was appraising him, looking at him the way Harry looked at some desirable piece of art he was about to acquire for less than it was worth.

He finished undoing his fly, pulled his cock out into view, then leaned against a chair while he undid his shoes. Shoes off, then he could pull his trousers down. Underwear off, and he was completely naked to Vaughan's gaze. "Like what you see?"

"Oh, yes, I think you'll scrub up very well."

He was about to say something about "you told me to get *un*dressed, not dressed up," when his 'smut detector' routine tripped in.

"Since when have you been fussy about having a shower before sex?"

"Since I decided I wanted 'freshly bathed virgin' for my next treat. Best way to get 'em clean is to do it myself."

Allard tried not to examine that remark. He was sure he was either going to find it amusing or erotic, and he didn't feel comfortable with either.

"Get along with you now," Vaughan said.

Oh, dear. He *did* find this competent, knowing version of Vaughan attractive, and he wasn't at all comfortable about the role *he* was playing in the scenario.

"I said get along," Vaughan said, without raising his voice. Standing up, he came to stand behind Allard and slapped him on the rump. Like an animal. Like a damned slow-moving *ruminant!*

Seething, Allard moved into the bathroom, muttering obscenities under his breath.

"A well-brought-up young thing oughtn't to know words like that," said Vaughan. "I can see I'm going to have to train you properly."

"Fuck off, Vaughan."

He was surprised to find himself slammed against the wall.

"Naughty boy. If you speak like that to me again, I will spank you."

It was a good thing he was at least slightly used to playing games. Otherwise, at that point he would have kneed Vaughan in the balls. On the other hand, he might have been too shocked to knee Vaughan in the balls.

Then he noticed Vaughan's expression and tone of voice. Vaughan was a bloody good actor. At least, he *hoped* Vaughan was a bloody good actor…

"Now, get in the shower," Vaughan said, letting go of him. "Don't turn the shower on. I have plans for you."

I hope he doesn't mind me standing about with my mouth open, looking confused. Actually, he probably enjoys me looking confused. I'm damn sure he enjoys me with my mouth open, but not when I'm confused.

Maybe Vaughan just wanted to humiliate him by not allowing him to do anything on his own?

Vaughan held up the douching head. "I want you *thoroughly* clean. Outside and in."

"I can do that for myself." He always had done it for himself before. He wasn't comfortable with the notion of Vaughan doing it for him.

"I'll be the judge of that. Bend over."

"I'd rather…"

"Bend over," Vaughan said, in a tone that suggested he hadn't even considered the possibility that Allard might disobey.

Allard bent over.

The feeling of warm water flowing in was familiar; the feeling of having no control over it was not. He found it strangely intimate, and was still trying to work out whether he was embarrassed enough to stop Vaughan when the experience ended.

"May I use the toilet?" he asked.

"Since you asked politely, you may."

Then he realised that there hadn't been the slightest trace of sarcasm in his question—or Vaughan's answer. It was more than slightly unnerving. It was even more unnerving to have Vaughan stand there watching. Not that he wasn't used to having to share bathroom facilities on occasion, but there was a difference between sharing and being monitored. He finished and got back into the shower.

He went to turn the water on.

Vaughan said, "Not yet."

"Why not?"

"I'm going to wash you." Vaughan unbuttoned his shirt, took it off, and laid it aside. Vaughan was very definitely *not* stripping for an audience. He came over to stand by the shower, picked up the soap, and said, "All right, put the water on."

Allard turned the water on. As soon as he was wetted-down, Vaughan started soaping him.

"That's the ticket," said Vaughan. "My nice, clean boy, inside and out."

Allard didn't say, *Don't be infantile!* There was no point.

"Nice, clean, *quiet* boy," said Vaughan.

"I hope there's a point to all this," Allard said.

"Oh, I think you've already seen the point."

Unfortunately, Vaughan was right. Giving up control completely was difficult—and tempting. Vaughan had asked him not to read up on the subject, and thereby removed any possibility that he could second-guess Vaughan's plan for the evening. He was in a new environment, and only his companion had a road map.

When he'd been soaped, Vaughan said, "All right, you can rinse yourself now."

"At least you'll let me do one thing for myself."

Vaughan laid a finger over his lips. "No cheekiness, now."

Allard rinsed without incident, until he moved to clean off his genitals and Vaughan stopped him.

"No playing with yourself."

"But I wasn't…" His voice trailed off as Vaughan took hold of his cock and stroked the soap off.

Well, that took care of his worry about whether he could get it up this evening. Now he just had to worry about the fact that he could get it up *because* Vaughan was controlling him.

He stood very, very still as Vaughan ran his hand over his balls, rinsing the last of the soap off. It felt astonishingly good, and he didn't want Vaughan to punish him for fidgeting by stopping.

Then Vaughan let go of them, and said, "All right. You can get out now."

He got out, and stood there dripping, feeling slightly silly and rather cold.

"Good," said Vaughan, and fetched a towel. One of the large, luxurious towels they'd bought a while back.

"You look so innocent," said Vaughan, "wrapped from head to foot in a big, white, fluffy towel."

Allard caught sight of himself in the mirror. He nodded sadly. Bad though it was for his dignity, he had to admit Vaughan was right. Having his hair all fluffed up wasn't helping.

Standing next to Vaughan certainly didn't help. He actually was average height—he just didn't look it when he was standing in bare feet next to Vaughan in boots.

Actually, Vaughan in trousers and boots next to him in nothing but a towel…was quite appealing. He looked more vulnerable than usual, and Vaughan looked competent and relaxed.

"You are a pretty little thing like that," Vaughan said.

Allard looked daggers at him before realising that he wasn't dressed to do so.

"Back into the bedroom with you."

Vaughan put an arm around his shoulder, steered him back into the bedroom, then left him standing in the middle of the floor while Vaughan rummaged in the cupboard.

Vaughan brought out a familiar-looking box. Allard sincerely hoped that it wasn't going to involve leather penis sheaths. He felt silly enough without the embarrassing reminder of just *how* naïve he'd been. He did not mention this to Vaughan, as it would only give him ideas.

"Drop the towel," Vaughan ordered.

He did so, and stood waiting.

Vaughan lifted something leather out of the box, then unfolded it. He was relieved to see that it was a strap, until he thought to wonder what it was for.

Vaughan came over to him and fastened it around his neck. "There. Now you're properly dressed."

"Is that all there is to it?"

"Oh, no. But the collar is just to remind you of your status."

Allard muttered, "Or lack of it," under his breath.

"Exactly."

Allard shivered slightly. If it wasn't that he trusted Vaughan, he'd be out of that door by now, without stopping to dress.

Vaughan got out the wrist-cuffs and put one on him. Allard tried to breathe slowly. This was exactly the point where he'd been terrified last time. He could do it. He was standing in the middle of the room, there was nothing to tie him to, and Vaughan, whom he trusted, was applying the wrist-cuffs without saying a word. He breathed steadily. Vaughan worked steadily.

"Well done," Vaughan said as he finished, with no mockery at all.

"I'm scared, Vaughan."

"I know."

And you're enjoying it, Allard thought. He didn't want to say that aloud.

"Give me the other hand," Vaughan said gently.

Allard had to psych himself up to it for a few endless seconds, but he managed to hold out his other hand.

Vaughan wrapped the other cuff around his wrist, then did it up by touch, watching Allard's face all the while. Watching his reactions.

Then Vaughan handed him a larger cuff and said, "Put this on your ankle."

He couldn't do it. He couldn't. Then Vaughan's hand was on his shoulder, pushing him down.

"Do it."

He knelt down on one knee and wrapped the leather around his ankle. He focused his mind on how to make it fit comfortably snugly, trying not to think about what it was he was fitting. He couldn't quite ignore the fact that he was tying himself up for Vaughan's use.

"Stand up," Vaughan ordered, "and hold out your hands."

He did so, wondering what was going on. He already had the cuffs on. Then Vaughan fiddled with one cuff, taking hold of the metal ring set into it, and clipped something onto it. He pulled Allard's hands closer together, and did something with the other cuff, then let go of Allard.

Allard found his hands linked together, as if he was wearing handcuffs. There was a metal bar a couple of inches long, with clips at each end, linking the leather wrist-cuffs together. "Vaughan!"

"Easy, Allard." Vaughan was holding him, not letting him go. But not letting him go from the cuffs.

"Let me go!"

"Oh, no, I've no intention of doing that," Vaughan purred. "I've waited a long time for this."

He nearly panicked at the idea that Vaughan had him helpless, was refusing to turn him loose. Then he remembered— safeword. Vaughan would ignore any pleas for mercy, unless he used the only one that counted in this context.

No, Vaughan wasn't abusing him. Knowing that helped.

He tried to get control of his breathing. His panic settled, a little.

Vaughan let go of him. "Now put the other one on."

He stared helplessly at the leather strap in his hand. "But how?"

"Try," Vaughan said.

He managed to get down on one knee again, although it was far more difficult with his hands cuffed together. There was just enough room between his hands, and enough movement at the fastening between cuff and bar, for him to be able to fumble the strap around his ankle. It fell off the first time he tried to do the buckle up, and he expected Vaughan to be angry.

"Try again," Vaughan said. "I can wait all night if necessary."

Well, it was better than being told he was an idiot, which was what he would have said if the situation had been reversed.

He managed it on the second attempt. He stayed on the floor waiting for instructions.

"I think you'll do quite nicely there for the moment," Vaughan said. "Now get my cock out."

He looked at Vaughan's trousers. Vaughan had specified 'get my cock out', not 'get my trousers down', so he left the belt alone and just tackled Vaughan's fly. It was a slow and difficult job with his hands linked together, but Vaughan didn't seem to mind. Vaughan's cock certainly didn't seem to mind, when it finally came to view. When he pulled it out, he snagged it slightly on the fastening. He winced in sympathy.

"I'm sorry I'm so clumsy, but I just don't know how to do this," he admitted.

"It's all right. I'm not going to hit you."

He looked up at Vaughan. He hadn't actually considered it was *possible* that Vaughan might hit him. The suggestion wasn't very pleasant.

Vaughan stroked his face with one hand. "It's all right, Allard. I wouldn't do something like that without discussing it with you first. We only talked about bondage. I'm not taking that as license for anything else."

"Remember, this is quite new to me."

"I know. And I like that. But this game does have rules, even if it seems strange to you. And a polite apology would be adequate, even to my offended cock."

"I did say I was…"

"I didn't specify words."

Oh. Well, this at least he knew how to do. He kissed it, licked up it, apologised profusely by kissing and licking at the place that might have been sore. Then licked again. Then wetted his lips, worked his mouth, and got going seriously.

He kept going until Vaughan tugged at his hair to stop him.

"That's…quite sufficient," said Vaughan. He looked less composed.

Allard felt more composed. "Isn't that satisfactory?" He licked his lips. Fellatio was an oasis of familiarity in this desert of strangeness.

"You're not going to get away with just a suck," said Vaughan. "I'm not going to untie you until I've had you. Thoroughly."

"Let me go!" said Allard. This time, he didn't really mean it. He was testing the parameters of this odd situation. Yes, he *was* free. Not free to move, not free to go, but free to say whatever he liked without it making any difference. In this room, he could say or do anything, and nothing would open the door to the outside world until he either used his safeword or they finished what they were doing.

"No. I mean to have you, my proud beauty, and I am not letting you go."

Ah. This was more familiar ground. He'd heard that appalling script before, and it didn't get any better with repetition.

He grinned up at Vaughan. "Don't we even get a new script for the occasion?"

"Cheeky little sod!"

"Well, come on, Vaughan!"

"Well, if it's a new script you want…" Vaughan picked something out of the box. A short chain. Before Allard could quite work out what was going on, Vaughan bent down and neatly clipped Allard's ankles together. "I think you'll make a very nice addition to my harem."

"Last I heard of it, I *was* your harem."

"Well, if I've got to make do with you, you'd better be very, very good. Now get up."

He tried to. It didn't work. He looked up at Vaughan for guidance. Vaughan appeared to be far too busy enjoying the sight of him sprawled on the floor to help.

"All right, now what do I do?"

"You ask me, very, very politely, to help you up. 'Sir' might be nice."

Allard remembered that Vaughan got fairly cross with anyone who called him 'sir'.

"Please help me up, Captain, sir."

"I think you need a lesson in manners."

Vaughan bent down again and grabbed Allard's cock. That didn't seem like much of a lesson in manners to Allard, given that Vaughan had promised no pain. He enjoyed Vaughan working his cock.

Then Vaughan took his hand away.

"I was enjoying that!"

"I know," said Vaughan reasonably.

Allard reached for his cock. It was a bit awkward with his hands clipped together, but he found an angle he could manage at.

"All right, Allard. Let me do that."

It was an awkward angle, so he moved his hands out of the way to let Vaughan do it for him.

Vaughan grabbed his hand, snapped something onto the bar between his hands, and then did something at his throat. He tried to tug his hand away from Vaughan, and something clinked. That was the point at which he realised he had an additional chain. He tugged at it. Yes, it was attached to his collar. What the hell—?

"You don't touch your cock until I give you permission," Vaughan said, in a tone of voice that suggested that this fact should be obvious.

He *could* touch his cock, but that was all he could do. He could only just reach far enough to stroke it with his fingertips. Suddenly, that knowledge made his cock the most important thing in the universe. It got harder. He vainly tried to stretch his erection to reach his hands—to reach *anything*—but didn't have much luck.

"You'll wait," said Vaughan, "until I let you."

"Bastard!"

"I've warned you once about your language, Allard."

"Bastard, *sir!*" said Allard.

Vaughan did not reply to that in words. He got a gag out and showed it to Allard.

Things could always be worse. If I don't shut up, they will *be worse.*

Allard was disconcerted. He *had* actually played at being gagged before, without being worried. What was different? Apart from the props (being tied up must make a difference), Vaughan seemed to be playing a slightly more serious game.

"Oh, yes," said Vaughan. "You've played these games before, but now I'm going to show you what it's *really* like. When I've finished, you'll be begging me to do it to you again. Hard and often."

Allard relaxed a bit. The script had improved, and Vaughan wasn't playing it for laughs this time, but it wasn't so dissimilar to what they'd done before.

"Please, not like this."

"Exactly like this, if I please. And it will please you, as well, once I've trained you properly."

That was what he was worried about.

"In fact, I think it *does* please you, even if you don't want to admit it to yourself." Vaughan leaned over, and stroked a finger intimately along Allard's cock. It wasn't enough. It wasn't anywhere near enough. He knew, even as he tried to arch into it, that Vaughan wouldn't give him any more.

"Tell me how much you like it, and I might give you some more."

"I like your hand on my cock—no, I *love* your hand on my cock! The rest of it I can do without."

"Oh, I think I can change your mind for you." Vaughan went to the box and got something out. "Spread your legs."

Allard didn't co-operate, of course. "You'll have to make me."

Vaughan said, "With pleasure." He went back to the box, and came back with a long metal rod.

Allard had just noticed the clips, looking remarkably like the clips on the shorter bar attached to his hands, when Vaughan rolled him onto his belly and sat on one of his legs.

"What the hell are you doing?" he yelled, trying to kick and then remembering the hobble chain. The leg he kicked with was grabbed firmly, and something happened at his ankle. Then his leg was forced back down, and something happened at the other ankle. He moved experimentally. Nothing happened.

Vaughan got off him, then came back and waved a butt-plug under his nose.

"No, thank you," said Allard.

"*Yes,* thank you," said Vaughan, lubing up the butt-plug. "Say 'thank you'."

"Fuck off," said Allard.

"I could always put it in the other end, and you hate the taste of this lube."

"Would it make any difference if I called you a perverted bastard, Vaughan?"

"No difference at all, no."

"Anyway, I thought you were going to put yourself up there."

"All in good time."

Vaughan went back to stand behind Allard. "You make a very pretty picture like that." A picture of how he must look popped into Allard's mind. Spread open, exposed, completely unable to do anything about whatever Vaughan might take it into his head to do next. Vaughan's property.

Then Vaughan made quite a performance of putting the butt-plug in. He did it slowly, teasingly, a little bit in, a little bit out. Just the sort of thing that would feel good if he did it with his cock, except it was unreasonable to expect any man to have that much self-control. Allard whimpered in pleasure in spite of himself.

"I told you I'd make you enjoy it," Vaughan said. "You don't get a choice in the matter."

"Please, Vaughan, give me some more." He didn't want to beg, but he couldn't touch his cock, and he needed *something*.

"And you tried to stop me giving you this," said Vaughan, tone full of huge fake surprise.

"I'm sorry. I made a mistake."

"Yes, I rather think you did." That lovely, lovely butt-plug was taken away.

"Please!" he wailed.

Vaughan was kind enough to return half of it. It wasn't enough.

He tried to thrust against the floor. The butt-plug was instantly removed.

"I have more stretcher bars here," Vaughan said. "I could, for example, immobilise your arms completely."

"Please don't, sir."

"Good boy."

He was shocked to realise he hadn't even *thought* about saying 'sir' that time.

Then Vaughan gave him the whole length of the butt-plug at once, and he stopped thinking at all for a few seconds. When he realised what he was doing, he was actually whimpering at Vaughan to move it a bit more. He shut his mouth firmly in case any more untoward sounds escaped.

"It didn't take much to break down your resistance," said Vaughan.

"I like you fucking me. It's just the circumstances I'm not enamoured of."

"Oh, dear. So I have quite a way to go yet before I have you begging to put the chains on. Good job I've always liked a challenge."

Allard felt uneasy. Half an hour ago, he'd definitely have said that the only reason he'd beg to put the chains on would be role-play to please Vaughan. At the moment, he wouldn't beg and mean it, but now he could see that there might come a time when he would.

"Vaughan…"

"Yes?"

"I don't think I like that idea."

Vaughan sat down where Allard could see him easily.

"That's all right, Allard. Changing your mind is my job." His expression softened slightly. "You didn't really expect to feel like this, did you?" he asked, more seriously.

"Isn't that what you liked about the idea?"

"Yes," Vaughan said, utterly sincere and utterly honest. "You don't like the idea that you like this, but you'll let me do it anyway."

"Could anyone do that to me? Make me want to be a slave?"

"Eventually," Vaughan said.

Now that really wasn't a nice idea. He sighed. "Sometimes I think you're *too* honest. It frightens me, the idea that anyone could do that to me if they tried."

"I think they'd have to try quite hard with you if you weren't trying to please them in the first place." Vaughan rubbed his shoulder. "Would you have let me do this to begin with if you didn't want to make me happy?"

That made him feel a bit better. This was still sex with Vaughan even if it was kinky sex. "Well, *are* you going to do anything to me?"

"Oh, I can think of *lots* of things I'd like to do to you."

"Do they involve cheese spread?"

"Now there's an interesting idea. Oddly enough…" Vaughan got up and walked out of his field of view. Allard was surprised—he hadn't exactly meant that as a serious suggestion, and he'd have doubted Vaughan would take it as one.

Vaughan came back with cheese spread—the soft sort in a tube rather than the less ductile triangular kind—and spread a little on his cock.

"I didn't actually mean that, Vaughan!"

"Don't ask for it if you don't want it. Now eat it all up. I put myself to the trouble of providing a tasty treat for my sex-slave, and it's a little untidy if you don't lick it off. I don't want cheese spread on my trousers, after all."

"Who would?" murmured Allard. He paused. "We have a slight physical problem here. I can't actually move."

"No, I suppose you can't," Vaughan said. "I'll see to that." He went and fiddled with Allard's ankles. Allard was greatly relieved to feel the weight of the bar drop away from him. It had been far more disconcerting than when he had been chained but still able to move his legs.

"Move your legs together." He did, rather relieved.

Then he heard clinking. Oh, god, that bloody chain again.

"You should be able to get to your knees now."

He did. It was a little tricky; his hands were attached to the short metal bar and that was chained to his collar, which made balancing something he had to actually think about. Once he'd managed to get to his knees, it wasn't too bad.

Vaughan presented him with a cheese-smeared cock. He hadn't slathered it on heavily, to Allard's relief, and at least it was right in front of his face; he didn't have to lean too far to get at it.

Allard leaned forward and licked tentatively, then got Vaughan's cockhead into his mouth and sucked with some enthusiasm. Actually, a savoury flavour went rather well with cock. He explored with his tongue, making sure he'd got all of it, before moving further down the shaft.

"I didn't realise till you mentioned it that cheese spread was one of your fantasies," said Vaughan. "Maybe we should serve this delicacy at the next cocktail party."

Allard spluttered and drew off. "Don't make jokes like that unless you fancy the idea of impromptu circumcision."

"What joke? It would go very well with all the other little delicacies. Cheese on cracker biscuits, pineapple cubes, little sausages on sticks…well, maybe not that last one."

"All right. 'Yes, master, it's a very big sausage'," drawled Allard.

"I'm going to teach you to say that without smirking," said Vaughan.

"But I do think it's a very big sausage. And a very tasty one. And I don't need to be chained up to think it."

"And you don't even need cheese spread, do you, pet?" Vaughan nudged himself towards Allard's mouth.

"No," he said, before his mouth was otherwise engaged. He cleaned every trace of cheese spread off, enjoying it, and eventually let go of Vaughan's cock.

"Allard," said Vaughan, "*was* the cheese spread one of your fantasies?" He sounded very slightly perturbed by this.

"Not until five minutes ago, no. I wouldn't mind doing that again some time, though. You bring out the pervert in me."

"Would you like a pervert in you?"

"Yes, please."

"Then you'll have to wait."

"Bastard!"

"That's an extra five minutes. Be grateful you've still got the butt-plug."

"I would be, if you'd only condescend to move it."

"Say 'please'."

"Do I have to sound as if I mean it?"

"Well, if I leave it long enough, you won't have to act, will you?" Vaughan grinned at him. "Stand up."

He couldn't. Maybe if his hands had been only cuffed, he might have been able to, but the extra restriction posed by the chain to his collar made it impossible to keep his balance. The hobble chain between his ankles certainly didn't help. He made one attempt, and gave up when he wasn't convinced he'd make it without falling over. This was ridiculous. He wasn't *that* tightly confined. If he'd been on his feet, he could have walked about readily enough; it was just moving from a kneeling to a standing position that was difficult.

"I can't," he admitted.

Vaughan just looked at him.

Then he realised what was expected of him. "Help me, please."

Vaughan took hold of him by his upper arms and pulled gently. He made another attempt to stand up. Yes, this time he could make it, with Vaughan steadying him. If he could trust Vaughan enough, trust him not to let go.

He took a deep breath and stood up.

"Well done," Vaughan said, and kissed him lightly.

He was on his feet, but he still felt unsteady, so he asked, "Hold me, please."

Vaughan put his arms around him and held him close. He leaned into the reassuringly solid bulk of Vaughan's chest. "Sorry, Vaughan. Give me a minute or two."

He'd offered to 'lose his virginity' in a BDSM sense, and it could have gone worse, but it was emotionally intense, and he kept seeing momentary flashes of 'virginity' pass by. The first time someone else gave him an enema before sex; the first time he'd let somebody chain him; the first time he'd admitted quite seriously that he was in someone else's control for sex. And when he'd stood up, he hadn't just been allowing somebody else to do things to him while he retreated into passivity. He'd had to act for himself, while putting complete trust in Vaughan not to let go.

If his hands hadn't been tied together, he'd have been clinging to Vaughan for comfort.

He'd have thought, before, that the props would have been the least important thing, and being tied up with chains would be much the same thing as being tied up with bits of cloth. He hadn't been prepared for the 'scene' to take on a life of its own, and he certainly hadn't been prepared for the possibility that he might enjoy it.

After a while, he pulled himself together a bit and moved back enough to see Vaughan. Vaughan's expression was a mixture of lust and tenderness. *It's not* just *that he likes me being afraid, and it's not the BDSM stuff. More than anything, he wants to be the cause and the solution to my fear.* Allard had known that for a while, but this was the clearest he'd ever seen it. It wasn't Vaughan fantasising about rape, but about seduction, and about a person who was afraid but willing to be led through the fear and out through the other side. For the first time, he had a tiny glimmer of perception that there *was* another side, something through the fear.

"Whatever *you* want to do," he said to Vaughan. "I know you'll take me further than I want to go, but not further than I can go."

"You do understand, don't you?"

Vaughan picked him up and carried him over to the bed like a bride being carried over the threshold.

He put him down very, very carefully, and chained him to the bed. Flat on his back, legs spread, arms above his head but not pulled tight enough to be uncomfortable. Then Vaughan stood back and admired his handiwork.

"You do look very nice like that," he said, and started caressing him.

Allard repressed the urge to be sarcastic or to ask Vaughan to get on with it. He was fairly sure that if he *did,* it would have no effect whatsoever. Actually, it was rather nice having Vaughan gently fondle different bits of his body that were not obvious erogenous zones. Vaughan was stroking all over him, taking possession of everything, not just his cock. Down one arm, gently fingering the scar where he'd been bitten by some obstreperous computer (he'd listened to one of the users who'd sworn blind the power supply was disconnected); across in a wavering trail down to near his nipple, then up to his throat just as his cock made the mistake of assuming it was the next thing on Vaughan's list of parts.

Not that his throat was objecting. Especially when Vaughan bent to kiss it. God, that felt good, and he wanted to grab Vaughan's head and hold him there. He was completely unable to do any such thing. He was completely unable to do anything but lie there and take whatever Vaughan was willing to give him.

What Vaughan was willing to give him was everything. No pettiness, no hurry, no rushing on to the next stage of the business; just total attention.

"It's nice having you in a position where I can ignore your demands to get on with it," Vaughan said.

"I was just thinking the same thing. Anyway, I was enjoying this too much to make any demands."

"That's true." Vaughan moved down, without hurry, and licked his cock.

"Consider me demanding," said Allard, rather tightly.

"You mean, all I have to do is touch the very tip of my tongue to the very tip of your cock, and you'll be begging for mercy?"

He didn't beg for mercy. He was too busy moaning.

Vaughan licked, again.

Allard got his breath back enough to say, "Please suck me!"

"Not just yet."

Vaughan moved up to kneel over Allard's chest, cock-tip waving just in front of Allard's mouth. "Why don't you show me what you'd like me to do to you?"

Allard licked. To his annoyance, Vaughan took his tasty treat away.

"I think I'll have you…" said Vaughan. He unclipped the chains holding Allard's feet, dragged Allard 'round so that his head was hanging back over the edge of the bed, and refastened his feet. Allard wondered just what Vaughan had been doing to the bedframe—there seemed to be rather a lot of fastening points available to chain him in any position Vaughan chose.

Then he had more interesting things to think about, or at least a more interesting thing. Vaughan's cock nudged at his lips. He opened his mouth wide enough to take it, sucked the head in. He set to work on showing Vaughan what he'd like Vaughan to do to him. Running his tongue around the tip, flicking it lightly, then sucking hard, encouraging Vaughan to give him a bit more length. He got another inch or two out of that, a satisfying mouthful. Not much control in this position, but Vaughan was holding still, letting him do as he liked with what he'd got. He sucked hard, enjoying the texture of cock against his tongue, then opened his mouth and breathed out, letting the light sensation tantalise Vaughan.

He wanted to grab with both hands, one hand on the shaft, the other on Vaughan's balls, but didn't have enough slack in the chains. He'd have to make do with what he'd got already, the length in his mouth. He couldn't even touch his own cock, aching with need. His pleasure depended on satisfying Vaughan with only his mouth.

He did his best, trying to push Vaughan beyond the limits of control. And then Vaughan pulled away quickly, leaving him empty.

"Any more of that and I'd have lost it," Vaughan said with a ragged edge to his voice.

"That was the idea."

"I still have plans for you," Vaughan said, a little more steadily. He walked down to the other end of the bed, undid Allard's ankles again, and pulled. "I think I'd like you properly on display now."

He'd thought he was already on display, what with being flat on his back with his legs spread. Vaughan seemed to have something else in mind.

Vaughan pushed and pulled until he was lying with his knees up and his legs apart. Maybe Vaughan was finally going to take that bloody butt-plug out and put something more useful in its place. Then the chains were clipped back on his ankles. He tested. Shorter length this time. He didn't have any slack in them. The only movement option was to try and scoot the rest of his body in the other direction so that he could lie flat. He tried it.

"Oh, no, you don't," said Vaughan. "I want your arse nicely on display."

Vaughan grabbed more chain, then grabbed his shoulders and shoved him back down the bed. Then he clipped one end of the chain to the collar, from what Allard could make out, and the other end to the bedframe. A second chain to the other side of the bed, and he was completely immobilised.

"Bastard!"

"You called?" said Vaughan, raising an eyebrow.

"Now what?" Allard said.

"Now for the next part of the programme." Vaughan moved back to the end of the bed, and removed the butt plug, twisting it as he pulled it out.

"Thank you," Allard said.

"Were you under the impression that I was going to replace it with my cock?"

"Well, yes. Unless you've got an even bigger and better butt plug to show off." He thought about it. Not a bad idea, if Vaughan was planning on delaying the climax. "Don't suppose you've got one that vibrates?"

"I was thinking of doing something else, as it happens." Vaughan went and rummaged in the cupboard. He came back with something long and thin. Three feet long, so it couldn't be something Vaughan was planning to insert in him.

More fiddling. It was a tripod.

Then Vaughan set a camera on the tripod, and started tweaking it. An old-fashioned camera, larger than he'd seen before. Manual focus.

Focused on him.

"Vaughan, no!"

"Yes. I want a record of this."

He started thrashing on the bed, fighting the chains. Only the chains weren't just for show, and he nearly choked himself. "Vaughan, I don't want this!"

"What you want doesn't come into it. I want it, and that's all that matters."

Couldn't Vaughan see that he really didn't want this, that it was time to stop playing the game? "Stop it, Vaughan, this isn't funny!"

"Keep still. I don't want to have to use a high shutter speed." There was a flash of bright light, and a loud click. "I think that's one for the Readers' Wives page."

That was when he panicked.

He forced it down long enough to remember, and screamed, "Money!"

Vaughan stopped fiddling with the camera, ran over to the bed, and released one of Allard's hands. "I'm sorry, Allard. I didn't realise you'd take it that badly."

"Other hand," Allard said.

"You should be able to do that yourself," Vaughan said, but he leaned over and unclipped Allard's other hand. *Oh, of course,* realised the more rational part of Allard's mind, *padlocks and slow ritualistic fastenings would be fine for getting into, but present problems if somebody panics.* It was a perfectly sensible rule, and Vaughan *had* set it up that way, and *did* respect the safeword when Allard had remembered it.

"Now I know what you meant about the safeword," Allard said quietly.

Vaughan touched his hand gently, and said, "It makes a lot more sense when it's demonstrated rather than explained."

"I wouldn't have thought, before tonight, that I'd like to say 'no!' and have it ignored."

"I'm sorry," said Vaughan. "I think I got carried away, or I'd have picked up on your reactions before you had to use your safeword." He looked puzzled. "But I didn't *expect* that to upset you. You've never been bothered by Harry. Annoyed, yes, but not bothered."

"That's different." He thought about why it was different. "Harry only does audio, and that seems to make a difference. Harry also will not willingly send the data off to be drooled over by strangers; nor will the girls. Somehow, the thought that an image of me could be out there, while I had no control at all over who saw me like that, makes my blood run cold."

"Willingly surrendering control to me is one thing. The idea of strangers wanking over pictures of you chained and exposed is another." Vaughan gently stroked his shoulder. "I wouldn't really send it anywhere. Not unless you said I could."

"You might not, but our horrible little brat of a computer would, and I'm not completely convinced I've managed to firewall him out of our private filespace. I want it deleted—now!"

Vaughan smiled. "I don't need to. It's an old-fashioned film camera. The image exists physically inside the camera and absolutely nowhere else."

"What are you doing with one of those? Just how long have you been planning this?" *I suppose I can discount the theory that he's been waiting for several centuries through the rise of digital photography.*

"It's been a hobby of mine for a while. You haven't seen the camera because I haven't had time to play with it these last few months. Nothing to do with you, of course." He grinned. "I haven't been planning this for very long. I've been fantasising about it for longer, though." He got up and put the camera away.

"What are you doing with that film?" Allard asked, wondering whether he should take the opportunity to undo the rest of his chains, run over, and destroy the camera.

"I'll destroy it, if you want. But I would like to keep one print just for myself."

Just in case I ever leave you? Allard wondered.

"One print," he agreed. "Keep it where nobody else can see it."

"Thank you," said Vaughan, sounding as though he meant that. He came back to the bed. "Shall we go on?"

"I'm not sure if I want to. Emotional catharsis is all very well in its way, but it doesn't make for a riotous night of sexual excess."

Vaughan lay down next to him. "What does, then?"

"Well, you could start by doing to my cock what I was doing to yours. As promised some time ago." Then as Vaughan started to move, he said, "I don't mind the hands and feet, but could you please remove the chain from my collar?"

"Certainly," Vaughan said, grinning. "Off the neck, as requested," he unclipped the ones from the collar, "and back on the hands."

Allard decided to be more careful in his phrasing in future. He didn't mind too much. Especially when Vaughan slid down his body and clamped his mouth on Allard's cock. A couple of quick sucks, and then Vaughan started kissing up and down the length of it, and...*pretending he's playing an oboe?* Allard thought incredulously. Yes. Complete with fingering exercises. Somehow, Vaughan didn't seem to be taking the business entirely seriously. Especially when he started practicing arpeggios.

Allard sighed, and smiled. Earlier on, when they'd both been taking the game very seriously, that would have ruined the mood. Now he was glad of it. "I hope you weren't planning on giving a public performance on that instrument."

Vaughan gave him the first couple of bars of *Minuet in G major,* and looked up at him and grinned. "They laughed when I sat down at the piano," he remarked mock-mournfully.

"Well, that one ought to be recognisable to anybody who's had the ritual music lesson inflicted on them, at least if they played a wind instrument. Oh, well, at least I'm not a recorder."

"What?" Vaughan said.

"Recorders are *so* common."

"You can't be a recorder," Vaughan said. "You've got all the nice fiddly bits to twiddle." He demonstrated.

"Yes, I feel better now," Allard said.

"Oh, good," Vaughan said. "Does that mean I can shove my cock down your throat now?"

"I don't feel like that position you were threatening me with earlier," said Allard, "but I am willing to be reasonable and consider anything comfortable for both of us."

"Who is supposed to be the top here?" said Vaughan.

"You," said Allard.

"Then I think we'd better get you back into a properly submissive mood," said Vaughan. "Now, what did you say about a vibrating butt-plug?"

"I think it was along the lines of 'please, sir'. Or else I just moaned."

"What a lovely idea." Vaughan went and rummaged in his box of tricks. He came back with something that definitely looked bigger than the last one. In fact, it looked bigger than Vaughan, at least in width.

Vaughan slapped a bit of lube on it, then touched the tip of it to Allard just underneath his balls, and stroked it down, switching it on halfway along.

"Yes, I think that's more-or-less what you said last time," Vaughan said, as Allard's moan got much louder in response to the toy becoming operational.

Vaughan had done an excellent job of re-arousing him with the 'musical performance', and his arse still seemed to be sensitive and interested after the previous teasing. He wanted something more substantial.

"Put it in me, Vaughan!" he demanded.

"Oh, I will." Vaughan touched the tip to his hole. "Eventually."

"Please, Vaughan!" he begged.

Vaughan gave him half an inch.

"Please, Vaughan!" he said, much more sincerely this time.

"Do you want this even more than my cock?" Vaughan twisted it and pushed it in a little more.

Allard frantically tried to work out what Vaughan wanted to hear in response to that, and fell back on the truth. "I don't care, as long as you stuff something in there!"

Another inch in, and the vibrator speeded up. Allard writhed.

"You really are quite an interesting sight when you're desperate. I wonder how desperate you can get?"

"Desperate enough to take something that size."

"Greedy, aren't you?" Vaughan said, and gave him the lot.

Allard jumped. He hadn't been expecting that, just more teasing. Then he realised he was being teased, because it still wasn't enough. "More!"

"Oh, I think you ought to do something nice to me first."

Vaughan walked around to where he could sit on the edge of the bed, releasing Allard's wrist but holding the chain, so that Allard had just enough slack to reach Vaughan's cock.

God, it was good to be able to get something in his hand at last. His own cock would have been better, but Vaughan's would do. He squeezed and tugged, enjoying the sensation of cock filling his hand.

"Very nice," said Vaughan. "I think I'll reward you."

Allard jumped, as the thing in his arse speeded up all of a sudden.

"Remote control." Vaughan grinned at him. "Might be fun to make you wear that during the day."

His cock *really* liked that idea. It wasn't something he'd ever really want to do—except that he did. He jerked at Vaughan.

"Don't pull it off," Vaughan said.

Allard was far gone enough not to even *think* of making a joke about that remark. He would only notice that when his language centres came back online later.

As it was, he waited eagerly while Vaughan shifted position, kneeling over him again. Only this time, he had a hand free, and he was able to grab his own cock just as Vaughan settled into position. Cold metal trailed across his skin, the length of chain still attached to the wrist-cuff. Vaughan's cockhead just in front of his mouth, where he could lick the tip. He struggled to reach it, then Vaughan thrust forward just enough, and he was able to suck and tug hard at the same time.

Vaughan groaned, thrust forward, nearly lost his balance, and pulled back—and came all over Allard's face.

The shock should have put him off. Instead, it put him over the edge. He felt himself go past the point of no return, squeezed and tugged and came.

It was the most undignified orgasm he'd had in some time: both of them were rather unprepared, he had Vaughan's come on his face, and a busily buzzing machine up his arse. It was rather unfair that the experience was absolutely glorious. He tried to stop shaking and whimpering, which took a while. Then he tried desperately to look slightly pained.

"You enjoyed that, then," said Vaughan.

"Apparently."

Vaughan got off him. He looked rather unsteady. Allard hoped he wouldn't end up with Vaughan sitting down heavily on him.

"Turn that damn thing off," said Allard, twitching irritably.

"Oh, sorry," said Vaughan. "I quite forgot it was there, though I bet you didn't." He switched it off obediently.

Allard scrambled up the bed a bit so that he could lie flat, and Vaughan pushed him over a bit so he had room to lie down.

* * *

After a comfortable doze, Vaughan got up and began to tidy Allard up.

"Did I actually go to sleep *chained-up,* Vaughan?"

"Yes. You looked very sweet."

Allard shook his head slightly in bemusement. He felt relaxed, but full of energy. He still didn't feel bothered by the chains, even now he had remembered they were there. Even worse, he didn't feel bothered by Vaughan remarking that he looked 'very sweet' in chains.

Vaughan finished wiping him down, and removed the butt-plug. It felt rather interesting going out. Apparently, his libido wasn't exhausted yet. Tired, but not exhausted.

Vaughan said, "Wasn't so bad, was it?"

Allard said, "Actually, it was quite tame compared to how afraid I was beforehand. Except for the camera, of course."

"I'm sure I can come up with something you won't think tame."

Allard said, "Me and my big mouth!"

"I was thinking of enlarging the other end."

"Vaughan? It's the size it is, whether you fuck it or not." Allard squirmed uneasily. He couldn't help noticing that it felt bigger now Vaughan had removed the butt-plug.

"Have you heard of fisting, Allard?"

"No."

"The human rectum can be stretched to take larger objects than a human penis. Quite a bit larger." Vaughan lifted his hand, closed it into a fist, and moved it about suggestively.

Allard gulped.

"Are you all right?"

"Scared, but all right. I don't think it's something either of us could get away with trying casually. I would want quite a lot of data before I considered it."

"There are books. It's not a rough-sex thing, for obvious reasons, but it is a thing people can learn to do. Actually, it's not done using a clenched fist, but an open hand that has to move in a very particular way."

"Have you…" Allard gulped. "…had it done to you?"

"Once. It's not something people try casually."

"Did it hurt?"

"Felt…strange. Intimate."

"Have you done it to someone else?"

"Yes. Several times. I wouldn't try it with you if I hadn't. And you're quite stretched from the butt-plug, which will help."

Allard said, in a small voice, "Does that effect wear off easily?"

"The muscle-tone sorts itself out after the experience. You'll wake up tomorrow feeling normal but perhaps sore, if we do."

"Could we do it as less of a BDSM experience?" Allard asked. "I'm still learning, and I feel I've had enough of a lesson for today on the parameters of submission."

Vaughan smiled at him. "Me, too. All right, we'll just focus on learning how to do it."

He removed Allard's chains, but didn't bother undoing the cuffs. Allard was comfortable with that. Vaughan had taken off enough of the regalia to make the point that they were now outside the scene, and he trusted Vaughan enough to know Vaughan would not force him back into it against his will.

Vaughan asked, "Want a couple of pillows? So that you can watch?"

Allard felt slightly doubtful about watching that happen to him, but sighed, and nodded. No sense in going into this half-heartedly.

"Allard," said Vaughan, "you have a naturally enquiring mind, so I thought you might find it fascinating from the academic point-of-view."

"True," he said.

"I'll go and find you a book," said Vaughan, "but not right now. I don't want to wait while you read the whole thing."

Allard was about to protest, then remembered *monaxonida* and his tendency to get distracted by the dictionary. "At least give me a précis of the more useful parts. I like to know what's going to happen."

"Lots and lots of lube, I work up to it slowly, relax and don't panic. There's a trick to how someone moves their hand. All the recipient needs to know is that it might *sound* impossible, but it isn't." Vaughan put a couple of pillows under Allard's shoulders so that he was propped up comfortably.

"Does it hurt?" said Allard. "It won't necessarily stop me if it does."

Vaughan looked at him. "It feels uncomfortable if you're not used to it, but if it hurts, it means it's being done wrong."

He nodded. That had been *exactly* what he wanted to know; there was a difference between pain as pain, and pain that meant something, and he always liked to know whether the appropriate response was to relax or stop doing what he was doing.

Vaughan checked his hands very carefully, and showed them to Allard. "Are my hands in a fit state to do this?"

Allard looked. No visible snags or sharp nails. "They look all right to me. Is this another of those ritual things that people do slowly and carefully?"

"Sort of, but it's as well to get it right anyway. If I had snags, or I didn't know somebody's medical status, I'd use gloves. Now the tools for the job have passed preliminary inspection, I'll get started."

The early stages were comfortably familiar. Vaughan lubed up a finger and slipped it inside. It went in easily, as it should after having a large toy in there earlier. Vaughan brushed it gently across his prostate, and he realised he was definitely ready to be interested in more sex, even if this was going to be a rather *strange* form of sex. He relaxed a little. His prostate didn't seem to be bothered about fine distinctions like whether this was normal or not.

"That's right," Vaughan said, "just keep relaxing." He withdrew the finger, slapped on quite a lot of lubricant, and tried two fingers. Allard couldn't actually see them going in, but he could see enough to make him feel more comfortable with what Vaughan was doing. He could see Vaughan, which was probably the point of the pillows, and did a lot to make him feel that he wasn't being subjected to an unusual medical procedure. Yes, this was definitely sex, even though he didn't feel a raging desire to come quite yet. He was just relaxed, and interested, and wanting to know what happened next. What happened next was three fingers. That toy *must* have been large: it took three fingers for Vaughan to be touching the sides.

Vaughan started fingerfucking him then, as opposed to simply dilating him. He wriggled, making sure he was in a good position.

"That's right," said Vaughan, "show me you like it."

He didn't have a problem with that. He settled down to enjoy the feel of Vaughan's fingers sliding inside him.

"Make me want it," he suggested lazily. "You're good at that."

"It's difficult to get up enough steam for the fantasy about you being a virgin if you go and make remarks about me being a sex-toy and you being a spoilt brat, you know." Vaughan kept his fingers working even through the long and complex sentence. Allard was rather impressed.

"I've never done this before, and you know that. Stop complaining."

"Oh, I'm sure you've done *this* bit before. I distinctly remember doing this…" Vaughan shoved a bit harder. "…to you last week."

He groaned with satisfaction. "Try four fingers," he suggested.

Vaughan muttered something about, "No, that's not how this is meant to go. I'm meant to really *surprise* you with the fourth finger." He added the fourth finger.

It did surprise him. It surprised him how much extra one added finger felt like. He was mortified to hear himself squeak.

"Good. Back on track," grunted Vaughan.

It felt extremely good, and extremely strange. No matter how much he tried to catalogue what he was *really* feeling, every time Vaughan shifted his hand slightly, the balance between pain and pleasure would change a bit. Not that it was really pain. Not quite. Then Vaughan pushed slightly deeper and it was undeniably pain. He yelped.

Vaughan pulled back a bit. "That hurt you. I'd better not try any deeper or wider than I was doing."

"You haven't finished it yet," said Allard. No matter how warped was the experience he'd set out on, he wanted to do it properly.

"Try to relax," Vaughan told him, and tested him carefully. Instead of the easy stretch of earlier, there was a sudden flash of pain.

"I can't seem to manage the damn thing!" Allard said crossly. "I *hate* when I know how to do something but can't seem to get it to happen. Just like data backup on an old Vax. I'd read the manual for that, as well."

"You're doing very well for me to manage four fingers. I have large hands."

Allard relaxed slightly and began to see the point of this strange activity. Being *able* to relax and let someone do this to him meant something.

He focused on how it felt with four fingers, which was more than he'd ever had inside him before. Vaughan was spreading them very slightly and relaxing again, but without going further, it didn't actually hurt. He was aware, to his surprise, of trusting Vaughan, who had known when to stop without actually being asked.

It was surprisingly erotic; it had taken him a while to realise that because the usual urgent desire to come, to move, to *get on with it,* was practically absent. Instead, it was a strange sort of intimate massage, performed in voluptuous stillness by a loving expert.

Vaughan eased a little further in. Now he felt wonderfully full. Allard relaxed. He no longer had any urge to ask for the thumb in order to cross the experience off his list as 'completed'. He'd like the thumb when he could manage it; it would make this even better. This was good now, smooth and deep; he would ask Vaughan for it again. In future, it might be his reward for giving Vaughan what he wanted in the way of BDSM, and never mind that when he'd got up this morning he'd had no conception about why *anyone* would want a whole human hand inside them—or even that it was possible.

"You look absolutely beautiful like that," said Vaughan tenderly.

"Why did you never tell me about this before?"

"Would you have believed me?"

Well, *no.* He would have started edging away from Vaughan the moment he'd mentioned the concept.

"I love this," said Allard dreamily. "I want you to do it again."

Why was Vaughan looking at him like that? Oh…

"So we tried the bondage, but the answer to converting a virgin was at your fingertips," Allard said, smirking slightly to cover his own mild embarrassment.

"Don't make me laugh when I've got my hand stuck up your arse," Vaughan warned him.

"Are we going to try for the whole hand?"

"Not this time," said Vaughan. "Even if we could manage it, it would take a long time, and we're both tired."

He thought about it. He was tired, and happy, and aroused-but-not-urgently-so. He was probably too tired to spend hours getting this right, and so was Vaughan.

"Mm."

Vaughan moved his hand very gently. "Have you had enough for now?" he said.

Allard thought about it. He wouldn't mind going on, but he wouldn't be disappointed if they stopped now. He said so.

Vaughan eased his hand out gently.

Allard sighed, almost regretfully.

"That would have taken a lot longer if I'd got all the way in," said Vaughan. "I'll just go to the bathroom and find some stuff to clean you up with. I had to use a lot of lube."

Allard was glad Vaughan had explained that. After the intimacy of the experience, it would have felt strangely distant to have Vaughan rush off to the bathroom without talking to him. The emotional connection was still there, even as he listened to Vaughan running the taps and splashing water around.

Then Vaughan came back to him, holding a large fluffy towel and a couple of wet flannels. "I'll just mop you down, pet."

"If you must," said Allard.

Vaughan cleaned him up very tenderly, taking care of every drop of lubricant with the flannel and then patting him dry with the towel.

Allard noticed, slightly surprised, that Vaughan was still wearing his trousers, although his cock was poking out in an interested manner.

Mm. He supposed hands hadn't *quite* made sexual organs obsolete.

His own rose to greet Vaughan's at the thought. He rather envied women the lack of transparent motivation.

"Not had enough yet?" said Vaughan.

"Apparently not."

Vaughan reached for his belt, undid it and dropped his trousers. "We'll soon fix that," he said, and sat down on the bed.

Vaughan's hand, which had introduced him to a new experience, was within reach. As Allard raised it, he noticed, with a small shock, that his own hand was still cuffed. But that didn't seem to matter. He kissed Vaughan's hand gently. "Thank you."

Vaughan stroked his face. "I think I ought to be the one saying that to you."

"Was I good?"

"You were very good indeed." Vaughan settled down on top of him and kissed him. The kiss seemed a continuation of the experience: all of him open and sexual and unhurried as he let Vaughan take him wherever they were going. Vaughan was right. They *had* been good. All they needed to do now was add the full stop of orgasm to the work-of-art Vaughan had created as a sexual experience.

The weight on top of him was precisely what he wanted. He rocked against Vaughan, cock moving delicately against cock as tongue slid against tongue. Just a little more…just a little…*there*…and falling over the slightest edges into an orgasm as gentle as a sigh.

He sighed.

Even as he wanted it never to stop, it was finally over.

"Will you hold me?"

Vaughan held him. The experience ebbed softly away without quite leaving him. He held Vaughan, as well.

Vaughan said quietly, "I find myself less worried that you're going to leave me, after that."

Allard sighed, and stroked his hair. A thought occurred to him.

"Just how much BDSM experience *have* you got, Vaughan?"

"Not as much as you seem to think. It was an occasional diversion, but it wasn't quite what I wanted, and then…five-foot-nine of wanton innocence walked into my life." Vaughan undid Allard's collar.

"I'm a complete innocent *compared to some people,* Vaughan, and apparently I can make them think kinky thoughts by wearing clothes and walking about. It's slightly unnerving."

"You left out 'bending down'," said Vaughan as he bent down himself and tackled the wrist-cuffs. "Anyway, it's the fact that you *don't realise* it's kinky that makes it so wonderfully effective."

"You remember the time we were testing computer communications, among other things. I have an uneasy feeling I tried to patronise you about your less-than-encyclopaedic knowledge of sexual practices. But I didn't even know about safewords." A thought struck him. "You've tied me up before, and you didn't mention safewords then."

"At any hint that you weren't comfortable, I'd have stopped," said Vaughan. "Apart from that, you've had a good illustration tonight about the difference between light play and being 'inside' the scene."

"You mean, we didn't laugh for most of it?" He sighed. "I think I'm the one with the less-than-encyclopaedic knowledge."

"Actually, you *do* have an encyclopaedic knowledge of sexual practices," said Vaughan seriously, as he undid the ankle-cuffs. "You just ran head-on into the difference between having read an enormous amount and having actually *done* some of them."

"I wish you weren't right about that, Vaughan."

"I'm glad I am." Vaughan lay down next to him and took him in his arms. "It's what makes you so appealing. Like I said, wanton innocence."

Allard realised there was no possible way he could get the upper hand in this particular conversation. The best strategy he could come up with was to go to sleep wrapped around Vaughan. So he did.

Buttered Bun

by Jules Jones and Alex Woolgrave

Drinking outside wasn't that much of a good idea on a chilly autumn evening in a street full of pollution-emitting vehicles. Allard had got out of the habit of considering weather, let alone pollution, in the long time they'd had between planetfalls.

Vaughan didn't look that comfortable, either, and Allard was fairly sure he needed a rest after a long day installing the new generators they'd just hauled across three star-systems. Allard and Karen had helped, of course, but Vaughan had been doing most of the work.

"Shall we see if it's more salubrious inside?" Allard said, picking up his drink.

"Good idea," said Vaughan, and picked up his.

It was still relatively early and the pub wasn't too crowded. Allard spotted a table well out of the draught from the door, and weaved his way around the intervening bodies. The table was probably intended for four or six people, and it would be well-mannered to wait for a two-person table to become free, but he was tired and he didn't really care.

They sat in silence and enjoyed the beer. It was quite good beer, really; they ought to stock up.

Vaughan had nearly finished his first half-pint, rather quickly, when a stranger slipped into the seat beside him and said, "You look as if you needed that."

"I did," Vaughan said politely.

"Is there anything else you might be needing?" the stranger asked.

Allard sighed. They always seemed to end up next to People Trying To Sell Things In Pubs. Occasionally they'd gone home with anything from a single red rose each to a wickerwork donkey that Harry, for some reason, couldn't resist.

"If you're trying to sell us tourist junk, no," said Allard, as politely as he could manage.

"I wasn't intending to sell you anything," said the stranger. "You're obviously from off-world, and I thought you might like a bit of extra company for the evening."

"Well, actually, no thank you," said Allard. "We're together."

"Allard…" said Vaughan. "I think he realised that."

Allard thought about it, then sat there with his mouth open. Was this man really suggesting…

"He's not *really* that thick," said Vaughan to the newcomer. "It's just that his mind has two modes: 'dirty' and 'clean'. If it was in the 'clean' one, he just needs to switch over."

"Whereas your switch has been welded in the 'dirty' position since puberty," said Allard sharply.

"Of course. I'm an engineer," said Vaughan, grinning.

Allard looked at him. Vaughan didn't actually look shocked.

Vaughan looked back at him, then said to the stranger, "Would you go away for a few minutes while I explain a few facts of life to my friend?"

"I'm not *that* bloody naïve!" snapped Allard, as the stranger nodded politely and got up.

"No, not quite," said Vaughan, "but I didn't think you'd be comfortable discussing it in front of him."

"Discussing what?" snapped Allard, and took a gulp of beer.

"Well—are we going to take him up on his offer, of course," said Vaughan.

He had already swallowed the gulp, fortunately.

"Don't choke," Vaughan said helpfully. "I'm surprised you're that shocked. Haven't you ever been in a threesome before?"

"Yes." It wasn't shock-horror, just shock-surprise, whatever Vaughan might think. "When I was young and foolish, and never had to worry about whether I could get it up a second time in one evening. Besides, actually doing it in front of Harry that time counts as a threesome, as far as I'm concerned."

"Would you like to? Properly, I mean."

Properly? "I'm quite happy with you, Vaughan." He looked at him. "Are you really interested in a three-in-a-bed romp?"

Vaughan looked embarrassed. This worried Allard. Considering the sorts of things Vaughan *hadn't* been embarrassed about in the past, what on earth was he about to come up with now?

"Well," said Vaughan, "not so much three-in-a-bed; more of a watching thing."

"Watching?" said Allard, not quite sure where this was leading. "Like with Harry?"

"Not *quite* like with Harry. I find the idea of watching you being fucked by a stranger quite erotic. Definitely that way 'round—I think it might bother me if it wasn't."

Allard stared at him for several seconds. Then he remembered to close his mouth.

Opening it again, he said, "Vaughan, I have been listening to your nervous maunderings about am-I-going-to-leave for months, and now you want to throw me into some stranger's bed?"

"Or up the wall," muttered Vaughan, blushing. "I think that sounds quite interesting."

"If this is some quid pro quo where *you* end up taking your turn with the stranger, *no*," said Allard firmly. "I do not want to watch you with anyone, on top or underneath or any other combination."

"No," said Vaughan, "I know you're a possessive little bastard."

"Then why? It doesn't make sense."

Vaughan shrugged. "Illicit thrill?"

He thought about it for a while. Vaughan was, perhaps, insecure in a different way. Vaughan had a distinct preference for being demonstrably the best his partner had ever had, in those little dramas he liked to play out. Maybe, if he was sure his partner would go home with him at the end of the evening, it might be a way of playing with an idea he found uncomfortable. Looked at that way, it made perfect sense.

Allard looked at their prospective partner, who was standing by the bar sipping a drink. He didn't seem unattractive. Reasonably tall and well-built, which he liked anyway, but with straight blond hair, so there would be no mistaking him for Vaughan. His voice was rich and mellow, and Allard was a sucker for nice voices. He'd spent quite a lot of time listening to Vaughan's political nonsense while tuning out the actual words. This man was quite an appealing prospect as a one-night stand.

More to the point, neither of them would ever have to see him again.

"All right," he told Vaughan.

Vaughan stood up, and beckoned the man over.

The stranger came over carrying two glasses, and set one in front of Vaughan. "I hope that suits you," he said. "You looked as if you would appreciate another one."

Vaughan sipped. "Very nice, thanks." He looked at Allard, and said, "Do you want something?"

Allard wasn't very far down his own glass of beer. "Not really," he said.

There was a slightly nervous pause, and the stranger looked at Vaughan.

"I think we've decided," Vaughan said. "Would it be sensible to set a few guidelines here? To be blunt, you fuck him, not the other way 'round, and I watch."

The man didn't seem in the least bit startled. "Oh, you're into HMW?"

"What?" Vaughan asked.

"Husband Must Watch." The stranger openly appraised Allard. "Suits me. He's a pretty little thing, and I don't mind an audience."

Allard was not quite as slow on the uptake as he had been before joining the *Mary Sue.* "Excuse me, but you're talking to both of us, not just him."

"Oh, sorry. I thought…"

Allard sighed. "Lots of people wear leather just because it's warm and hard-wearing, you know. And he was the one giving the terms because it was his idea."

"Ah. You wouldn't be interested in playing, then?"

Oddly enough, the thought was slightly intriguing. No *more* than slightly. Allard's tastes in BDSM were virgin fantasies, both as virgin and as seducer, and catering to Vaughan's occasional whims because he liked pleasing Vaughan. Playing with strangers could be dangerous. "Fucking, yes. Playing, thanks for the offer, but no. It doesn't do a lot for me."

He caught a very slight, private smile from Vaughan. He was pleased that Vaughan took that as the gift it was.

"If you don't like it, no problem," said their new playmate agreeably enough. "It's always useful to get these things sorted out before the clothes come off, isn't it?"

"Quite," said Allard, relaxing a bit. The stranger obviously seemed to mean that. "When and where?" Allard asked, thinking he was a bit out of practice at negotiating.

"My place is quite close," said the stranger. "You might as well finish your drinks. You two look as if you need to relax a bit. What have you been doing?"

"A transport and install job," said Vaughan. "Basically, hard work and heavy lifting. You're quite right that we need to relax."

"Oh, you don't just haul cargo, then?"

"Actually, hauling cargo is a sideline," said Allard. "We sell our expertise, and sometimes we fetch things to use our expertise *on.*" *Viable computers, junk computers, wine collections, antique flintlocks, coffee machines—anything weird that one of us knows something about.*

"So you're consultants?"

"You *could* say that," Vaughan said. "Actually, we're from a syndicate ship."

Allard watched for the blank look—yes, there it went. Vaughan drew blank looks more often than not when he mentioned his hobbyhorse, but it never discouraged him.

As Allard had expected, Vaughan hastened to fill in the blanks. "Syndicalism is a form of shared ownership by the workforce."

"Ah," said the stranger. "I think I *have* heard of that. So you're syndicalists." To Allard's disgust, the man looked interested.

"No. *He's* a syndicalist," Allard said. "I'm just along for the ride."

Vaughan said, "A very good ride you are, too."

"So you're his…ah," said the stranger to Allard.

"Maybe I should just have a card printed," said Allard disgustedly. "Everyone jumps to that conclusion. No, this just happens to be a syndicate that was willing to accept an outside consultant."

"Especially as his attitude to management is even more malevolent than that of most syndicalists," Vaughan put in. "But he is a bloody good ride. *Off-duty,*" he added carefully.

"So what do you actually do on the ship," the stranger asked Allard, "if you're not part of their system?"

"I do my job," Allard said, slightly surprised that it needed saying. "They needed a good computer man more than they needed more political verbiage, which they can create at will, anyway."

He watched Vaughan decide not to rise to the bait.

"Oh," said the stranger, as if enlightened. "You're a techie. That explains the leather and attitude."

Good. This man knows the signs, thought Allard.

"Can you actually tell me more about syndicalism?" the stranger asked. "How does it work if you don't believe in management?"

Allard hastily disconnected his brain from his ears and listened to the sweet flow of Vaughan's voice. It was even better now—two warm, mellow voices in counterpoint, and he had no need at all to pay attention to what Vaughan was saying. After all, he'd heard the speech once, months ago, and he had no need to listen to what would certainly be more of the same.

Eventually, he heard his name, and switched mode hurriedly.

"Thought that would get your attention," Vaughan said. "Thirty minutes of syndicalist theory don't leave a mark on his brain," he told the stranger, "but as soon as we get onto 'let's go and fuck Allard through the bed', he's with us again."

Allard thought for a moment. Would it be more embarrassing to admit all he'd heard was his name, or more embarrassing *not* to admit it? Then he said, "I didn't actually notice the word 'fuck'. That's part of your normal description of what to do to corporate management and why you're a syndicalist. I *did* notice my name."

"Well, shall we go and fuck you through the bed?" Vaughan asked politely.

"Are you going to take it in turns, then?"

"Sounds like an excellent idea," said the stranger.

"I will very politely let our new friend go first," said Vaughan.

"You're very civilised about sex," said the stranger, glancing at both of them.

Allard was startled. It was the first time in a long time anyone had called him 'civilised' about *anything.* He must be slipping. Vaughan certainly didn't apply that term to his sex drive—'greedy little bastard' came first. Usually literally.

Civilised sex also included letting your shipmates know you were going to be later than expected.

"We'd better call the ship," he said. "It would be embarrassing to have a search party come looking for us." He glanced at Vaughan. "Especially if it was Harry, who would certainly *come* while looking for us."

Vaughan explained. "Harry is one of our shipmates, and a voyeur. Need I say more?"

The stranger laughed and said, "Better call, then. Unless you fancy anyone else dropping in."

Allard got out his phone and called the ship. He was grateful when Claire answered. The 'nudge nudge wink wink' would be slightly less tasteless.

"Vaughan and I have found something else to do," he said. "We'll be back late. By the way, did Karen let you know she will be back late, as well?"

"Yes, I gathered that somebody offered to show her his weapons collection," Claire said. "With anyone else, I'd assume it was a version of 'come up and see my etchings', but with Karen, they probably will spend some time drooling over his weapon collection before she drools over his weapon."

Only slightly *less tasteless,* Allard thought. "You've got a filthy mind, Claire."

"It gets a lot of practice on this ship," said Claire. "By the way, would you like to give me the address you and Vaughan are going to, to screw in private, in case I need to find you in a hurry? I promise I won't tell Harry."

He sighed, and asked, "Where are we going?" and repeated the address to Claire. At least, if they *had* misjudged this person, other people knew where they now were.

"Oh?" said Claire, "That wasn't Vaughan. Picked up a friend, have you? I'm surprised at you, Allard!"

"Why does *everyone* have the mistaken impression I am: a) Vaughan's tart, and b) too innocent to notice that someone's trying to pick me up?" asked Allard, a little sensitive on this point.

"Because you are, dear," Claire said. "You didn't even notice the first few times one of us tried to make you feel welcome, you were rude to Karen when she decided being blunt might get your attention, then you went to bed with Vaughan and haven't fucked anyone else since. At least, not that we've noticed. Unless you're counting Harry."

Well, yes, he did count Harry, that one time at least, but he could see why others might not. Or had Harry still not confessed to the women about that?

"I take it Vaughan is with you," Claire added.

"Yes, Claire. My lord and master is with me, and suggested this particular little diversion. Maybe Harry is contagious." At least Claire cared enough to check that he wasn't getting into trouble.

"No, I don't want to watch," said Claire. "I'll settle for hearing all about it afterwards. Let me know when you get back."

Actually, he'd been thinking about Vaughan wanting to watch, but it was a happy accident that Claire had misread that. He didn't really want her to know that much detail.

"Have fun," said Claire, and closed the call.

"I really don't like you using those terms, even as a joke," said Vaughan. "I am—sometimes under protest—captain of the ship as a legal requirement. I am *not* your lord and master."

"No, dear," said Allard politely. He kept his face straight for about three seconds before smirking.

"Annoying little sod," said Vaughan.

"Yes, dear," said Allard, rather more sincerely.

"There's one way I'm happy to force you to shut up, and I'm not doing it in public. Come on," said Vaughan, and led the way.

"I think I'll go back to my first opinion on you two," said the stranger.

"As long as you remember," said Allard, "*he's* the sub!"

"Some of the time, at least," said Vaughan.

The sun had set while they'd been in the pub, and it was cold outside now, not just cool. Allard shivered, wishing he'd brought a coat. His leather jacket was thick enough, but it didn't keep his legs warm. "How far are we going?"

"Just around the corner. I go to that pub because it's my local, not because it's a pick-up joint."

"Oh."

The man looked at him. "Didn't you realise?"

Vaughan said, "It was the first one we saw that we liked the look of. All we were looking for was a drink."

Quick grin in response from their host. "And you got more than you bargained for. Ah, well." He looked more closely at Allard, and then draped an arm around him. "Don't worry; I've got good central heating."

Allard was surprised at how odd it felt to have someone he didn't know put an arm around him. The *Mary Sue's* crew were all fairly tactile people; he was used to being touched, hugged. But this was different. This was the first time in months he'd known it was the prelude to sex with someone new. He enjoyed the warmth, even though it wasn't his shoulders that needed it. Then they were standing in front of the street door to a block of flats.

Not particularly salubrious flats, it had to be said. Somebody owned a tomcat, and nobody owned a deodorant.

"I apologise for the scenery," said their new friend, leading them inside and up a staircase that Allard was pleased to note had not been used as a urinal, human or feline. "It's really not too bad inside, it's just that I moved here to be near work and I've never bothered with the externals."

Allard could sympathise with that. He relaxed slightly as the stranger opened the door to reveal a small but nicely decorated flat. One wall was filled with bookcases holding a selection of paper books, recordings, and storage devices for at least three different sorts of computer. Enough of a geek to make Allard feel at home.

He wandered over to inspect the bookcase, and decided he liked this man's taste.

"You're not visiting a library, Allard," said Vaughan. "We're here for something else."

Allard sighed. "Where's the bedroom, then?"

"I apologise for my companion's manners," said Vaughan to the stranger.

"Excuse me!" said Allard indignantly. "You pointed out that our friend here might want to get down to it rather than discussing literature; therefore, I'm trying to be thoughtful."

"Is he always like this when he wants a shag?" asked the stranger.

"He's quite right," said Vaughan. "He *is* being polite."

Allard smiled at him, very slightly.

Vaughan went on. "His boundaries for what's polite and what's rude are just set slightly differently to most people's. From his point of view, you invited him back because you want sex—therefore, it's rude of him to be looking at your bookshelves; therefore, it would be politer to go to bed."

"Yes," said the stranger thoughtfully, "I see that. Incidentally, thank you for reminding me there's a reason I don't normally shag hard-core techies. Mainly because I'd need an emotional phrasebook."

"Now we've got that sorted out," said Allard, "do we shag?"

"Stop pouting, Allard," said Vaughan.

"Why?" asked the stranger interestedly. "I mean, it makes him even more attractive. Seriously. I do quite fancy a shag, with him standing there offering it on a plate, and pouting."

"Well, where *are* we going to do it, then?" demanded Allard crossly. "On the bed, on the floor, or on a plate? I'm too old to do it anywhere but in bed."

Without answering, the stranger went to the bookshelf and picked up a book. "Well, if you want it on a *plate*," he suggested, opening the book to the middle with a flourish.

Allard looked at the title. *Rude Food.* He looked at the centrefold. It was an arrangement of meat and vegetables that looked…like meat-and-two-veg. The sausage especially was very phallic.

"No. Nobody is going to eat mine, except metaphorically."

The stranger looked at Vaughan.

"He has a tendency to use multisyllabic words until you shag him hard enough," explained Vaughan.

"Right, then, we'd better get on with it," said the stranger. "This way."

He led the way into a bedroom with a nice, big bed. The bed had lots of pillows on it. Obviously, the man had sorted out the basics—the bed would have been big enough to entertain both him *and* Vaughan, if they'd agreed to it. There were also some comfortable chairs, suggesting that this was not the first time the man had entertained friends as well as shags.

"This is very nice," said Allard. "And by the way, have you had your shots?"

The man picked up an oldish but still usable medi-reader from the bedside table, and ceremonially brushed his thumb across it. There was a quiet beep and a green light, and he passed the medi-reader to Allard.

Allard, then Vaughan, submitted themselves to the brief medical check, which was unsurprisingly clean—they did normally keep up with shots against contagious diseases.

"Good," said the stranger. "I do like to know that my acquaintances aren't right out of the gutter."

"So," said Allard, "do we."

"I like that, as well," said the stranger. "Good, clean fun is fine, but it's best to keep it that way on all sides."

"As our friend Harry would say," Vaughan added with a grin, "it's best to have fun without your bits turning green and dropping off later."

"Harry?" asked the stranger. "Oh, the voyeur one. Voyeurism is taking safe sex a bit far, I think. At least if voyeurism is *all* you do. Quite a turn of phrase, has he?"

"You could say that," said Vaughan. "Now, I suppose we'd better adjourn to the bed, since Allard is obviously gagging for it by now."

"I am not! I was showing a polite interest, as you said."

"Good," said Vaughan.

"What do you mean, 'good'?" said the stranger.

"If he's *really* desperate," said Vaughan confidingly, "he tends to catch me with his elbows and swear at me. It can only be a good thing if we start slowly and work our way up."

"Excuse me," said Allard coldly, "there are about to be three of us in this…arrangement, although I am beginning to feel less and less interested the more I listen to you carrying on."

Vaughan looked more serious and came over to him. "All right," he said, "I *do* know when to stop, you know." He kissed Allard gently. Allard found that rather more embarrassing than the teasing, but appreciated the kindness. This wasn't a combination of feelings he was unused to with Vaughan.

"That looks like fun," said the stranger, and came up to them rather cautiously.

Vaughan stepped out of the way, and the stranger put his hands on Allard's shoulders and kissed him very carefully. Not with the tender affection that Vaughan did, of course; more as if he had the manners to be reasonably cautious in a new situation.

Allard found the experience rather disconcerting. He hadn't been kissed sexually by anybody other than Vaughan in quite a long time. The other crew members had kissed him, of course, as a member of the 'family'. Well, sort of… He'd been quite aware that several of them would have made a play for him if he hadn't been with Vaughan; but he'd been with Vaughan, and the others had been aware of that. Rather like being an attractive, distant, *married* cousin, he supposed. They'd considered him unavailable.

He'd got used to being aware that people found him attractive when he didn't have to do anything about it. It was disconcerting to realise that he'd somehow slipped into a situation where he *did*…

Not that this chap was a bad kisser; it was just strange to be in this position with anyone other than Vaughan. The man was a little taller than Vaughan; Allard had obviously become used to the exact stretch he needed to do to reach Vaughan's mouth, because this was slightly different. As he reached out to embrace their new friend, Allard realised that the other man was also slightly thinner than Vaughan. Every slight difference felt intensely strange—not 'wrong', but unexpected, as his every muscle had to adjust to this being a different person.

He tasted of mint, slightly. Vaughan just tasted of…Vaughan. Maybe this man used a different toothpaste—or maybe he'd become so accustomed to Vaughan, he no longer noticed what Vaughan used, any more than he noticed what *he* used. Frightening thought; how quickly had Vaughan become the unnoticed background-colour of his life?

The stranger reached for the buttons on Allard's shirt, and broke the kiss to say, "Shall we undress?"

Allard glanced at Vaughan. Oh, dear. Vaughan was clearly not comfortable with this, and equally clearly Not Going To Say Anything About It.

"All right," said Allard, still watching Vaughan.

Vaughan's expression lightened a bit. He evidently found it easier to cope when Allard was concerned about him.

'Shall we undress' evidently meant, 'Shall *I* undress *you?*' After a quick assessing glance to discover if this was all right with Vaughan, Allard relaxed a bit, and let the stranger uncover him inch-by-inch.

He even put up with Vaughan giving the stranger occasional helpful hints along the lines of 'there's a button there', 'that clips on the left', and 'you won't believe this, but there are three other layers under that'.

After a few minutes to establish that the stranger was allowed to take the lead, Allard reached out and began to unbutton his shirt. Plenty of buttons to undo slowly and teasingly; not often the case with Vaughan, unless he'd dressed-up for a night out or had been wearing A Suit for a business meeting. This gentleman had a natural, relaxed, slightly formal style. He rather liked that, for a change.

About three buttons down, he discovered a thatch of thick blond hair on their new friend's chest. Considering Vaughan was naturally smooth, warm, and hairless, this felt, for a second, about as surprising as finding breasts on his partner. Not that he had any objection to either breasts or chest hair (although not on the same person); it was just unexpected after getting so used to Vaughan.

He twiddled about at it with his fingers.

"Ouch," said their new friend. "Tug, don't pull."

Allard adjusted his actions for more exact tolerances, and continued.

After a while, it occurred to him that he was still overdressed for the occasion. He stopped playing with the stranger's exotic pelt for long enough to push his own unbuttoned shirt off.

"Very nice," said the stranger, looking at him appreciatively. *No, that's not how it works,* thought Allard for a moment. *I was looking at* you. *You can look at me next.* He realised that was a rather stupid way to think about it. They both looked at each other.

"Can I see if the lower half is as tempting as the top half?" asked the stranger.

"Tight trousers he wears," muttered Vaughan, "everyone already knows."

Being near enough to the bed, Allard threw a pillow at Vaughan's head.

"That's not in the scenario," said Vaughan mildly.

"It's Husband Must Watch," said Allard. "Nowhere in that does it say Husband-Does-Not-Get-A-Pillow-Chucked-At-His-Thick-Head-If-He-Makes-Stupid-Comments." He paused. "If we wanted a running commentary, we could have asked Harry. And the girls."

"How do you *ever* get any work done on your ship?" marvelled the stranger.

"Once I've screwed Allard hard enough, I get 'round to the work," said Vaughan.

"Shut up, Vaughan," said Allard.

"No. He's just come up with an excellent idea," said the stranger, and began to unfasten Allard's trousers. Well, *try* to unfasten them, at any rate.

"It's that weird twiddly bit that looks like a decoration," said Vaughan helpfully. "You just sort of click it to one side."

Armed with this knowledge, the stranger was more successful. "You know," he said to Allard, "you *weren't* promising any more than you could deliver. I approve of truth in advertising." He evidently did. He started rubbing Allard's cock up and down in an is-it-really-this-big sort of way. Allard liked that. He hoped he was looking smugly virile, but it was probably just the usual stupid grin he got if he was enjoying himself too much to keep an eye on his expression.

"I see you can handle him," said Vaughan. "He likes it if you rub it through his knickers for quite a while until he's desperate, and dripping. Then he likes it if…"

Allard cut through the stream of nonsense effortlessly. "If this is merely going to be a re-run of exactly what *you* do to me, why the middleman?"

"I have no intention of following a script," said the stranger, "but it's useful to know what a person really likes and really hates."

"Allard has horribly ticklish armpits," said Vaughan. "He hates it when you do…this!" Vaughan made a dive for Allard.

In escaping him, Allard fell backwards on the bed.

"Very helpful, thanks," said the stranger, grabbing Allard's shoes and pulling them off before pulling his trousers (and the loosened underwear) all the way off.

Allard was now stark naked and sprawled on the bed, wondering exactly when he'd become the star in some low-budget porn flick, and wondering how this stranger managed to get the choreography so neatly right on the spur of the moment.

Then the stranger fell on him, kissing and groping, and he forgot to think about that. His mouth opened, and his thighs opened, and all he had was a simple response to good, rough, uncomplicated sex. This man had not a clue what he liked, but was going to do his damnedest to give it to him anyway. He hadn't expected that to excite him, but it did. Here he was, in front of Vaughan, performing yet another of Vaughan's peculiar fantasies, and enjoying the moment of exhibitionism.

His eyes were closed, and he could see a very clear image of Vaughan, blushing and breathless with arousal at him, admiring his thighs opening and the stranger's fingers disappearing inside him. Vaughan always liked him unambiguously eager.

He was ready, and the stranger's cock poised against him and started to slide in. Vaughan must be watching the stranger's cock disappearing into him, into that part of him that *Vaughan's* cock knew intimately and carnally. He could almost feel Vaughan's gaze. It inspired him.

He panted. He moaned. He came out with streams of dirty, noisy nonsense about do-it-hard and fuck-me-now and need-that-cock. Far more than he'd have bothered with normally, but then Vaughan *knew* what he liked; and at least half this wanton display was aimed at Vaughan anyway, because if Vaughan wanted a bit of a slut, he was going to get one. It seemed odd, role-playing a slut instead of a virgin, but it was just as true and just as false.

As the stranger started ploughing him in earnest, he hadn't the breath for that particular game, but the vision of Vaughan's eyes watching him didn't leave him.

Down to the short strokes, for both him and the stranger. He wanted to come. He wanted to open his eyes. He wanted *Vaughan* to see him come.

So he opened his eyes.

Vaughan was watching him. Vaughan was aroused, very aroused, but he wasn't happy.

Allard felt trapped, literally and figuratively, beneath the stranger's weight. He knew he couldn't actually stop and run to Vaughan to comfort him, but he was in agonies of social embarrassment at misjudging the situation.

And he was, at last, *quite* sure that if he could run off (on his own or with someone else), he wouldn't, because he was with Vaughan now.

What a time to discover one was seriously faithful.

Well, it didn't look as if Vaughan was finding the realisation comfortable, either.

Damn. He was gritting his teeth and trying to think of circuit diagrams to stop his body doing what it was trying to do, but that wouldn't work forever.

Suddenly, Vaughan stumbled forward to the bed and held his hand out.

Allard reached out.

Tightly enlaced, fingers between fingers in that warm, familiar grasp, Allard fell helplessly into his orgasm, forgiven and accepted and *known.* There was a cock in him, a weight on him, but he could feel Vaughan's grip, and he could hear Vaughan murmur, softly, "Allard," and that was all that mattered.

Worth knowing, his mind burbled to itself. *If we ever go to a very strait-laced planet or run out of lubricant, we can apparently have sex by holding hands.*

The stranger grinned tiredly down at him. "That was amazing!" he said.

Good. He came as well, then.

"Move over," said Vaughan. Not to Allard, to…

"Oh, my god," said Allard, in a quiet awed whisper to Vaughan. "I have been faithful to you for almost a year, celibate for months before that, and now I've just been fucked by someone without even knowing his name."

"Tawson," said the stranger helpfully. "Paul Tawson." He moved aside as requested.

Vaughan said, quietly, "Do you know what you look like, Allard? Absolutely debauched."

"Good. Get on with it," said Allard.

"No foreplay?" Vaughan asked.

"I'm not going to come this time, but I'm quite prepared to feel very good. Afterglow shading into sex, with plenty of cuddling," Allard explained. "Also, if you don't get on with it, I'll just doze."

Vaughan took him, at his word.

Allard enjoyed it, as he'd expected, without coming. He was stretched, so it didn't hurt. All he had to do was cuddle Vaughan, which he loved; and the three or four quick, hard strokes Vaughan managed were quite good enough.

Vaughan must have been *very* turned-on, even if he hadn't quite liked the experience, Allard thought sleepily, as all three of them piled together on the big bed and went to sleep.

* * *

When he woke up again, it was dark.

He was used to Vaughan being insatiable, but Vaughan usually managed that without having four hands.

No, this *wasn't* a dream. He was in bed with Vaughan and—somebody else. What a ridiculous idea. It must have been Vaughan's.

He'd probably slept through at least some of a delightful cuddle, and Vaughan was beginning to get more purposeful. Not that he minded, of course. Vaughan knew just how he liked to be worked up to it slowly, and Tawson's cock was rubbing suggestively against his buttocks.

"Can I—?" murmured Tawson.

Oh. The poor devil had obviously figured out he was the gooseberry, or three's-a-crowd, in this bed.

"Vaughan?" asked Allard.

"Mm?" said Vaughan, eyes still shut, rocking happily against Allard.

"Tawson wants to know if he's included in this particular dance or should sit it out," said Allard.

Vaughan opened his eyes. "Sorry, Tawson. I expect you've figured out that we're not exactly experienced at this."

"That's all right. I just like to know where I stand." Tawson sounded as if he meant that. Allard was in a position to know that Tawson's cock certainly knew where it stood.

"I don't mind your fucking him if I can kiss him," said Vaughan. "Probably doesn't make sense, but…"

"Aha," said Tawson cheerfully, "I'm the dildo."

Allard began to wriggle against him, making sure Tawson's cock knew it was welcome.

There was something pleasantly effortless about this sort of sex. They hardly needed to move much from their entwined sleeping position, Allard was stretched and lubricated, and all they had to do was…

Tawson slid in.

…start.

Vaughan started to kiss him, and wriggle suggestively.

It was a much more friendly, relaxed fuck than earlier, but that didn't mean it was unexciting. Pressure inside him at the same time as he had frottage—or was that sodomy, with a side-order of frottage? Very illicit, and he'd got a wonderfully kinky dildo who didn't seem to mind at *all* being treated as a mere sex object (well, Tawson was good at that), and there was nothing to do but wallow in his own greed without feeling guilty. Like having a huge box of chocolates without having to share them with Vaughan. Or like having a huge box of chocolates while Vaughan watched him...lick them, and taste them, and nibble them. Vaughan was nibbling *him* now, on the nipple. He seemed to be making an embarrassing noise. No wonder.

Tawson kept working away inside him while Vaughan worked away *outside* him, moving up to kiss him now. The combination was delicious. Like the box of chocolates. Or was *he* the box of chocolates, being offered 'round? Nipple-flavoured chocolates...the trouble with free-association was that you couldn't turn it *off*.

Couldn't turn *him* off, either. Or Vaughan, or Tawson. This was wonderful. It was never going to happen again, so he intended to enjoy it to the utmost while it lasted.

He liked being in bed with tall men who could cover him all over. Every stroke behind worked him against Vaughan's ready cock in front, every probing stroke of Vaughan's kissing tongue seemed to push him back firmly onto Tawson's cock. It seemed to go on for hours. Inside-outside, fucking-rubbing, holding-kissing. All at once, nothing left out. It had always just been a brace of cocks before, however plump and fine. This time, another had been provided for him. One inside, one outside, and his own caught breathlessly in the middle, like his own body caught between these two men.

It was rather as if Vaughan had somehow cloned himself and was taking care of him from both sides at once. A Vaughan sandwich, with a warm, damp, panting layer of Allard in the middle, quietly melting. He quashed that thought. He was fairly sure one wasn't supposed to think of toasted sandwiches while having sex.

What one thought of was how nice it felt having a cock up him and another pressing against him, all heat and weight and…

He *was* going to melt. Not at all quietly.

He pulled out of the kiss long enough to have a good, hard, noisy come, and then peacefully lay there while his dancing-partners arranged him for the end of the figure.

"You first, Tawson," said Vaughan, moving back a bit, and Tawson obediently came, cock wet and shuddering inside Allard.

Vaughan moved forward, making sure he was rubbing against Allard's belly, not his cock, while Allard murmured sweet inflaming nothings about how Vaughan was the *best,* the very *best,* even now he'd some basis for comparison, he *knew* Vaughan was the best…and Vaughan groaned, pressed against him, and came.

"Shall we go to sleep now?" mumbled Vaughan.

"Mm," said Allard sleepily.

"You do realise it's only about nine o'clock?" said Tawson. "It looks later because it's winter, but I don't think any of us have had dinner yet."

Allard's stomach made itself heard in answer to that.

He ignored it.

Vaughan said, "We'd better get some food. Otherwise, Allard's stomach is going to keep me awake all night."

I should hit him with the pillow again. I really should, thought Allard.

"I'm hungry, too," said Tawson. "I'll go and throw enough for three people into the microwave."

"Pizza!" suggested Vaughan.

"If you're going to indulge in pizza while we're on-planet," said Allard, "we're going to order it from a decent food place that makes them fresh."

"No," said Tawson firmly. "Getting one made and sent over would take too long, and I have a casserole in the freezer. Made fresh last weekend, so it's real casserole that didn't come in a little square packet."

Allard said, "I suppose that's a passable use for a microwave, heating up real food."

"Sounds nice," agreed Vaughan, "and I can quite see you might want to get your inconvenient techie sex-partners out of the way and put your feet up."

"Casserole it is, then," said Tawson, crawling out of the bed. "The shower's over there. I'll just clean up and then go and put dinner on."

When Tawson had had his shower, he put on a dressing gown and got going. Allard and Vaughan spent a few minutes cuddling and listening to kitchen noises.

"This is nice," said Vaughan.

"It's a normal human reaction to like to listen to someone else doing the work," said Allard, feeling the words twist slightly on the way out. They were meant to be a garden-variety cynical remark, not a double-entendre. He hadn't even been sure Vaughan would like to refer to it now it was over. "That…didn't come out the way it was intended. I'm sorry."

Vaughan held him close. "I don't regret it. I don't want to do it again, ever—well, it's an idea, but we might not be as lucky with picking a reasonably civilised chap next time, so we probably won't. But even though it made me feel uncomfortable, it was a *hell* of a turn-on, and it did reassure me, in the end."

"That I am with you because I choose to be with you?"

Vaughan kissed him gently on the lips. "Yes. That even if you screw about with someone else, you'll come home to me."

"That was a bit of a shock to me, as well," said Allard. "I knew I had no intention of leaving you, but there's a difference between knowing something as a theoretical proposition and getting a practical example."

At this point, Tawson cleared his throat.

The kitchen noises had stopped, and the throat-clearing was in the room with them.

"Yes?" said Allard, making the best of it.

"I'm glad you enjoyed it," said Tawson.

Allard looked at Vaughan, and shared a momentary shrug. 'Enjoyed it' sounded like a rather inexact description, even though they *had* enjoyed quite a lot of it.

"I hope you enjoyed it, too," said Allard belatedly, wrenching his attention away from Vaughan to glance at Tawson.

"Well, I thought I was in for a night of cheap sex, but it ended up more like marriage guidance counseling," said Tawson.

Allard tried not to look guilty.

Vaughan probably tried *to* look guilty.

"Don't worry," said Tawson. "It leaves less of a bitter aftertaste than cheap sex, I should think, and it's something different." He grinned at them. "Do I get to be best man?"

Vaughan looked at Allard. Very carefully, he said, "We haven't discussed that option yet."

"Oops, put my foot in it again. Casserole's nearly ready, anyway."

"I suppose we'd better get up and get washed and dressed," said Vaughan.

"The shower's big enough for both of you to get in together," said Tawson.

It was. Five minutes later, they were sitting in the kitchen while an extremely savoury-smelling casserole was dished up.

While they ate, Tawson asked Vaughan questions about syndicalism. "It's a very interesting arrangement, and it seems to work for you two."

Allard raised his eyes to the heavens. "It is *not* a group marriage," he said firmly, and switched off his attention for the *nth* time since he had met Vaughan.

Then he thought of some of the middle-management types he'd had the misfortune to find in a few of the companies he worked for. Actually, syndicalism didn't seem so…

Shuddering, he muzzled that thought. Obviously, too much exposure to sex, or Vaughan, was softening his brain.

As soon as they got back, he needed to have a conversation about algorithms with Mark.

Tailpiece

by Jules Jones and Alex Woolgrave

It was an unofficial tradition on the *Mary Sue* to spend the hour or so before dinner having a more-or-less serious conversation about anything that needed talking about *except* work.

Especially the day after they'd finished a strenuous job. Allard was glad of that. He was actually quite tired even today.

"Well, Allard?" Harry piped up. "Have you decided yet?"

Decided? What decision?

"Well, it's a year and a day since you joined us provisionally," said Vaughan. "We were rather hoping you'd come to a decision."

Oh. That decision.

"In some cultures," said Claire, "that's a form of legal marriage. It's reasonable of us to consider the question of whether you're going to join us properly."

The rest of the crew nodded, and looked at him.

"It isn't a deadline," added Karen gently, "but we do think you ought to give the idea serious consideration. You don't have to sign up for the whole belief system, but we all do feel you're part of the 'family' by now, and we'd like to think it goes both ways."

He'd made a remark, down-planet, that it wasn't a group marriage. It was unnerving to feel that, in some senses, this *was* more like a marriage contract than an employment contract. Not sexually, of course—he was rather grateful not to be handed 'round after meals to all willing participants. There were, however, shared *emotional* responsibilities he'd been completely unaware of when he'd blithely joined this group of lunatics under the impression it was (more or less) an ordinary job.

"I'm going to have to think about this," he said. "It's a serious commitment."

Unlike the last few people he'd worked for, they took that at face value and accepted it.

"You really don't have to take the lot onboard," said Claire. "I was just about as sceptical as you when I joined this bunch, but there were pragmatic reasons to join in."

You're not reassuring me, Claire. That just implies that the syndicalism virus is irresistibly contagious.

"What pragmatic reasons?" he asked.

"Well, for one thing," she said, taking a sip of her coffee, "there's a certain barrier between you and everyone else until you have a share in the same ship. They're not nasty; they just don't behave as if you're necessarily going to be there in a few weeks' or months' time."

Allard thought about that. Yes, they all drank and chatted and worked with him in a perfectly friendly manner, but he *had* noticed them shutting up when they were discussing the yearly Ship's Party and he came up to them. He'd just assumed that he was visibly not the Life and Soul, etc; he never had been at any of the other places. It *could* just have been that they saw no point in talking about a party he might very well not still be there for.

"Even if you don't ever believe in the political system," said Claire, "it's still a much better way of working—and a convenient way of arranging the legal paperwork."

"The *normal* way of working involves getting a boss in to mess things up, far as I can see," said Harry. "We just leave out that stage and get on with the work." He moved his feet into a more comfortable position on the desk.

Allard looked at Vaughan. Vaughan didn't say anything for a minute, and then said, "Do you remember the last place you worked at?"

"Unfortunately, yes," said Allard.

"I remember it, too. I helped you clear your desk out. I didn't like it, either. Do you want to go back to that sort of system?"

Allard didn't say anything. His silence was probably as clear as an outright confession.

Vaughan said, "Remember, I worked in a corporate environment for years. When I tried this, I could not imagine how I'd stood it for so long. I wouldn't have gone back even if the *Mary Sue* went bust and I had to hitch a lift on my next ship."

Allard said, very quietly, "I still need to think about it."

"We didn't mean to push you," said Karen.

"You didn't. I'm just not sure if I'm capable of that level of commitment." He looked 'round at them. "That's not a reflection on you as much as it is on me."

"Oh, I've read about this," piped up Mark. "There are all sorts of books about men who're like that."

What, *Men are from Earth, Their Colleagues are from Alpha Centauri?* Allard wondered. No, even the vast flood of self-help books he'd seen weren't *that* specific.

"It's all right for you," he muttered to Mark. "You *wanted* to join all this."

Apparently, Mark had finally learnt something about tact. He kept quiet.

"It doesn't matter if you think about it and decide 'no'," said Karen, "but you must think about it and make a decision. You can't drift indefinitely."

You didn't see my last six jobs, Allard thought. 'Drifting indefinitely' would have been quite a good description.

"What are we having for dinner tonight, then?" asked Harry.

Very smooth change of topic, Harry, Allard thought. Actually, he enjoyed eating dinner with the rest of them most of the time. In his last job, he'd taken active steps to avoid going to lunch with other people. It was partly a function of being on a spaceship where people *did* do things together, but if he'd really wanted to avoid people, he could have.

"Pizza," suggested Allard, and grinned.

"Not again," said Claire. "You don't have to live down to the stereotype by having pizza for every meal."

"Not every meal," said Vaughan. "He gets very upset at the idea of cold leftover pizza for breakfast."

"What *does* he like then?" leered Harry. "Sausage?"

"I'm not answering that on the grounds that if I incriminate myself, Allard will throw something at my head," said Vaughan.

"Just like normal meal-times, then," murmured Claire.

"Oysters?" suggested Allard hopefully. "I don't think we've ever had those for dinner on-ship."

"They don't freeze well," said Claire, "and you can't say you need them from what Harry tells us about your sex life!"

"What is that?" asked Mark curiously.

"My sex life is not a spectator sport," said Allard with dignity.

"Why, whatever gave you that idea?" asked Claire.

The conversation degenerated into the usual amiable argument. Listening with half-an-ear to the flying banter ("How can anyone want butterscotch Instant Whip on Weetabix for pudding?"), Allard decided that, for some (possibly masochistic) reason, he was actually enjoying himself. He liked these people. If he wanted to stay with them, he was going to have to give some serious thought to this.

But no power on earth was going to make him eat Instant Whip on Weetabix.

* * *

He opened his door to Vaughan, slightly mistrustfully, an hour or so after dinner. "You haven't turned up to add to the previous conversation?"

"What, about uses for Instant Whip?"

He hit Vaughan with the pillow. "The other conversation, about your pet subject."

"No," said Vaughan innocently. "Interesting as it was, thought you'd rather fuck."

"Ah. You're trying bribery and corruption."

"Yes," said Vaughan cheerfully. "Did it work? Although, now I think of it, I've spent ages corrupting you, so I hope it did."

He smiled back. Vaughan had a quite unfeasible degree of charm when he was just being himself rather than making a speech. "Not sure if I'm up to 'corrupting a virgin'," Allard admitted. "It sounds like hard work. Shall we just fuck?"

"But that's the same thing without the script," said Vaughan.

"Vaughan, your scripts are *terrible*. I just want to get into bed with you and enjoy myself, and you, in a more relaxed fashion. Oh, that reminds me…can the cameraman stand down for the evening?"

There was a muffled "Yeah, OK," from the two-way audio pick-up Harry had installed under the bed to remind them he was there at odd moments.

"Thank you, Harry, and good night," said Vaughan. He turned to Allard. "I'm surprised he was even listening. I'm sure he thought I was going to come and talk to you, and he's usually good about not listening to private conversations."

"He's also good at guessing when one or other of us, as he puts it, 'fancies a shag'," Allard said.

"Do you fancy a shag, then?" said Vaughan, not bothering to wait for an answer before he started unbuttoning Allard.

"Fortunately for you, yes," Allard said, reciprocating. This was one thing he'd miss very badly if he left this job, although he was reasonably certain that if he left this job, Vaughan would follow him.

"I got the nipple first," said Vaughan, pinching it gently.

"This is not a race."

"Oh? I got the impression you wanted a quick fuck and a good night's sleep."

"Not quite. A good fuck, a cuddle, and a good night's sleep," suggested Allard, undoing Vaughan's trousers.

"Hmm. Don't want *much,* do you?" said Vaughan.

"Considering what I'm undoing, that's a very ill-judged phrase," said Allard.

Vaughan looked at him carefully. "You really *are* tired, aren't you?"

"Mm," said Allard. "I'll try to keep awake."

"Maybe something less demanding than fucking?" suggested Vaughan.

"Are you calling me demanding?" Allard said.

"Not at the moment, but I can if you like," said Vaughan, picking him up and depositing him on the bed. "Your turn to fuck me through the bed, considering you've been underneath twice lately."

Allard groaned hollowly. "Too energetic."

"All right, does that mean I fuck *you* through the bed?"

"Vaughan, it's the concept of fucking each other through the bed that's a little too energetic for me right at the moment," Allard complained. "As in, I'd actually have to move about whichever way up I was." He decided not to make any comments about Vaughan squashing the breath out of him. He actually quite liked Vaughan being solidly built, and he'd hate to drive the man into unnecessary dieting.

"What *do* you want to do?" Vaughan asked, undoing Allard's trousers and tenderly caressing the contents.

"Don't want to do anything," Allard muttered sulkily, thrusting equally sulkily into Vaughan's hand—how dare Vaughan make him want it when he just needed to rest!—and half-hoping Vaughan would take him at his word and let him sleep.

"Then I'll have to," murmured Vaughan, bending down as he spoke, so that the last word of that was breathed against Allard's cock. "You're leaking a bit; I'd better tidy you up to let you sleep." The tip of Vaughan's tongue traced that betraying dampness and removed it.

Allard moaned.

"You're not helping, you know. You seem to be getting wetter."

"That's because you're licking me," Allard managed.

Vaughan snorted. "Don't believe a word of it!" he said, before tonguing Allard 'round and 'round and up and down, again. The tip of that tongue scooped and stroked, and then rested while the broad sweep of it curled affectionately 'round him. Then Vaughan kissed the tip of Allard's cock, and Allard felt himself swell and push as those lips moved back slightly and the lips parted to swallow him in. He could feel himself coming up firmer as Vaughan began to move; feel the rounded, plump tip of his own cock move into the wetness of Vaughan's mouth past the sucking circle of the lips, and…

Vaughan stopped. "You're still a bit wet there. Are you sure I'm not licking you too hard? Should I go and find a towel to mop you with?"

Before he could think of something to say, Vaughan was licking his way up him again. He sighed, moaned again, and twisted his fingers absently in Vaughan's hair.

Vaughan began to play with his balls, with some skill. Nudging and teasing as the tongue worked its way up Allard's shaft.

"Don't pull my hair," Vaughan said, in a pause, "or I'll stop licking."

Allard untwisted his fingers very gently from the curls he was exploring. He thought about Vaughan's solemn, careful face when working on some spare part or other. He'd have difficulty watching that in future without thinking about his own *un*-spare part.

As promised, Vaughan didn't stop licking. As he worked his way slowly up and down, with an engineer's careful attention to detail, he licked and pulled at Allard's cock, cupped and teased at his balls, and kept going without settling down to work on the business end.

"I can't help noticing," Allard said crossly, "that it's still extremely wet."

"Is it really?" marvelled Vaughan disingenuously, and stopped what he was doing to lie on the bed with Allard. "Have a taste, just to make *sure* it's still wet," Vaughan said, and kissed him.

Allard began to move against Vaughan, feeling and hearing the restless rubbing of half-clothed and extremely interested flesh as he stroked his tongue in Vaughan's mouth. He could taste himself in the kiss already.

He gave a little sigh of disappointment as Vaughan withdrew himself from the kiss and stopped lying on him. Obviously not too tired to enjoy a man's weight on him, after all.

"I've still got to tidy you up," said Vaughan.

"So you have."

"I'm good with self-lubricating parts," Vaughan went on. "All you have to do is work them smoothly until they really *want* to move…"

"'And they call it easing the spring'," Allard murmured gently, quoting a poem that could possibly be misinterpreted as pornographic in a couple of places.

"'We can slide it/Rapidly backwards and forwards'." Vaughan capped his quotation absently. Allard would have admired that if Vaughan hadn't been busy sliding him rapidly backwards and forwards.

"It's getting wetter," Vaughan said, withdrawing his discourse from the realm of literary quotation and back toward fact.

"Mm," said Allard. "You'd better clean it up, then."

Vaughan bent down to get to work in earnest. This time, as he licked up to the tip, he didn't lick down the other side. For the second time, his lips popped open around Allard's eager cock-tip, but this time, he didn't stop. Instead, his mouth slid smoothly into place until he had the full length commanded by mouth and hand working in perfect, pitiless unison.

Allard felt the full intensity of it close over him, unstoppable. He gasped and shuddered and pulled Vaughan's hair and kept shaking and poured himself out until he was finished.

Vaughan swallowed, rather ostentatiously. "I think that's taken care of it," he said, after a moment.

"Mm," Allard said, agreeing with that.

"Are you too tired to take care of mine?"

He reluctantly dragged himself back to reality, resenting Vaughan for making him do so. Then he decided that that was probably a little unfair. "I have no objection to you rubbing against me, as long as I'm not expected to move."

"How very gracious of you." Vaughan took hold of his hand. "Am I allowed to move you?"

Before he could answer, Vaughan moved Allard's hand. It was wrapped firmly around Vaughan's cock, and then moved briskly up and down.

Actually, this was rather pleasant. He had the fun of wanking Vaughan without any of the work. He peeled his eyes open to check what was going on. Vaughan was kneeling next to him. Vaughan noticed him looking, and rubbed a little harder.

He grinned at Vaughan.

Vaughan came. Messily.

"You're cleaning that up," he said sleepily.

"It's your room," Vaughan said.

"It's your mess." He shut up, because Vaughan was, in fact, mopping up the mess. And Vaughan might point out why Vaughan was the only one to have made a mess.

"Anyway," Vaughan said, "I suppose it's our room. It's just that this is the one of the two rooms that has most of your junk, while most of my junk is in the other half of our two-room suite."

What would they do if he was a formal member of the syndicate? "I suppose I'll keep the same cabin even if I do join the ship?" he asked. This was the room that had been assigned to the nominal passenger/consultant, not that it was actually any different to any of the other cabins.

"Of course," Vaughan said. "I prefer to sleep in the same bed as you, but we have enough days on different shifts that I'd rather not *have* to sleep in the same bed as you."

Yes. He and Vaughan had definitely moved in together, even if they retained separate cabins for practical reasons. "We could always see about putting in a connecting door. If that doesn't seem too much like a French farce."

"No structural reason why not, I should think," said Vaughan.

Practical and romantic. I like it, Allard thought.

He cuddled up to Vaughan. "It's nice," he said drowsily, "when we *do* sleep together." He settled down for a nice doze on Vaughan's shoulder. There was silence for a few minutes.

"Allard?"

"Mmm?" he said.

"I'm not trying to nag, or anything," Vaughan said, "but why *do* you get so nervous at the idea of joining the syndicate?"

He stiffened. He didn't like this being dragged into the bedroom, and he'd have thought Vaughan was above that.

Vaughan stroked his back, a soothing glide of warm hand down stiff muscles. "I said I wasn't trying to nag. I'm just trying to understand. You wouldn't still be here if you hadn't enjoyed the last year—you've had at least three job offers that I know of. I know it's not simple greediness—you'd have made more money as a partner than as an employee." Another long stroke down his back. "And you don't spend most of your salary, as far as I can tell. No, I haven't been prying, but I haven't actually seen you spend much money. I assumed you were investing it. Why not simply treat a share in the syndicate as an investment, if you don't want to buy into the philosophy?"

"A very large investment," he said. "Too many eggs in one basket, and I'm not comfortable with that." He faced the truth of it. "The eggs in this basket aren't just financial. If it did all go wrong and I had to leave, I'd be a lot more bitter about any financial loss. Especially if it was on a scale where I'd *have* to find another job immediately or dip into capital, rather than being able to live on the income from my investments for a while."

"You've got *that* much money tucked away?" Vaughan grinned at him. "You obviously have been well paid for your talents."

"I was well paid, I invested both luckily and wisely, and it wouldn't be a very *good* standard of living, just something I could put up with for a few months if the alternative was spending half my waking hours with people I actively hated rather than just didn't like."

Vaughan stroked his face. "Yes, I can see that if you've spent the last few years knowing that you really can walk away without even having another job lined up first, it could be very stressful to give that up. It's not just the worry about how long it would take to disentangle your money, is it?"

"No." Maybe he should have had this conversation with Vaughan before. Vaughan seemed to understand, better than he'd expected. "And it's worse now that I have an emotional stake in this job, not better."

"Of course, you could just marry me on a planet with community-property laws," Vaughan said. "That way, you'd legally have joint title in my share of the ship. That should satisfy the others that you've made the emotional commitment to the ship."

"Although you'd legally have joint title in my money," Allard said, before his brain caught up with the conversation.

He stared at Vaughan. "Would you repeat that?"

"Will you marry me?"

This, he had *not* expected. "I thought you'd stopped worrying about me being about to up and leave you at any point."

"Yes," said Vaughan. "Now I feel more secure, I can ask you to marry me because I want to, without thinking you'll feel pressured to agree just so as not to make me feel insecure."

He thought about it. He was surprised to find that this was less frightening than being asked to join the ship once and for all. He'd already made the emotional commitment to Vaughan; if he chose to leave the ship rather than join the syndicate, he'd do his damnedest to prise Vaughan loose, as well. Not that he'd have to try very hard, even though it would be a wrench for Vaughan.

And Vaughan had let him think about it in silence, not pressuring him, not trying to persuade him.

"Yes," he said.

"Thank you," Vaughan said simply, and pulled him into an embrace.

He lay against Vaughan, feeling the warmth of Vaughan's body, the warmth of Vaughan's emotion. This meant a lot to Vaughan, more than he'd realised. More, he suspected, than Vaughan had quite realised.

It meant a lot to him, too.

After a while, they moved apart again, resting comfortably within easy reach of each other. Vaughan said, "We do need to sort out a few practical details, like when and where. It would be nice if it was a year and a day after we first fucked, but we probably need more time than that to make arrangements if we want more than a quick, practical ceremony with just our shipmates as guests."

"*I* certainly do," Allard said. "It's over a year since I've seen any of my family. It's a good excuse for a get-together. Anyway, if we're going to the bother of making it legal, we might as well do it properly." He turned to Vaughan. "You do realise my mother will insist upon a full formal Church wedding."

"I didn't realise you *had* a mother," Vaughan said mildly. "I thought you were hatched. By the AI running a fertility clinic, which got broody on its own account and stole some of the stock."

Allard glared at him. "For your information, my mother is an extremely distinguished mathematician; but in her sentimental moments, she's always wanted me to make a good marriage."

"Somehow that explains a lot," said Vaughan. "Do I count as a 'good marriage'?"

"Let me see," said Allard. "Own ship, teeth, and hair. Plus the fact that you're sufficiently unconventional to keep even an unreformed hippie like Father happy. If he comes to the wedding, of course. I wouldn't put it past him to forget if he happens not to be on the same planet as Mother at the time."

"I'm sorry I asked," said Vaughan. "And it's only a part-share in a ship."

"It was a lovely relationship," said Allard regretfully, "until you started talking about my family, which is none of your bloody business."

Vaughan kissed him. Allard suspected that this was because he couldn't think of any other response to the situation, but it was nice anyway.

"I'm quite happy with the idea of a Church wedding," said Vaughan.

"You are?" He hadn't thought Vaughan was the type.

"Oh, yes." Vaughan's eyes acquired a distinct gleam. "The idea of listening to your trembling voice repeating your vows as you wonder what is going to happen to you in my arms, carrying you off from the reception when I just can't wait any longer, and then ripping the white, virginal bridal robes off your quivering body on our wedding night…"

"Even my mother isn't sufficiently romantic, or demented, to imagine me in a white bridal gown."

"Can you get one anyway? In ivory? For the bedroom," Vaughan specified unnecessarily. "Anyway, it's really supposed to symbolise chastity, not virginity, and I don't think I have much to worry about on that score."

Allard agreed. The only time he'd strayed had been at Vaughan's determined instigation, which was odd, now he thought about it. Not odd that Vaughan had had a peculiar fantasy, but odd that it had been such a romantic experience for both of them.

Not many people could have essentially made the decision to marry their partner while being soundly fucked by a third party.

Jules Jones & Alex Woolgrave

Jules Jones is a material scientist by day, writer by night, whose publishing credentials include such gems as European Union research reports. Thrilling though these might be to at least three readers, Jules believes that variety is the spice of life. Writing erotica provides an adequate amount of variety. However, Jules has found that it's better not to mix the two styles of writing, though—it's very embarrassing when your manager points out that the file you were working on during the lunch hour has found its way into the project folder…

The Occasionally Spotted Woolgrave is Jules Jones' partner-in-crime and can frequently be heard shrieking across the Atlantic: "Oi, Jones, which way up are the boys at this point?", "Trousers, what trousers?" or "That's not a POV shift—it's an experimental literary device!"

Woolgrave cannot visualise. At *all*…

Fortunately, Jules Jones believes in expressing one's Inner Editor, and is good about spotting completely impossible positions or characters undressing more or less than once.

In fact, Jones comes up with the plot and half of the dialogue, and Woolgrave adds regrettable knob jokes and the *other* half of the dialogue.

It seems to work. We think.

Check out these other titles, also available in print
From Loose Id®

WHY ME?
Treva Harte

THE PRENDARIAN CHRONICLES
Doreen DeSalvo

TAKING CHARGE
Stephanie Vaughan and Lena Austin

SHE BLINDED ME WITH SCIENCE FICTION
Kally Jo Surbeck

FOR THE LOVE OF…
Kally Jo Surbeck

Printed in the United States
79372LV00003B/52